Operation Grab Bag

A Frank Sweeney Adventure

Will Ponner

Copyright © 2018 Will Ponner

All rights reserved.

ISBN-10: 1718861206
ISBN-13: 978-1718861206

DEDICATION

This book is lovingly dedicated to my mother, Patricia Catherine Ann Sweeney (her maiden name), a mother to nine children, a grandmother to twenty three, and great-grandmother to two (currently). She is, quite simply, a treasure. Mom continues to demonstrate faith, family, fun, and forgiveness to all of us.

She is a truly remarkable and sweet woman who has lived a wonderfully full and uncompromising life on this earth for 90 years. I love you, Mom, and all of us are incredibly blessed and thankful to have you as our mother and mentor.

"Her children rise up and bless her; her husband also, and he praises her, saying: Many daughters have done nobly, but you surpass them all. Charm is deceitful and beauty is vain, but a woman who fears the LORD, she shall be praised". -Proverbs 31:28-30

A portion of the proceeds of this book will go to providing honor flights to Washington, D.C. for our military veterans.

CHAPTER 1

October 28, 1932

"We'll only have about four minutes. We have to move fast." Gino Garcetti was nothing if not thorough. All of 5'7, his dark eyes matched his short cropped hair. He had a permanent five o'clock shadow, which he felt made him more attractive to the broads. At 25, Gino was entering his twentieth year of crime. It all started with swiping candy from Ralph's, a small store on the west side of St. Paul. He graduated to breaking and entering by the age of ten. By fifteen, as cars became more popular, he began stealing and re-selling them. By his twentieth birthday, he had three bank jobs behind him. When it came to casing banks, Gino was already legendary. He was meticulous in his planning, going over every detail repeatedly. He and his two accomplices had hit nine small banks over the past couple of years. All of them had been in or near Minneapolis, and they had never even come close to being caught. The key was doing your homework and getting in and out as quickly as possible, even if it meant not getting all of the money. "Don't be greedy," Gino preached to his partners. "There are plenty of banks to hit, but you can't hit nothin' if you're in the slammer."

Today was different. They were going after something much bigger. And it was not in Minneapolis. Gino had cased the brand new 1st National Bank in St. Paul for weeks. There was so much fanfare about the new building that getting a copy of the blueprints was a breeze. By far the largest bank in the city in size and, more important, in deposits, the bank stood 417 feet tall and was the tallest building in the city. It also had the first connecting skyway, up on the seventeenth floor. The skyway connected 1st National to the smaller Merchants Bank. 1st National was 32 stories high. Gino reminded himself if they had trouble, the last direction that he wanted to go was up. He hated heights, and the thought of falling 32 stories terrified him.

He had studied everything about this monstrosity for days on end. As he did so, he began to take note of patterns that he saw. He noticed that there was only one guard on each shift, and that the guard in the morning was much older and seemed to move more slowly than his younger counterpart who had the afternoon shift. He also had thick glasses.

"When we make our move, we should make sure that we knock his glasses off. That way he won't be able to identify us," he reasoned.

He also took note of the employees at the bank. Many of them were older, middle-aged men who didn't appear to be all that observant of their clientele. They kept their heads down and worked, talking little to each other or even to their customers.

"It's a very quiet place," he thought. The one different thing that he noticed was that there were two female bank tellers. He had never seen that before. And one of them was quite a looker, too. "Some other time," he told himself. "No distractions. Stay focused on the task."

After this job, they would take a break and head down to Chicago. From there, they'd drive to Oklahoma and wait out the winter. There would be plenty of broads along the way.

He knew that he was breaking the rules on this one, but the money was just too good. And though he wouldn't admit it to anyone, there was something that appealed to his ego. This was the largest and newest bank in St. Paul. It had not been hit by anyone yet. There was a reason for that, of course. The Chief of Police of St. Paul had an unwritten agreement with the criminal element in the city: Do your "business" outside of the city and you could live in St. Paul in peace. Violate that rule, and you would feel the wrath of the St. Paul Police Department. While this job might stir up the Chief, he would cool off in a few days. Besides, since most of his brethren honored this arrangement, St. Paul's finest would be soft and less attentive to the banks in the city. So long as no one got hurt and they left town right away, the St. Paul cops would let it go after a while. They'd be mad about someone breaking the rules and crossing over to their city to do their crime, but so long as no one else broke the rule, everything would work out. Besides, Gino and his team would be laying low down south until the heat let up.

OPERATION GRAB BAG: A FRANK SWEENEY ADVENTURE

And truth be told, he really wanted the big boys in Chicago to take note of him. Hitting the 1st National would certainly send a message that the Garcettis weren't small time anymore.

There are two reasons most robbers get caught when they are hitting a bank. First, they stay in the bank too long because they want to get all of the money. Second, they don't have a good escape route. Unlike most guys, Gino started his planning backwards. He would always begin with the escape route. Regardless of whether the job was successful, you still had to get out of the bank. On this job, Gino came up with a great plan. While they would come in the front door like all of the customers, Gino noted that there was a side door that opened onto Robert Street. They could park the car right outside of the side door and make a quick escape from the bank through that same door. The plan had come together nicely.

"Remember, each of us has a job to do. We will fail if one of us forgets to do his job. So don't mess it up."

"Gino, we got it, we got it," said his younger brother, Joey. Even though he was two years younger, Joey was three inches taller than his brother. But there was no doubt as to who was in charge. "Me and Joey know what we're doin," Jimmy Martini mumbled boringly. Jimmy was big in size and short on brains. Not only was he lacking smarts, he was lazy. To Gino, that was a deadly combination. But he was Joey's best friend and had protected Joey when they were kids. They'd managed to do nine jobs without a hitch, so something must be right about this team. Gino gave Jimmy the "You are such a moron" look.

"We've been through this a hundred times, Gino," whined Jimmy. "We got blueprints of the joint and we know when the old guard takes his break to walk down to the corner to get his newspaper every day. Plus, it being in St. Paul, no one will be looking for a bank to be robbed. They've been beefing up all of the banks in Minneapolis, not here. We can do this job in our sleep."

"That's just when you make mistakes!" roared Gino. "You want to get the respect of Dillinger and Barker and the rest of 'em? You gotta do these jobs and do 'em flawless!"

After an awkward moment of silence, Joey looked at his older brother and quietly repeated, "Gino, we got it."

An hour later Gino pulled the car up by the side door of the bank. Joey and Jimmy exited the car and slowly strolled the 50 feet toward the front of the building, waiting for the guard to exit the bank, as he always did at 11:30AM.

The weather worked in their favor. Late October in St. Paul can often be as cold as January in other cities. Given the fact that the high was only going to be 30 degrees, all three men had long overcoats on. The long coats allowed Joey and Jimmy to easily hide their shotguns. Gino packed a Winchester revolver that he kept in his coat pocket.

Gino left the car a few seconds later and turned up the collar on his coat to hide his face. He slowly walked in the opposite direction toward the street corner. As he stopped to look in the window of a nearby shop, he noted the guard holding the door open for a good sized young man as the younger man entered. The guard stopped to greet his young friend. As the guard and the young man chatted, Joey and Jimmy hesitated slightly, but then proceeded into the bank while the guard stepped to the side of the door to talk longer with his friend. Gino watched them talk for almost another full minute before the guard shook the young man's hand and began walking toward the street corner.

Gino turned his back on the scene and continued to walk toward the corner as well, counting the ninety seconds that it would take for the guard to get to the corner. Gino calculated that it would take the guard about an additional forty five seconds to buy the newspaper, a bit longer if Gino could stall him. This made up the roughly four minutes that he figured that Joey and Jimmy would have to hit the bank. His job was to make sure that the guard took longer than four minutes to get his newspaper. The fact that the guard had stopped to talk to the younger man could only help give additional time to his cohorts.

CHAPTER 2

The day started like any other for Jack Sweeney. Jack was living his dream. A cop's cop, he had followed in his father Michael's footsteps and joined the St. Paul police force. An intense but fair young man, Jack was a spitting image of his father when his father was his age— jet black hair and steely blue eyes that, depending on his mood, shifted from hard and unforgiving to as soft as the color of the Pacific. He had matured into a fine detective who had learned the give and take of a police officer's job.

He was a natural leader of his men. It didn't hurt that he was the oldest of the four Sweeney children. Since his dad was a cop for many years, that meant a lot of time alone for Maggie and her four children. Jack had to grow up quickly and not only be his mom's helper, but the man of the house when his dad was away.

Michael worked his way up from patrolman to detective, and eventually was named Chief of Detectives for the city of St. Paul. After being in that role for several years, Michael departed the force to venture out on his own. No one was at all surprised when Jack followed in his dad's footsteps and joined the force. Six feet tall with broad shoulders, Jack starred in high school as an athlete. Several of his teammates ended up joining the force with him. Jack started as a patrolman five years ago, and he had recently been promoted to detective. As a testimony to his character, not one of the other fellows thought he had been given preferential treatment when he made detective so quickly. Jack simply was an exceptional cop.

While he loved his life on the force, he didn't want to see his younger brother follow him into law enforcement. There was no doubt that it was a dangerous job, especially in St. Paul in 1932. John Dillinger was known to have a hangout in the city, and everyone knew Ma Barker and her two boys made St. Paul their home for most of the year. Truth be told, it was common knowledge that the Chief himself was on their payroll. This didn't sit well with Jack, and it certainly didn't sit well with his father, either.

The advent of the machine gun had really evened the playing field when it came to cops and robbers. The bad guys (and gals) were bad – nasty bad - and almost prided themselves on taking down an officer or two in the midst of a bank robbery or a moonshine transaction.

"Two cops in one family are enough," Jack would say at the family dinner each Sunday night. Everyone agreed. Except Frank, 12 years Jack's junior, who idolized his older brother. Last Sunday night, Frank expanded his argument to include his logic behind his pat answer: "But there's only one officer now, Jack. Dad left the force years ago to start his armored car business. So we will need another Sweeney on the force to bring us back to two cops!"

Jack looked down the table to his father, who smiled and shrugged. "Frank, you will have plenty of time to decide what you will do. You keep running the football the way that you did today, and the Gophers will want you!" smiled Michael.

Frank grinned at his Dad, but wanted to go back to the topic at hand. Evelyn, the next child in line behind Jack and the oldest of the Sweeney girls, quickly passed the meat to him and Frank temporarily forgot what they were talking about. Jack mouthed a silent "thanks" to Evelyn.

Katherine, the next in line after Evelyn, saw the exchange between her two older siblings and smiled, but kept the secret to herself. Maggie watched her Irish brood with pride. Each of her four children were young people of faith. And besides loving them, she really *liked* each of them. She watched Michael's reaction to all of the banter. He was beaming with pride. Maggie and Michael exchanged a glance that only a married couple with children can relate to. It was that look of "We've done all right, haven't we?"

When Jack first came on the force, Frank was so proud that he told everyone he knew (or barely knew) about his big brother. Jack smiled as he thought about Frank's creative ways of always bringing his brother's occupation into a conversation. His mind drifted to his family and how thankful he was for his parents and siblings. The Sweeneys were a close knit family that were fiercely protective of each other. He always looked forward to the Sunday night dinners, when everyone came together for a night of great food and lively conversation. And this coming Sunday would be even more special, because he was bringing a young woman home to meet his family for the first time. That is, assuming she would say yes to his invitation. Given all of Jack's success on the athletic field and on the force, one would think that his social life would be every bit as stellar. Not so. It wasn't his looks. Or his personality. With that easy smile and a curiosity that made him a great conversationalist and an excellent listener, one would expect him to have no trouble when it came to women. At least that was what his sisters and his Mom always pointed out. Jack, however, wasn't so sure.

Kathleen Geraghty was one of only two female tellers at 1st National Bank in downtown St. Paul. A redhead with a wonderful smile and an even better laugh, she had met Jack when he came to the bank to deposit some money. Over time they began to talk and found out that they had a few things in common, not the least of which was their proud Irish heritage.

For all of Jack's natural leadership and bravery, he had to admit that when it came to Kathleen, he was a bit…timid. He had never been serious with a girl before. And he really hadn't even dated much in high school. As he was leaving his parents' home last Sunday, he had mentioned to his mom that he might be bringing a girl home for dinner next week.

Maggie Sweeney was every bit as Irish as her husband. Her maiden name was Flynn, and her dark hair and fair complexion reflected her spirited Irish personality. She may have been born in Iowa, but she was a Minnesotan through and through. She loved her children with every inch of her 5'2 frame, and she wasn't afraid to show it. She and Jack were very close, probably due to all of those nights alone while Michael was working his way up the ladder at the force.

Maggie was the one who held the family together when Mike was out working all of those nights. And then when he started the Sweeney Detective Bureau and the armored car business, there were even more nights away. So when her eldest son told her about this special girl that he wanted to bring home, Maggie tried (and failed) to remain nonchalant. She could barely contain her excitement. "This family is ready for an expansion," she said to herself. Jack had never brought a girl home, so this one must be special. She resisted asking a lot of questions, wisely deciding to wait until Sunday night when she and Mike could meet this young woman in person.

She did ask one question: "What is this girl's name, Jack?"

"You'll be happy to know that she is German, Mother," said Jack with a twinkle in his eye.

"German?" shrieked Maggie.

"Yes, if you consider "Geraghty" to be German." smiled Jack. "And her first name is even worse: Kathleen! Kathleen Geraghty! Can you believe it?"

Maggie, exasperated, said, "Jack Sweeney, you are every bit as bad as your father!"

Jack chuckled and hugged Maggie tightly. "Don't worry, Mother. I think you'll really like her."

Michael was just walking into the room and asked, "Who will your mother really like?"

"A nice German girl, Michael," said Maggie, as she winked at Jack.

CHAPTER 3

As Jack entered the bank, he said hello to Patrick Clancy, who was a retired cop that worked at the bank as a security guard. Clancy was on the police force even before Michael started out as a patrolman, walking a beat downtown. He was a bespectacled, older man who had pushed past 70 years of age. His holster carried a gun that had never been used. "How's your dad, Jack? From what the papers say, Sweeney Detective Bureau is doing very well in protecting people's money. He's a hero around the cities, given how his boys have managed to stop all of those holdups."

"He sure is, Mr. Clancy," replied Jack, beaming with pride.

"As much as he loved being a cop, I think he really enjoys the detective and security business."

Michael had left the force 15 years ago and had become a very successful businessman, especially after designing the first armored car in America.

"Well, I'm sure it pays better than a cop's salary," said Clancy. "I have to work this security job because my pension isn't enough. I'm not sure that you know this, Jack, but your father helped me get this job. I'll always be grateful to him for that. The extra cash really helps, especially since my wife took ill. It's been wonderful here. Wonderfully quiet, anyway. Seems like all of the bad stuff continues to take place across the river, which is fine by me."

"I'm sure you were more than qualified for the job, Mr. Clancy. My dad speaks highly of you. He said that you were always a cop's cop, and there's no higher praise than that. He told me many times how you taught him the ropes when he was just starting out."

Clancy's eyes grew moist and he was silent for a moment. His voice broke as he said, "Coming from your dad, that is quite a compliment, lad. Please make sure to tell him that I asked after him."

"I will. It was good to see you, sir."

"You too, Jack." As he watched Clancy shuffle down the sidewalk, Jack made a mental note to tell his father about Mr. Clancy. "Wow. Another guy that Dad helped that I never knew about," he said to himself.

"I wonder how many men like Clancy that Dad has helped?" As he pondered this, he entered the bank.

CHAPTER 4

Joey and Jimmy entered the bank unnoticed. The noon rush hadn't started, and it being Wednesday, it should be a light day anyway. The middle of the week was typically slower for foot traffic. But the Sweeney armored cars would come later in the afternoon to take the cash to the reserve bank further into the city. In other words, the bank would be flush with cash this morning. The two thugs each made their way up to separate tellers and quietly handed each one identical type written notes.

Jack told himself that he had to ask her today. After all, it was already Wednesday, and he didn't want to insult her by waiting too long into the week. As he entered the bank, he continued to rehearse how he would ask her to dinner at his parents' home.

He saw Kathleen from a distance, busily packing a large amount of money into a bag. He saw the teller next to her doing the same thing. It took a second – but only a second – to process what was going on.

Gino waited for Clancy to get to the newsstand, then subtly stepped in front of him to engage the newsboy for a newspaper. The boy gave him a newspaper and Gino fumbled around for the nickel to pay him. After he finally produced the nickel, he asked the kid for a pack of Lucky Strikes. The boy produced the cigarettes, and Gino again fished for a dime for the cigarettes. He stalled as much as he could, then thanked the boy and turned to open up the cigarettes. Clancy was behind him now and obviously hurrying to get his newspaper. Sure enough, Gino calculated that he had bought his two accomplices another minute or so. Clancy made his purchase and turned to walk back to the bank, and Gino followed just a couple of steps behind. When Clancy was only steps away from the bank, he heard a gunshot, followed immediately by another two shots. Clancy started to run toward the entrance of the bank, but he only took two steps before being knocked out by a vicious blow to the back of the head.

Jack assessed the situation and put together a plan in seconds. He made his way to a large desk off to the right of the robbers. They were still waiting for the tellers. Incredibly, no one else in the bank had noticed what was going on. Kathleen was focused on filling the bag with cash, as was the other teller. Kathleen looked up for a second and saw Jack. She made eye contact with him for only a moment and subtly shook her head, telling him to not do anything. As the robbers turned to go, they produced a second pair of identical notes that told the two tellers to not move or say a word, or they would be shot. Joey and Jimmy started to make their exit. They walked rapidly toward the side door that led to Robert Street and their getaway car.

Jack waited until he had a clear shot. He yelled for them to stop and to drop the bags. Carrying the guns under their long coats turned out to be a disadvantage for them. Jimmy turned to open his coat and Jack immediately shot him in the shoulder. Joey dove for the ground and Jack led him perfectly, catching Joey in the chest. By now Jimmy had his gun out and fired, hitting Jack squarely in the abdomen. Jack was knocked back and fell against the wall. He was hit badly, and he knew it. He tried to keep his senses while he assessed his wound and the situation.

Gino raced into the bank with his gun drawn. He saw his brother lying dead and Jimmy writhing on the ground. He grabbed the bag near Joey's body and went over to Jimmy. Jimmy started to talk and Gino shot him dead. He picked up the second bag and saw the young man who had been talking to the guard. The young man was bleeding heavily from the stomach and was trying to reach his gun, which he had dropped due to the force of the shotgun blast. Gino quickly moved toward him to finish him off. As he raised the gun to fire, his knees were kicked out from under him. Stunned, he looked up to see a young red haired woman trying desperately to grab his gun. He shoved her away and turned again to fire on the young man. Before he could pull the trigger, his head exploded. Kathleen looked up from the ground to see Jack with the gun in his hand and his face glazed over. He slowly dropped the gun and closed his eyes. Then everything went black.

CHAPTER 5

The morning of October 28, 1937: 5 years later.

Colonel Robert von Greim tried to look confident and assuring. The former characteristic came to him easily. The latter quality is what he needed to work on – especially now. He was sent to Ireland on a mission, and this was his fourth – and final – attempt. This effort was the last piece of the puzzle. Von Greim was Hermann Göring's right hand man, even though the two men hated one another. He found Göring to be a talentless and vile little man who had wormed his way into Hitler's good graces. And Göring found von Greim to be egomaniacal and yet obsequious to those in authority who could help him.

The Fuhrer – well, technically Göring - was about to name von Greim the head of research for the Luftwaffe, Germany's air force. A few years earlier, Göring had asked von Greim to help him rebuild the German Air Force, and in 1934 he was appointed to command the first fighter pilot school, following the closure of the secret flying school established near the city of Lipetsk in Russia. The Fatherland had been forbidden to have an air force under the terms of the Treaty of Versailles of 1919, but the Fuhrer had no intention of adhering to such an unreasonable demand, so the military had to train its pilots in secret. Von Greim was the natural choice for the assignment. He was a decorated combat pilot in the Great War and was respected and admired for his courage. Tall and thin with deep set eyes and a long nose, von Greim was a driven man who believed that he had paid his dues. He had met the Fuhrer – what a glorious day that was – many years ago when Hitler boarded his plane to attend a Party meeting in

Berlin. There was a mutual respect from the outset, and von Greim dedicated his life to his beloved Fuhrer and to the Party.

Still, he had not been successful in breaking into the inner circle. Göring was his main obstacle there. "Hermann is threatened by me," he had told himself many times. There was jockeying and politicking at all levels of the Nazi Party. One man had to prove his loyalty and outdo the others, so there was a constant "one-upmanship" between the men in power and the wannabes. Von Greim was too arrogant to see himself as a wannabe. He was a man in waiting. And Herr Göring was not helping him.

The man seated across from him at the table looked unsure. Again. "He's still not convinced," thought von Greim. Nevertheless, he pressed on.

"So, Dr. Conway, do we have an agreement?" Von Greim's cold eyes of steel stared directly at Dr. Edwin Conway. He smiled his most winning smile at the brilliant engineer.

Edwin Conway looked at the man across from him. He was a strange man, there was no doubt about that. The opportunity on the table was intriguing, to be sure. To be able to do research in the very field that he had dedicated his life to, that also kept him sane…who could ask for anything more than that? It would give him an opportunity to not have to continue to think about Hannah, his recently departed wife. Still, there was something that was holding him back. A small voice wrestled with him whenever he considered this option. And this had to be the third or fourth time that von Greim had come to see him.

"Your offer is both generous and flattering, Colonel. And I appreciate you making the trip to Dublin. However, I am not sure that it is something that I can commit to at this time," said Edwin.

They sat in Edwin's office just outside of Dublin. Edwin had built a very successful career as an aeronautical engineer. He also was a gifted author and a sought after speaker on all things related to aviation. Von Greim had read every book that Edwin had written; he attended Edwin's lectures, and he had made up his mind that Edwin Conway was the man that he needed for his project.

"But Doctor, we have been through this many times. I've spoken with you for almost a year now about this opportunity. We need your expertise to assist in not only protecting the Fatherland, but sharing this eventual technology with the rest of the world so each country can protect itself in the event of a war. Dr. Lippisch would consider it a personal favor if you would work with him again."

OPERATION GRAB BAG: A FRANK SWEENEY ADVENTURE

Alexander Lippisch was a designer of leading edge aerodynamic aircraft. He and Edwin met at a flying consortium years ago that was conducted by none other than Wilbur Wright. Up until they met Wilbur, both men were headed into the same career path: Edwin wanted to study automotive engineering and Lippisch was going to design automobiles. Their lives changed forever upon meeting one of the famous brothers from Ohio.

Von Greim decided to take a different tact. "I know that you lost your wife not so long ago," continued von Greim. "I am very sorry for your loss. Perhaps a new adventure for you in Germany would be just what you need?"

Von Greim was not going to tell him that he was on strict orders from Göring himself to employ whatever means necessary to get Conway to Germany. The project needed Conway's expertise in this particular area of technology in order to change the inevitable war that would come. But this project was like no other, and the combination of Lippisch and Conway working together would be critical to not only speeding up the process but seeing it through successfully.

"Thank you for your concern, Colonel. My daughter and I miss my wife. She was an amazing woman, and we lost her almost eight months ago. We had a wonderful marriage and a real partnership. Leigh and I are still working through the process of not having her with us."

Edwin and Hannah were married for 29 years. Most of their married life had been spent in Ireland, outside of Dublin. Edwin had studied at Oxford for several years before moving back to his home country. He and Hannah didn't pay much attention to politics. They were both focused on Edwin's advancing career. Their life together had been marked by tragedy. After suffering through two miscarriages, Hannah gave birth to a son.

They named him James and called him Jimmy. One more miscarriage followed. One year after that, Leigh came along. Edwin and Hannah knew that Leigh would be their last child.

They were able to put the past behind them as best as they could, and focused on the two children that they had been blessed with. Edwin's reputation as the top aeronautical engineer in the country grew. He spoke all over Europe and was widely recognized as one of the very top experts in aviation. Everything was fine until Jimmy went off to study at his father's alma mater in England. He was a bright young man who was in a hurry to make his mark on the world. The university years flew by. The fall of Jimmy's senior year, the whole family couldn't wait to be reunited during the holidays. Edwin had arranged his schedule to be off for a couple of weeks. The family was going to go to the Swiss Alps to ski after Christmas.

Edwin found a beautiful tree and he, Hannah and Leigh spent a night decorating it in anticipation of Jimmy's homecoming.

The three of them arrived early at the train station. Hannah had made Jimmy's favorite cookies for him and had a few in a bag for him for the ride home. They found out later that the train had left London on time with Jimmy on it. It had made only one stop along the way, and that was only for fifteen minutes. The train arrived in Dublin, on time, without Jimmy. That was almost a year ago. They never stopped searching. There was no explanation for it. Then Hannah fell ill. It seemed like a fever that wouldn't go away. After several weeks and numerous visits to different doctors, she slipped in and out of consciousness. When she was semi-conscious, she kept insisting that she had seen Jimmy, that he had visited her late one night and assured her that he was fine. Each time that she was even marginally coherent, she told Edwin and Leigh the same story: Jimmy had slipped into her room late one night to hold her and tell her that he loved her, but that he had to leave. She eventually fell into a coma and passed away a few days later. What had been a very happy family had been reduced to a father and his daughter.

Leigh was always the apple of Edwin's eye. She reminded him so much of Hannah that he often mistakenly called her by her mother's name. She loved to read and write and was well versed in both. Edwin was looking forward to getting back to his home to have dinner with his daughter. If only this bore of a man would leave him alone. The offer was, in fact, quite generous. And it did challenge him in all of the ways that he loved to work: being on the cutting edge of innovation and creating something that had never been done before. The commercial opportunity for this technology was almost exactly what Edwin himself had envisioned several years ago.

On top of that, Lippisch truly was exceptional as a designer. There were few who could match his capabilities, and the two of them together really could make aviation history. But something just didn't feel right to Edwin. He certainly did not care for von Greim. He knew nothing about Göring. And this Hitler fellow was becoming more outspoken. Still, the Great War had ended only 20 years ago. Surely with the reprisals against Germany, no one wanted another war, least of all the Germans. "Maybe this might be something for me to do for a time. Leigh will be finishing school soon anyway. I could really use a challenge to get my mind off of Hannah. And Jimmy." He felt guilty even saying that to himself, but maybe it really was time for something...different. Still, he hesitated. Something just kept holding him back. What was it?

He was about to tell von Greim that he would once again give consideration to his offer when the German officer interrupted his thoughts.

It is amazing what a couple of sentences in a conversation can do. The world changes on such comments. Wars have been started. New products have been born. Relationships have been restored. Or severed. Certainly, Edwin's world changed that day. In a matter of seconds, Edwin Conway went from one of the world's foremost aeronautical engineers to an employee of the Third Reich. There was no argument. There was very little negotiation, if you could call it that. Von Greim had played the trump card. And he had won.

CHAPTER 6

Colonel von Greim let out a sigh of relief when he got in his car. His driver didn't notice it. Or if he did, he was too smart to show it. With the pressure that he was getting from that madman Göring, he had no choice but to do what he ultimately knew would force Conway to agree to come to Germany. Von Greim was no fool. He knew that Hitler was preparing the entire country for war. And von Greime relished it. He believed Hitler to be godlike. He thought back again to the day that he had met the future leader of the Fatherland. It had been 17 years ago when Hitler was in charge of propaganda for the German Army. Von Greim actually flew Hitler to his many different stops. He knew that this one man could raise the Fatherland back to its rightful place as the leader of the world. He longed to be part of Hitler's inner circle. And he had risen quickly, with the culmination being hand selected by Göring to head up this secret project. The Fuhrer must have approved, had he not? "Göring will eventually self-destruct," thought von Greim. Von Greim was a soldier and a pilot – "a superior pilot," he reminded himself. "I am one of the most decorated pilots in German history. By the Great War's end I accumulated 28 victories and was awarded the Bavarian Military Order of Max Joseph," he boasted to no one. This award made him a Knight, or Ritter, and allowed him to add both this honorific title and the style 'von' to his name. Thus Robert Greim became Robert Ritter von Greim.

Yes, Göring also had flown, but he certainly did not have the skills – or the medals – that von Greim had accumulated. Göring supposedly had 22 victories, but many believed that that number was inflated. "He probably bribed someone," thought von Greim. "Besides," he told himself, "The Fuhrer needs people more like me: thoughtful, strategic, and loyal no matter what the cost." Göring was too much of a politician. And it was

OPERATION GRAB BAG: A FRANK SWEENEY ADVENTURE

rumored that he was addicted to morphine. It started when he was shot in the hip during an air battle in the Great War. It was so bad that at one point the great Göring was put in an asylum and restricted in a straightjacket.

The other reason that von Greim was so sure that he would be promoted soon was that Göring was stretched too thin between the SS and the Luftwaffe. "If I can make this project successful, my future would be secure. There is no telling where I could end up," he told himself. Perhaps he would become Vice Chancellor? No, the thought was too great to consider. At least for now. He simply had to determine how he could deliver this new technology. That was where he needed to focus for now. Göring would be taken care of at some other point, either by his own hand or someone else's.

As the car made its way to the Dublin Airport, Colonel von Greim smiled once more at his shrewd plan. Surely the Fuhrer would admire his craftiness. Perhaps he would celebrate tonight with Elsa, his longtime mistress. Of course, she mustn't know the reason for the celebration. It was quite common for the officers in the Third Reich to have a mistress or two. As a matter of fact, if a man didn't have a mistress he was almost looked down upon. Knowing that Göring would stop at nothing for political advantage of any kind, he wouldn't be surprised if Elsa was a plant for Göring. "Maybe that's why so many of us have mistresses," he mused. Upon reflection, he doubted that she would do that to him, but it was a good reminder to trust no one. Göring was the shrewdest of the shrewd. Yes, Elsa deserved a nice night out. And so did he.

CHAPTER 7

Unlike her brother, Leigh chose to stay in Dublin to study, specializing in American History. She stood 5'6 with brown hair that almost matched her eyes. Those beautiful brown eyes were often filled with mischief. She loved to laugh and she could give it as well as she could take it. She had inherited her father's razor sharp mind and her mother's discernment and empathy. Leigh assessed people and situations quickly and usually came up with the right analysis, always erroring on the side of grace.

Though she had never been to America, she loved reading and learning about its origins. She thought that someday she might teach in her native land about this magical country an ocean away. She would love to see the United States. Both of her parents had relatives that had moved there many years before. She had cousins that she had never met that were Americans. She wondered what they looked like and what sort of accent an American would have. The Depression was in full swing in the U.S., and from what Leigh had learned, Franklin Roosevelt's policies had not done anything to get the country out of the economic mess that it was in. She mused about how this Depression was impacting her relatives there. Some of them were farmers in one of the Midwestern states. At least one was a policeman. Leigh chided herself for not remembering which one. "Fine teacher you'll be, Leigh Conway! You can't even remember where your relatives live!"

Edwin was protective of Leigh, and she understood why. She would do anything for her father. While she was sweet and kind, do anything to threaten her dad and you would see a very different side of her. Theirs was a comfortable but tight relationship. After all, it was just the two of them now. She had a couple years of university left to complete. Now that her mother was gone, she would focus on finishing school and seeing after her father. She realized with no regret that she likely wouldn't stray far from her dad. Over the past few months, she had arrived at the conclusion that her life would be far different than what she had imagined it to be just a year ago. She would never leave her father alone. He was her hero and, though he might never admit it, he needed her. And she needed him. Yes, it was just the two of them now.

She heard the back door creak open at the usual time. She had already prepared his favorite dinner that night: a huge bowl of potato soup followed by leg of lamb. Since her mom had passed away, she made it a point to keep as much of the house as "normal" as possible, and that included the meals. She just thought that it gave her dad one less thing to miss about his wife.

She caught her father's eye as he walked into the kitchen. The look on her father's face betrayed the fact that he was deeply troubled.

CHAPTER 8

Hermann Göring sat at his desk in his palatial office in Berlin, plotting his next move. The Nazis had gained control of the German government several years earlier, and with that control came power. And Hermann Göring knew not only how to grab power, but how to use it.

He was rebuilding the Luftwaffe at a very good pace, and his SS thugs were doing their jobs, intimidating and arresting anyone who dared question the regime. Some paid for their sins in prison, while others endured a more permanent fate. He didn't really care either way. He was systematically helping to find every Jew in Germany and either had them put to work or put to death.

He stood up to stretch his stout frame and look out of his window. His was one of the few offices with a window in this particular building. He had insisted on such an arrangement. One of his many interests was mountain climbing, so to be confined in an office with no windows would have been torturous. The number of interests that he had was matched only by the number of titles that he had carried over the years. And those titles that followed his name were indeed impressive. He clearly had Hitler's ear in all things strategic. And just as important, he had Hitler's trust, which afforded him almost limitless power.

He turned back to his desk, and his eye caught one of only two pictures that decorated his work area. Of course, the larger of the two framed photographs was that of his boss, who happened to be the head over all of Germany.

The other picture is the one that he chose to focus on for a moment.

It was a photo of his second wife, Emmy Sonnemann. They had only been married for three years now, and were expecting a child soon. His first wife, Carin, had died in 1931. She had been a sickly woman, saddled with tuberculosis, epilepsy, and a weak heart. The weak heart is what took her.

In contrast, Emmy was full of life and energy. An actress from Hamburg, Emmy was fast becoming the equivalent of the First Lady of Germany. Pictures of her were everywhere, mostly because she had played hostess to so many events involving the Fuhrer.

In the meantime, Hermann was accumulating a fabulous amount of wealth. He had systematically been "collecting" art and jewelry from virtually every Jewish home and business that was commandeered by the Party. He felt no guilt over it. He felt no guilt over anything.

Hermann Göring was, in a word, a survivor. He had a lot of experience in it, starting as a child. His father was the consul general to Haiti, and he and Hermann's mother were living there when she got pregnant. Just before she was ready to have Hermann, she flew back to Germany so her son could be born in the Fatherland.

Right after his birth, Hermann's mother left and went back to Haiti for three years before returning to see her son. Once back in Germany, his mother began a long affair with Hermann's godfather, a wealthy Jewish physician who ended up letting the family live in a small castle outside of Nuremburg. From there he was sent to boarding school, which he hated. He feigned an illness so he could come home. He eventually enlisted in the military, where he was rejected as a pilot candidate. Ignoring the order to be removed from pilot school, he eventually flew in the early days of the Luftwaffe, and was awarded many medals for bravery in combat.

After the Great War, he was involved in the Beer Hall Putsch in 1923, Hitler's first attempt at gaining power of the German government through a failed coup attempt. Almost everyone ended up in jail, or worse. But in typical Göring style, he fled to Austria and remained untouched. One way or another, Hermann Göring had always managed to survive.

Asked by Hitler to create a four year plan to rebuild – and re-arm – Germany, Göring wasted no time in grabbing power, so much so that many viewed him as Hitler's number two man. He was a man of action and was ruthless in doing whatever it took to accomplish his objectives.

He had already set up the Gestapo and, having stabilized it, gave it to Heinrich Himmler to run. Himmler was handpicked by Göring, in large part because Himmler was the only man who was as cruel and as shrewd as Göring himself.

It was likely that he would have to give the Luftwaffe to someone else to run, at least at some point. But not now. And he would not be giving it to von Greim, no matter how much he begged him or politicked for it.

Just mentioning that name brought Göring back to reality. He expected to hear from that idiot von Greim at any moment. The egomaniac had better have gotten Edwin Conway to move to Augsburg. If he hadn't accomplished this, then Göring would begin the process of planting seeds of doubt in the mind of the Fuhrer about von Greim. Hero or no hero, the Great War ended many years ago. Besides, he secretly thought that von Greim had inflated his victories so that he could be recognized with more medals. "Probably bribed someone," he thought.

There was a knock on his door. "What is it?" he barked.

"Sir, Colonel von Greim is calling for you."

"Put him through."

"Yes, sir!"

A few moments later, his phone rang.

"Yes?"

"Herr Göring, this is Colonel von Greim."

"What do you want?"

"I am calling to tell you that Dr. Conway will be joining us on the project. He will be in Augsburg within four weeks."

"What took so long?"

"He just needed to be persuaded, Herr Göring."

"It's about time, Colonel."

"Yes, sir. We can now move ahead with the project."

"Yes, we can Colonel. Expectations are high from the Fuhrer himself. I doubt that you would want to…disappoint him."

"On the contrary. My intention is to delight him."

"See that you do that. Anything less than that will be...extremely unacceptable. And consequential."

"Give me the resources and you will not have anything to worry about, Herr Göring."

"Prove to me the viability of such a project and you shall get your resources, Colonel."

Silence.

"Good day, Colonel."

"Herr Göring?"

"What?"

"Heil Hitler!"

"Yes. Heil Hitler!"

With that, the two men raced to hang up first.

Göring's face contorted in disgust. "What an imbecile!" he said to no one. "This project will finally sink him."

Von Greim stared at the phone. "A complete idiot. He has underestimated me, and he will pay for it. This project will allow me to catapult right over him."

Göring smiled a bit, in relief. "Ah, finally. It's time for my shot. I shall need two today. One because of my hip, and one because of von Greim."

CHAPTER 9

October 11, 1942

Minnesota fall days are almost always cool and crisp, and this day would be no different. "Minnesota" is an Indian name that means, "Land of sky blue waters." Today was one of those days that gave evidence to the wisdom of the Indians. The leaves were radiant in their splendor, as if they had been painted on the sky's canvas. Children would collect the most colorful leaves, paste them in a book, and give them to their mothers, who would feign shock and comment on what a beautiful job their children did. The fall in Minnesota was the warm up act for the main event, called winter. While the fall was beautiful and eased Minnesotans into the cold season, winter would arrive unannounced and stay for as long as it pleased.

As much as Minnesota is known for some wonderful things – all of those lakes, wonderful summers, and beautiful falls – it was known for something else, especially in the 1920's, 30's, and early 40's. Some of the most notorious criminals in the country resided in Minnesota for at least part of the year. Ma Barker, John Dillinger, Baby Face Nelson…all of them called St. Paul home during the Spring and Summer months. It was only when they left before winter that the city could afford a sigh of relief. And all of the police forces in the state could take a break and re-group for the next year of crime. That is, all police forces, except one. That one particular force never had to worry about any serious crime in its city.

The tall man with broad shoulders, thick silver hair and a silver mustache to match leaned against the window and looked out at the children playing football across the street. He was grateful that they could play safely in a neighborhood like his. About 7 years earlier and only a few

OPERATION GRAB BAG: A FRANK SWEENEY ADVENTURE

blocks away, John Dillinger was involved in a shootout with the St. Paul Police. Maggie was always concerned about whether or not their home was safe from these ruthless criminals. She was even more concerned after Jack had killed the three thugs that day. She feared retaliation from the Garcettis, but her husband knew better. There was an unspoken code between the gangsters and the cops: Keep the families out of it.

He was in his favorite spot: his office at home on the 900 block of Hague Avenue in St. Paul. His two story home with the welcoming front porch had allowed for many fond memories and family gatherings. That is, until he lost his oldest boy. There had not been much laughter or many pleasant memories made since that awful day. He made himself think of other things. It was much easier to think about all of the criminals and the close calls than it was to think about Jack.

Michael Sweeney started down memory lane by running through a mental checklist of all of the Chiefs of Police in St. Paul over the years. Some were decent men. But a fair number were not. The most corrupt of all of the chiefs was John O'Connor, who had implemented "the O'Connor system" in the city. The system consisted of three rules: Gangsters needed to "check in" once they came into town; they needed to do their crimes outside of the city; and they needed to pay O'Connor and other officials to look the other way. Not necessarily in that order.

Most of the time the money was exchanged at the Hotel Savoy in downtown St. Paul, only a few miles from where Mike and Maggie lived. The system stayed in existence long after O'Connor retired. The guy who collected the money on O'Connor's behalf was a local gangster named "Dapper Dan" Hogan. Hogan was a legend in mob circles during the Prohibition era. He served as the go between for O'Connor and all of the criminals who were coming into the city. Of course, word spread of such a system, and it brought many more gangsters to St. Paul. Crime spiked in all of the surrounding cities. And the bribe money increased as well.

It got so bad that the citizens began to rise up and insist on change. The end of Prohibition in 1933 only exasperated the problem. No longer being able to make money on illegal booze, many criminals turned to kidnapping local rich businessmen and holding them for ransoms. And they robbed more banks.

All of the corruption and the influx of crime made national news, which got the attention of the feds. A brave local journalist named Howard Kahn, together with Commissioner of Safety Henry Warren, hired a detective from Chicago named Jamie Wallace. Wallace wiretapped the St.

Paul Police Department, and not too long after that, it was all over. Cops went to jail. Public officials went to jail. Gangsters went to jail, or they left the state. A new regime of police leadership was brought in and changes were made. O'Connor never went to prison. Hogan was killed by a car bomb. His murder was never solved. After over 30 years, the O'Connor system was finally history.

Jack Sweeney's death in the 1st National Bank was another turning point for the city. The city of St. Paul got a lot more serious about protecting the banks when Jack was killed on that awful day.

Mike would never forget the long lines at the funeral home, the church, and the cemetery. It was the longest and most painful day of his life. All of the people who came were well intentioned. What could one possibly say to a mother and father after their son had been cut down?

Jack wasn't the only person who acted heroically that day. If Kathleen Geraghty had not grabbed that Garcetti kid, more people would have died. Her action allowed Jack to fire one more shot that took Garcetti out before he could kill anyone else.

As the family made their way down the aisle of the Cathedral at Jack's funeral that day, Maggie saw a beautiful young woman sitting by herself, near the back of the church. She was quietly sobbing. Somehow, Maggie just knew that this young woman was Kathleen. Jack's Kathleen. Maggie stopped behind the coffin, reached out and took Kathleen's hand, and had her walk down the aisle with the Sweeney family. She sat with the family during the entire service. She was considered a Sweeney from that day on. Mike smiled sadly at the memory, reminding himself that Kathleen would be coming for dinner tonight. She had never married, and he had more than one talk with her about "moving on." So far, no soap. His thoughts drifted back to Jack. Again.

"He was simply at the wrong place at the wrong time," Mike told himself for the hundredth time. That thought was always followed by, "He died a hero. He saved many lives that day." All true, but there was little lasting comfort in that. "Let someone else's son die for others. Let someone else's son save lives. All those people have gone on to get married, have children, have grandchildren, start careers…and my son is still gone."

Jack's death obviously impacted everyone in the family. The house became quieter. Dinners were less lively. The kids spent more time in their rooms. Maggie made a huge and constant effort to hold everyone together, and she succeeded, at least in some ways.

The family remained close, just more withdrawn. When not in their rooms, Evelyn and Katherine hung around the house more with their mom. Frank had poured himself into sports and had excelled in each of them.

And what about Mike? "How have I responded?" He asked himself. The answer was that he threw all of his energy into the business. Sweeney Detective Bureau thrived, ironically in large part because of John O'Connor. Businesses and municipalities were so fearful of the gangs that they took every precaution possible to ensure that their people and their money were safe. His businesses – the armored cars, the detective bureau, and the security services – all went through a huge growth spurt as the gangsters ratcheted up their game.

In the early 20's, the best (and only) defense that a bank had when they had to move money was to employ deception. Typically, a courier would wear plain clothes and use a suitcase to hide the money. He would then take public transportation – a street car or some other means – and deliver the money to its destination while "hiding in plain sight." That idea had a whole host of potential issues, one of which was that it was terribly time consuming. One man could really handle only one suitcase at a time. And with so many people on the take, it didn't take long for word to spread as to who was carrying what. Michael saw the problem – and the opportunity – and opted to leave the force in 1920 to design the first armored car in the country. The outcome of this adventure was called The Sweeney Detective Bureau, which, among other things, provided armored cars and armed guards to handle the transfer of money for banks and businesses. There was another division that provided private detective work, and a third one that offered private security services. What began as one idea had morphed into three different but related businesses, and it all started over twenty years ago.

While all three businesses thrived, the armored car is what Sweeney Detective was really known for. Continuing to protect people and their money all of these years later was his way to honor Jack.

Still, all the money in the world could never be a substitute for his loss. Nothing would ever make up for losing his son.

He allowed himself a few more moments of reflection. These moments were rare for him. He was not a man given to such introspection. He was a man of action. Nonetheless, he seemed helpless to stop for some reason. Today was the tenth anniversary of Jack's death.

"No doubt that must be driving all of this," he thought.

After starting as a patrolman, Mike worked his way up to a detective position, and after a few years, Chief of Detectives. He was credited with solving hundreds of crimes, from robberies to murders. His name was in the paper regularly and he was quoted extensively, all of which he hated. He just wanted to be a cop. He only served as Chief of Police on an interim basis, at his own insistence. He wanted no part of compromising his principles in order to appease criminals. Or politicians. Because any police job with the title of Chief in it was named by the board of commissioners, it had morphed into a political position. And one thing that Mike Sweeney could never be accused of was being a political animal in any sense of the word. He disliked the politicians almost as much as he did the criminals, and often wondered out loud to Maggie if anyone could really tell the difference between the two. "One group are born liars and the other group are paid liars," he would say.

While he was thankful for the experience of being a cop, he was more thankful that he no longer was one. Even though he threw himself into the business in large part so he didn't have as much time to reflect on Jack's death, it was true that he loved the three entities of his business. Most of his detectives and security guards were former cops who had worked for him at one time or another, so the business still had the feel of a police unit. Even the war hadn't slowed things down. "I suppose we will always have crime as long as we have people," he mused aloud.

His easy smile and piercing blue eyes reflected a sense of humor that was either dry or mischievous, or both, depending on who was his intended victim. But those same eyes could not hide the pain – the absolute worst pain that a parent can experience – of losing a child. As much of a toll that Jack's death had taken on him, he had seen the result in his wife's life, too. He and Maggie rarely spoke about Jack. It was just too painful. Instead, they focused on their other kids. It was just much easier that way.

Maggie was much more withdrawn since Jack's death. Naturally cheerful and outgoing, she had to force herself to get out and mix with people now. Anyone who knew her well noticed the difference. Maggie had tried to keep a stiff upper lip – after all, she was every bit as Irish as he was – yet there was an unspoken but acknowledged pain that they would share for the rest of their lives. The way the couple dealt with his death was, for the most part, to not talk about it.

Occasionally late at night when neither could sleep, one of them might mention Jack. There would be a short conversation, but then the subject would inevitably be changed. Sometimes late at night he would awaken to hear her sobbing quietly on her side of their bed. As he pondered all of this, he knew that tonight would be another night of hearing Maggie crying quietly into her pillow. And him pretending to be asleep. Their son was a combination of both of them, and they both loved him dearly.

But they each suffered their grief separately. Privately. He just didn't know how to comfort Maggie, and perhaps he somehow had communicated to her in his silence that he neither wanted nor needed her comfort when it came to Jack. But deep inside, in his weaker moments, he wished that he could let her into that corner of his heart that was hidden away from everyone. The irony was not lost on him: Michael Sweeney, Chief of Detectives who had to tell countless numbers of people that their loved one was dead; who reached out a hand and hugged them in their most desperate hour; who attended more funerals than he could even count; this same Michael Sweeney couldn't comfort his own wife...and he couldn't comfort himself.

He choked back a sob and looked at the sky to clear his eyes.

Jack had one goal as a little boy, and that was to be a cop like his father. Maggie, for whatever reason, kept the newspaper clippings that had covered the story. She had gotten close to Mrs. Clancy – her husband Patrick Clancy was lost that day, too. He had been struck so viciously from behind by Gino Garcetti that the coroner couldn't determine if the blow to the back of his head had killed him, or if the collision with the sidewalk that occurred on the front part of his brain due to him not being able to break his fall had done it.

While Michael coped by throwing himself into his armored car and security business, he could never really stop being a cop. He wondered almost daily what Jack had seen when he first walked into the bank. How much time did he take to assess the situation and read it? How had he decided to position himself where he did, so he would have the optimal shot at stopping the robbers while simultaneously keeping all of the people in the bank safe from stray bullets? And in Mike's darkest moments, he wondered what Jack's last thoughts were. Did he know that he was dying? Probably. Michael shut his eyes to the thought and made himself, once again, think about something else – anything else.

He began to think of his own father, who had long since passed away. His father and mother had both emigrated as children to the U.S. in the late 1850's with nothing but the clothes on their backs. They were just one of the many that were impacted by the Great Famine, commonly called the

"Potato Famine," in other countries. Ireland lost almost 25% of its population as a result of that famine. The ones who didn't die tried to emigrate elsewhere, and many ended up in the U.S. His father couldn't read or write when they came here. After 5 years of scraping and saving, they bought land south of St. Paul and began to farm it. The crops came along well and the family got by. His parents loved their new country and were fiercely patriotic. After all, if they hadn't made it to America they likely would have lived very short lives in Ireland, and their kids almost certainly would have fared no better.

"Has it really been ten years since Jack's been gone?" Mike asked himself. He did a quick personal inventory: He would soon be sixty, which didn't seem possible. Maggie was two years younger than he was, but she looked the same to him. Except for her eyes, which betrayed pain on most days. Time itself reminded him that it had been much longer than yesterday. He moved a little slower, thought a little longer, and cherished time a little more.

Michael was not enjoying the beauty of this particular day. As a matter of fact, with the exception of seeing the kids playing football across the street, he hadn't even bothered to look outside for most of the morning. The reason for his lack of interest in the scenery was about to sit down before him in the form of his old friend George Parker. George and Michael were detectives on the St. Paul force a generation ago. Dubbed the "Twin Sleuths," by the local papers, Michael and George had put a lot of people away. They were fiercely loyal to one another in those days. Given the amount of corruption, it was difficult to know who you could trust and who might get you fired. Or worse. When Michael walked away from his Chief of Detectives position, George resigned as well. While Mike wanted to start his detective business, George wanted to move on to more responsibilities on a larger scale. He was a few years younger than Mike, and felt like he had several good years left in him to serve in a grander capacity. So after fifteen years on the force together, the two friends parted ways. Because of their success, the F.B.I. had come calling. J. Edgar Hoover saw an opportunity to aggressively expand the Bureau's reach on a national scale by taking on organized crime at the Federal level, and the Twin Sleuths were the perfect pair to help him. Mike had politely rejected the Director's offer, but George readily accepted. This meant moving to D.C. for a couple of years, followed by assignments in New York, Chicago, and Miami. His last stop was back in D.C., where he had worked his way up to a Deputy Director. While the two friends didn't talk as much as they used to, there was still an iron bond between them. There is something permanent about two men covering each other as bullets would rain down on them.

"Mike, it's so good to see you. Sorry I was late. I had to wait for a military transport plane. There aren't too many of those around for those of us fighting the war stateside."

"Well, Georgie, the world has been kind to you. Although working for Hoover can't be any picnic. The average citizen probably hasn't noticed much, especially because of the war. But he's done a massive power grab over the years by giving the F.B.I. carte blanch across the states. The guy must be an egomaniac. They even have their own radio program that promotes the Bureau. And what's this malarkey about "The F.B.I. always gets their man?" "Come on, George. Hoover's in every episode. What does that say about him? I can't believe the President puts up with all of that." Michael paused, loading his pipe with tobacco. He murmured as he tried to get the pipe going, "I always thought Hoover was a bit…strange."

Parker looked at his former partner with mocked astonishment. "I have no idea what you mean, Mike. J. Edgar Hoover is a great American," he stated in a monotone voice.

Michael just chuckled and shook his head. "You always were better at the political nonsense than I was. Just to put your mind at ease, you're safe here. There are no listening devices. I have the house checked every week. That is, unless one of Hoover's boys has been in here the last couple of days." Now it was Parker's turn to laugh.

After a couple more barbs, Parker shifted in his seat. "OK," thought Mike, "Here comes the pitch."

George leaned forward. "Listen, I know that today is the tenth anniversary…"

"Thanks, George", said Michael, quietly. "Can I get you something to drink?"

Parker knew his old friend well enough to take the hint. Mike really didn't want to talk about what happened ten years ago. It seemed like it was yesterday, especially as he looked in his old friend's eyes. "The pain is as fresh as ever," he thought. George opted to accommodate Mike's wishes. "Well, it's 5:00PM somewhere, right, Mike? How about a glass of wine?"

It was Michael's turn to observe his partner. Parker's eyes betrayed his own sadness about Jack's death. The Parkers and Sweeneys had gotten together almost every week back when the kids were young. Mike and Maggie were godparents to George's oldest boy. George was surprised at how fresh the wounds still felt after all of these years. But his sadness was even more profound at this moment, because of what he must ask of Mike. "The timing couldn't be worse," he thought. To ask his best friend on this day of all days...

As Michael poured him a glass of wine, Parker couldn't help himself. "This stupid, awful war," he mumbled.

"What did you say, Georgie?" asked Michael.

"Huh? Oh...nothing, Mike."

They reminisced about their days starting out on the force, and some of the more difficult arrests that they had made together. They caught up on their fellow cops; who was still on the force and who had retired; who was corrupt and who wasn't. Unfortunately, the list of the former was longer than the latter.

After a while of this exchange, Mike brought them to the business at hand. "So, Georgie, what's the occasion? An FBI man doesn't fly half way across the country to talk about the old days, especially with a war on."

Parker smiled. "You're right. No, an agent certainly doesn't waste the Bureau's time and money doing something like that." He hesitated for a moment, trying to figure out the best way to move into the real reason for his visit. Finding no clear path, he decided to dive right in. Mike Sweeney was a no nonsense guy, and he always wanted to hear things straight up. George would oblige him, no matter how difficult it would be.

"Mike, what I am about to share with you can go no further than the two of us. I know that I can trust you, but I need to preface my remarks by getting your assurance that what I am about to share with you will remain confidential – forever." Michael was taken aback. George Parker was a lot of things, but one thing he was not was someone who had a flair for the dramatic. He had never seen his friend like this. "Of course," he said, somewhat warily.

"First of all," began George, "I am no longer with the FBI. Roosevelt just signed off in June on a new organization called the Office of Strategic Services, or O.S.S. This is a far reaching organization that is just in its infancy. There was a lot of intelligence being developed, but it all resided in each governmental department. Hoover was not going to share a lot of information with the Navy, and the Navy wasn't going to go out of their way to give a lot of their findings to the F.B.I, or anyone else, for that matter. You basically have a bunch of departments competing with one another. Mike, it's crazy! These people are all putting their personal agendas ahead of the best interests of the country. Well, maybe they aren't doing it intentionally, but it surely is the consequence. Bill Donovan has had the President's ear for a while about this, and he finally convinced FDR that he needed more of a centralized intelligence office that can gather information and share it as needed with the most relevant departments. Donovan is heading it up. I am reporting directly into him."

"Wild Bill Donovan?" said Mike. "Wow. They are obviously serious if they are getting him involved." Bill Donovan was a legend within the inner circles of Washington. A decorated World War I hero, he was the recipient of virtually every military award that there was. After the war he became a well-known attorney in New York and dabbled in that state's politics, even making an unsuccessful run for governor.

"Donovan isn't even a democrat, George. Roosevelt must be very unhappy with the intelligence efforts if he is willing to hire someone outside of his own Party."

"Ha! Boy, you can say that again," snorted Parker. "It's just chaos, Mike. Too much bureaucracy, too much politics, and too many personal agendas. The President recognized this and knew that he had to do something about it. To his credit, he wanted the best man period, and Donovan is the best man."

"What does the O.S.S. do? It sounds a bit...clandestine," said Michael.

"That's exactly what it is," replied Parker. "We are tasked with all kinds of things that I can't talk about, but you get the gist of it. We are getting killed – literally – because we are so far behind on the intelligence front. The Brits are well ahead of us, and they are willing to train us and share what has worked for them. This is a different war than the first one. Technology has improved, and not just militarily. We need to get a lot more sophisticated and do it quickly. Churchill is fascinated with all of it, and I have to admit that they are using all of it brilliantly. They have hundreds of experienced people that have been in place well before the war. And they are all over...France, Spain, Poland, the Netherlands, and Switzerland; even right in Germany. And like I said, the Brits are willing to help us get caught up."

"What sort of help?" asked Michael.

"You name it, we're working on it," answered George. "Time is critical on all of this. We will be implementing propaganda strategies, code breaking, setting up spy networks…" he paused here and looked directly at his friend of almost 30 years- "Even dropping our spies behind enemy lines."

Michael caught his glance and the change in tone.

Michael's hand clenched his glass so tightly that he almost broke it. "No!" "No, George!" "You have no right!" George looked at his old friend with sad, somber eyes. After a full minute of silence, George said, "You're right, Mike. I don't have the right to ask you. But I am not the one asking. This is an operation that has been approved by the President himself. It will directly impact the war and the results of the war. It will save hundreds of thousands of lives if it is successful, and it will cost hundreds of thousands of lives if it is not. We will likely lose the war if we fail."

Michael stood and walked to the windows. "What in the world could be so important to the war?" he demanded.

"I cannot tell you. What I can tell you is that Ireland is neutral, and we need someone of Irish descent who can pass for a man who has lived in Ireland. And I can tell you that we do have an asset on the ground to assist him. That is all that I can tell you about this mission. Frankly, I have already told you more than I should have. The country will forever be in your debt, Mike. And we know that yours is not the only family to have suffered a cruel, inexplicable tragedy. It seems like the whole city has those gold stars on every door, and the war is not even a year old."

Michael stayed at the window so his friend wouldn't see the tears forming in his eyes. After a minute, he said softly, "Georgie, what are his chances of coming back?"

There was a pause equal to the previous one before his friend answered. "You know that I can't lie to you, Mike. It's probably 50%. But I can assure you of one thing. Given that I am the officer assigned to this case, I will do everything in my power to get him home safely. He's your son, and he's my godson. I wish there was some other way…"

The two men said nothing. Mike was processing all of it, and his old friend knew that it was best to give him time to do so. Michael finally turned to George. "I know that I don't have a say in any of this. He is already serving his country and I am immensely proud of him for that. You didn't have to come all this way to tell me this. You could have just contacted him directly. He's over in Europe now anyway. Thank you, Georgie."

For only the second time in ten years, George Parker teared up as he shook hands with his old friend. "I'll be in touch," he said, as he turned to leave. Michael Sweeney merely nodded as he stared out the window. He had to once again turn away from his friend for the same reason that his friend had turned from him.

Later that night, as they lay in bed, Maggie expressed disappointment in missing George. She had been shopping downtown. She asked her husband what George had wanted to see him about. "Oh, he was just in town on some F.B.I. business and wanted to check in on me," said Michael. He was thankful that Maggie couldn't see his face in the dark. But she didn't need to. Somehow, Maggie knew. She just knew.

CHAPTER 10

November 12, 1942

The tall young man with his father's bright blue eyes and athletic build found himself with a rare few minutes to relax. Frank Sweeney sat in the mess hall enjoying a bottle of Coke. His large hands easily wrapped around the bottle of soda, hiding the label. He found himself unconsciously squeezing the bottle like a baseball bat. And of course that brought him back to so many great memories...hitting homeruns down at Lexington Park, catching doubleheaders, and all of the usual dugout and locker room banter that was a part of the game. He knew the Cardinals were looking at him, and the Yankees had also had a couple of scouts come to most games. All of that changed on December 7th of last year. He wondered where all of his teammates were now. Some were undoubtedly in the Pacific theatre, and he knew at least a few were over in Europe now as well. Like him, every single young man enlisted right after Pearl Harbor. The guys were scattered throughout each of the branches of the armed forces. He wondered if any of them had ended up like him – a pilot. This last thought brought him back to present day.

He had just completed his final training on the Spitfire. Most of the American pilots based in England would have to wait for the U.S. built P38 fighter to make it through production. That could be awhile, although no one really knew what an angry country was capable of producing when the need arose. And there certainly was a need. Fighting two different wars in two different parts of the world was unprecedented in modern times. In the meantime, the Spitfire was more than capable. R J Mitchell, the Spitfire's designer, learned his trade during WWI. He was conscious of the fragility of the early planes, and always considered pilot safety in his designs.

Even when designs were optimized for speed, Mitchell never sacrificed his concern for the pilot. At least that's what the blokes told Frank and the other American pilots. The Spitfire proved to be a robust and adaptable design. The problem was that there were not enough qualified pilots in England to fly these planes. Enter the Americans, who lacked planes but had plenty of young men. They not only needed to learn how to fly, but they needed to learn how to fight in a machine that they had no knowledge of and no experience in handling. And one other little detail: none of the pilots had ever experienced combat thousands of feet in the air.

Despite the challenges, the Americans found the training to be first rate. The English knew this plane inside and out, and made sure that the Yanks who were sent over knew it as well as they did. Frank was impressed with the Englishmen's fearless attitude and their use of humor to calm each other's nerves. Although they were understated in their appreciation for the U.S. jumping into the European theatre, the Americans understood that their cousins were a proud people. And having bombs rain on their city night after night tended to harden one's feelings. Given the will of the English and the steel resolve of their Prime Minister, Frank and the other pilots felt that England had a real chance to survive this thing and eventually win it, with America's help, of course.

Frank reflected on how he got here. His story was very similar to most of his fellow pilots. As a matter of fact, for many of the young men from the U.S., this was their first time away from home. Getting to know the English ways and manners took some time, but they eventually caught on. They acquired a taste for tea, and the more formal English way of life. The English people went out of their way to welcome them, putting many of them up in their homes as they learned to fly at the local air bases. Many of the pilots were athletes. Most had played baseball and football. Of course, it took them awhile to understand that the English version of soccer was called football in the country. Frank was excited to finally complete all of the training. A few of his buddies washed out in trying to pass the rigorous testing. They wouldn't be sent home. They would just have to qualify to fly an easier transport plane.

The only things to do in England were to fly and sleep. Given the urgent need for pilots, he was getting a lot more flying in than he was sleep. As much as he enjoyed being in the air, he wasn't the stereotypical flyboy. While most of the other pilots were cocky and talked tough, Frank was quietly confident. He was his father's son, to be sure – not looking for a fight, but always ready, just in case. He knew his capabilities and didn't really feel the need to tell anyone else about them. But if challenged, he would defend himself without hesitation, and do it very well.

As he enjoyed his few minutes of privacy, he read his mail. There was a letter from his sister Katherine. She was the most faithful sibling to write him. Staunchly Irish, she was disappointed that Ireland had decided to remain neutral in the war. She just couldn't understand how the old country would sit this one out, given the stakes. His Mom wrote almost daily, although he might not see the letters for weeks, when they would come in bunches. Occasionally his father would write, or stick a note in the envelope that contained his Mom's letter. The letters from his parents were always different. Mom wrote about what was going on with the family, the weather back home, and the news around the city. Dad wrote mostly about the detective agency with a few lighthearted observations about Frank's siblings. Mom always ended her letters with "I love you." Dad's letters typically ended with. "Keep your head down," or words to that effect.

As busy as he was, he still missed home. People who grow up in Minnesota tend to stay in Minnesota. The Sweeneys were no different. He only heard stories about his grandparents who came over in the 1850's. His dad told him that they couldn't read or write initially, but they worked hard at both and were able to eventually communicate in both ways quite well. Still, they must have done a lot of things right. Michael Sweeney sure turned out well.

The different ethnicities in the Twin Cities tended to stay within their own circles. Even the Catholic churches reflected these unique pockets. St. Michael's and St. Joseph's were the Irish churches; St. Matthew's was the German church, St. Louis was the French church, and St. Stanislav ministered to the Poles. Each church had a grade school attached to it, and the nuns and priests were very much involved with the kids. Summers were spent on the family farm in South St. Paul. Dad and his siblings all contributed to keeping it up, and Frank and his cousins all pulled farm duty all summer long. While the days were long and the work extensive, they all loved pulling together to keep the farm active and productive.

He had already decided that he would move back to St. Paul after the war. Assuming that he made it back, of course. Unlike most of the other guys, there was no "H.T.H." (Home Town Honey) waiting for him. He was 24, so there was still lots of time. The Sweeney men tended to marry a bit later anyway. Besides, not only was there no one back home that he was serious about, there wasn't anyone back there that he was even particularly interested in. Sure, there had been some opportunities. Frank would get dragged along by his buddies to dances and other social gatherings, but there was no one that really struck his fancy. He wondered if he would just be a bachelor for the rest of his life. In some ways, that sounded all right. But he would be the one who would have to keep the Sweeney name alive.

OPERATION GRAB BAG: A FRANK SWEENEY ADVENTURE

"That will be a topic for another day," thought Frank.

He loved to fish. When he was a boy, the family would sneak off to Poplar Lake, a small lake in western Wisconsin about an hour's drive from St. Paul. When he was older he would borrow the car on a Saturday and head up there with a couple of buddies and catch northern pike, bass, crappie, and sunfish. His dad was more of the hunting type, often going for small game in South Dakota. But he had wonderful memories of fishing with his dad and Jack. Jack. It was ten years ago now, wasn't it? He flashed back in time to that day. He remembered being told by his teacher Miss Pettigrew to go home, even though it was only 1:30PM. When he asked why, he was told to just put on his coat and hurry. He made his way home and, as he opened the front door, he saw something that he had never seen before or since. He saw his father on his knees, wailing into the couch. His mother was standing over his father, sobbing into her hands. Frank made himself think about something else. But he kept coming back to that day and the days that immediately followed. Death had come to the Sweeney household in a very cruel way. He had never seen so many people in one place than when the funeral was held at the St. Paul Cathedral. Police cars were everywhere. The mayor of the city came to the funeral. Even Governor Olson attended. As is the case with so many tragedies, everyone was extremely supportive for the first couple of weeks. And then, well, life re-appeared. People got busy and stopped calling. Others weren't sure what to do or say, so they said and did nothing. His mother and father rarely mentioned Jack after the funeral. It was simply too painful. And it was the Irish way.

Frank poured himself into sports. Consciously or unconsciously, he wanted to give his parents something – or someone – to be excited about. It was his way of coping, and helping his family cope. He went on to be a three sport star at Cretin High School in St. Paul. His favorite sport was baseball. He was an excellent catcher and dreamed as a child, as most boys do, of playing in the major leagues someday. After high school he went on to play baseball at the University of Minnesota and even played for the St. Paul Saints, a minor league team. After that, he went to work for his dad's detective agency, escorting and guarding the armored cars to and from banks. He enjoyed the job immensely, even if his dad made sure that there were extra guards involved on every run that Frank made. When the war broke out in December of last year, he was one of the first to enlist. His father asked him to wait, but Frank and his father both knew that it was a wasted request. Within weeks of enlisting, he was sent to Fort Bragg, where the Army Air Force was based. While there, he learned the basics of flying. The training was rudimentary, but at least he got a few hours under his belt.

After a couple of months, he was shipped over to England, where he began training in earnest on the Spitfire seven days a week, eight hours a day.

His thoughts drifted back to Jack. Jack would be 36 now? "Yes, that must be right," he mumbled to himself. "I wonder what he would look like now. He was sure sweet on Kathleen." Frank smiled, wistfully. "I'm glad that we embraced her into the family. They would have had a few kids by now."

He was lost in thought as he continued to ponder the what-ifs that would inevitably enter his mind when he thought of his brother…

"Hey Frank? You OK? Frank?" Frank looked up to see Len Guerra, one of the other pilots. "Hey Frankie, a penny for your thoughts! You looked like you were dreaming with your eyes wide open!"

"Sorry, Len. I guess my mind was somewhere else."

"Listen, Frankie, we're heading over to the dance hall. Are you coming? Some band is playing the latest Glen Miller music. Whatta ya say?"

Frank tried to clear his head. "Um…no thanks. I think I'll sit this one out."

"C'mon, Frank. Now that we've tested out, we don't know how long it will be until we're doing real missions! This may be the night that you meet the love of your life! I'm telling you, English gals go for the Irish lads, especially the 6'1, 180 pound guy with the dark wavy hair and blue eyes to match."

Frank chuckled. "Len, up until the physical description, I thought you were describing yourself."

Len was 5'9 with dark hair and a permanent five o'clock shadow. He could afford to lose a few pounds. Len was from Wantagh, New York. "Oh, that's really funny, Frankie! You ought to tour with Hope and Crosby! Come on, let's go out. All of the boys are going. It will do you some good."

"No soap, Pal. I have some letters to write and then I'm hitting the sack early."

"Suit yourself, pretty boy. But don't blame me when I invite you to my wedding, and the bride is the girl that I met tonight."

"Keep dreaming, Len."

With that, Len Guerra left. Frank would never see him again.

CHAPTER 11

Frank had fallen asleep and was enjoying a dream about playing baseball at Lexington Park in St. Paul. As he was about to swing at a belt high fastball, he felt someone shoving his arm. He couldn't swing because now someone was really rocking him. He couldn't stay in his stance. Who was doing that? Then he started to hear a voice: "Get up! Captain Sweeney! Get up!"

He opened his eyes to a corporal who was trying desperately to wake him. Frank came to and jumped out of bed, already getting into his flight suit. "What are we doing, Corporal?"

"I don't know, sir, but the Colonel told me to get you up immediately. "He wants to see you on the double."

Colonel John McKenzie was a marvel in this man's Army Airforce. A tall Texan with deep brown puppy dog eyes, he spoke quietly but confidently and just didn't fit the stereotype of an officer. He never raised his voice, nor did anyone ever hear him cuss. His men loved him and, just as important, respected him. He was a father figure to each of them, and they knew that he would always be straight and fair with them. But he was also tough. He rode his men hard in preparing them for battle. If one of the planes flew out of formation, the entire squadron would have to go back up. If another missed its target on a practice run, everyone would be sent back out until it was all done properly and proficiently. And McKenzie himself would go up with them, just to show them that he was willing to work just as hard as they were. As Frank hurried to the Colonel's office, he kept wondering what all of this was about. He knocked on the door and heard the familiar voice say, "Enter!" As Frank opened the door, he saw

OPERATION GRAB BAG: A FRANK SWEENEY ADVENTURE

McKenzie sitting at his desk with a pipe in his mouth, finishing his signature on a document.

"Captain," smiled McKenzie, "You better get ready on the double. I'm told that you have a very important guest that you have to meet tomorrow morning in London. And given that we can't fly you there, Corporal Gillstrom will be driving you. It's about 5 hours to London from here on a good night, so you better get a move on. The corporal is securing a jeep as we speak."

Frank looked at the Colonel, confused and still trying to wake up. "Sir, may I ask who it is and what this is about?" Colonel McKenzie looked at him with his tired eyes, and said. "You can ask, but I can't tell you a thing. I'm as in the dark on this as you are. There are only two people who know about this in all of England and that is the two of us. Gillstrom just knows that you are heading to London for some classroom training for targeting German cargo ships. No one is to know anything other than that. Frank, I'll be honest with you. It sounds like someone high up is pulling some strings here. But that is only speculation on my part. Good luck, son."

"Colonel, I...thank you for everything that you have taught me here. I don't know how I ever could have made it here if it hadn't been for you and the incredible training-"

McKenzie interrupted him: You are going to make one heckuva pilot, Captain. Best of luck and Godspeed." With a confused look on his face, Frank nodded to the Colonel and saluted. Colonel John McKenzie saluted back and tried his best to look reassuring. "Lord, protect that boy," he prayed. With that, Frank made his way out of McKenzie's office and into the war.

CHAPTER 12

Leigh awoke with a start. She hadn't been sleeping very well lately. Living in Germany was…different. Augsburg was about as different from Ireland as one could imagine. Her father announced five years ago that he was moving to Germany to assist an old friend, and he insisted that Leigh move with him. They had decided to make an adventure out of it. He worked long hours at a research facility and she taught English to German school children. These weren't just any children, however; they were the children of some of the most powerful men in all of the Third Reich. It was a special school deemed necessary by Himmler, who believed that the next generation should be fluent in English, because the Nazi Party would need to understand their future captives' native tongue.

Because of her father's reputation and her excellent tutelage, Leigh and Edwin were treated almost like royalty in German social circles. Many weekends were spent socializing with local political figures and wealthy industrialists. But when the war broke out, things became much more serious. The parties became more…purposeful. And the attendees changed. She found herself socializing more with the local military elite. The local politicians had either been neutralized or shipped off into military service. Leigh noticed her father working more and more hours. The only good news was that most of the Allies' focus (at least until now) was taking place in the northern cities in Germany. Her father never talked about what he was working on, but she was beginning to piece a few things together. It was obviously something important, given his long hours at the laboratory. And it must certainly be aviation related, otherwise why would the Germans have wanted him so badly? Just as she had done from her early years with her mother every morning, Leigh slipped out of her bed and onto her knees. She spent a few minutes praying...she prayed for strength for the day; she prayed for her father and God's safekeeping of him; she prayed for Jimmy, as she did every day, that by some miracle he might still be alive. She prayed for each of her students. Generally, they were kind and sweet, just like the children of Ireland. And she prayed for the war. Specifically, for the allies to do all they could to defeat the very fathers of the children she taught.

CHAPTER 13

Frank's all night drive to London was uneventful. He and Corporal Gillstrom made small talk for part of the trip, but the jeep wasn't exactly conducive to a deep conversation. It wasn't conducive to a cozy snooze, either, but Frank tried, nonetheless. Despite Corporal Gillstrom taking a couple of wrong turns that Frank pretended not to notice, they arrived in London around 5:30AM. As Gillstrom navigated to the hotel, he told Frank that Colonel McKenzie had ordered that Frank arrive in the city in street clothes. Being that it was still dark, Frank changed right in the jeep. He neatly folded his uniform and put it carefully into a small suitcase that he had brought. He was told that there would be a room waiting for him at the hotel.

Gillstrom stopped at a corner. Confused, Frank said, "Why are you stopping, Corporal? I don't see any hotel." The corporal didn't meet the captain's eyes. He said, "Sir, my orders are to drop you off a couple of blocks from the hotel. It is straight down this street. It's only a 5 minute walk. When you get into the hotel, please go to the front desk and identify yourself by the name in your bag as part of your new I.D. At the bottom of your bag, you will find your identification. You may want to familiarize yourself with it before you register. You are to ask for your room and specify that you want to stay in room 301. Everything will be in order."

When he reached for his bag that contained his uniform, Gillstrom said, "No need for that, Captain. Colonel McKenzie's orders."

Frank stared at Gillstrom. "No uniform? A new I.D.? And you drop a superior officer two blocks from his intended dwelling? What's going on here, Corporal?"

"Sir, I don't know. I was told to ask no questions and to answer no questions. I couldn't even tell you what your I.D. says, because I was told not to look at it. I have followed Colonel McKenzie's orders to the letter."

They sat in silence for a full minute as Frank collected his thoughts. Finally, he said, "Thanks for the lift, Corporal."

"Good luck, Captain." Frank could see genuine concern in the man's face. He wondered if Ramsey saw that same look when he looked into Frank's face.

CHAPTER 14

The Burlington Hotel was a fairly nondescript dwelling. One of the older hotels in London, it was decorated with black drapes – the blackouts were a nightly occurrence in the city these days – and there was no doorman or concierge. They were all fighting the war.

After checking in under an alias, George Parker waited in room 305. While it would be great to see Frank, he desperately wished that it could be under different circumstances. He had argued with himself over this assignment from the moment that Donovan sprung it on him. Bill Donovan was a lot of things. He was certifiably brilliant. He had built his law firm in New York into an international powerhouse. He was a decorated war hero from the Great War. No one could ever question his patriotism. And when Donovan had presented his vision for espionage and intelligence to the president, those few people in the know were not surprised that Roosevelt, a liberal, had insisted that Donovan, a conservative, be tapped for the top job. George took some solace in the fact that the war itself had certainly united the country.

Within weeks of his appointment, Donovan had pulled George into his office for a discussion around a mission that Donovan had been kicking around. After hearing him out, George had agreed, albeit reluctantly, that it could very well work. And as difficult as it was to think objectively about this, George also knew the perfect man for the job. Even then, he wrestled with whether or not to bring it to Donovan. "This job is going to kill me," he muttered to himself.

OPERATION GRAB BAG: A FRANK SWEENEY ADVENTURE

So secret was this new organization that only five people of any notoriety knew about it: Roosevelt, J. Edgar Hoover, the Director of the F.B.I., General George C. Marshall, the Army Chief of Staff, and Admiral Edward Stark, Marshall's counterpart in the Navy. And, of course, Donovan himself. George could only imagine how the meeting went between these five men. They would have needed a ballroom to hold all of their egos. But to his credit, Roosevelt corralled each of them and told them to line up under this, because it was truly in the country's best interest. Donovan confided to George: "You should have seen Hoover's face when Roosevelt told him that we would be tapping into the F.B.I. for the initial recruits!" "Wild Bill," as he was known, alternated between a scornful laugh and outright rage as he told the story to George.

The sleeper was Stark, because most of the intelligence work that had been done had reported into the Navy until now. A man of impeccable character, Stark vowed his cooperation from the beginning. And rather quickly after that, each of the men had agreed to play ball. Perhaps that was an indication of the stakes in all of this. It is difficult enough to fight one enemy on foreign soil. But to have two wars – two very different wars with two very different enemies – that would tax any nation, and in this regard the U.S. would be no exception. This was why George landed where he did with the decision. At the end of the day, the nation's survival was at stake, and the country needed the very best men and women available to secure victory. George knew that his godson would be uniquely qualified. As he was flying back from St. Paul to Washington to pick up Donovan for their flight to London, George reflected on his conversation with his good friend Mike. He was initially surprised that his former partner didn't fight him more on his plan. But as he thought about it, he realized that Mike Sweeney had quickly ascertained the stakes as well. Mike knew that his son's godfather – Mike's closest friend - would not put Frank at risk unless there was something of critical importance to the country. And Mike Sweeney was every bit as much a patriot as he was.

CHAPTER 15

Burghoffs was the largest night club in Augsburg. With over one hundred tables and a huge dance floor, it was the place to be on weekends for many of the city's citizens who wanted good food and a place to dance. Most of the military command frequented the establishment on a regular basis as well.

"Herr Conway! How good to see you again!"

Colonel von Greim was in full character tonight, thought Edwin. "I must play along! I must not betray my utter disdain for this man," he told himself as von Greim approached. "Hello Colonel," said Edwin, doing his best to sound warm.

"And Fraulein Conway, what a pleasure it is to see you again!" he practically screamed.

Leigh, trying to hide her discomfort, forced a smile and nodded, "Colonel."

"Edwin," said von Greim, "How is it that such a beautiful young woman remains unattached? Did you have her hiding back in Ireland her whole life?"

Edwin kept his pasted smile on his face and said, "Leigh is very dedicated to her work. Her teaching position here keeps her quite busy."

"Well then, we should do something about that. Fraulein, may I have this dance?" Von Greim dramatically bowed and extended his hand.

Leigh gave her father a "Please get me out of this" look, but he subtly shook his head. "Why, thank you, Colonel. It would be my pleasure." And off they went, waltzing to some unbearable German tune.

"You dance beautifully, Fraulein."

"Please, call me Leigh."

"Very well. "Tell me, Leigh, do you like it here in Germany?"

"It is very different than Ireland, Colonel. But I think the differences between people in different countries are sometimes exaggerated. I taught children from Ireland and now I am teaching children in Germany, and I see many more similarities than I do differences."

"That is interesting, Frau – er…Leigh. With your country being neutral in this war, I would think that you would have noticed more differences."

"How so, Colonel?"

"Well, Ireland's children – and I mean no disrespect here – have no real common goal to unite them. They are just living for today with no eye toward the future. Take the children that you and people like Fraulein Eggold teach. They are naturally gifted. In fact, all of Germany's children have a great future to anticipate. Indeed, great things will be in store for them as they grow. They have the most brilliant man in the world as their leader, and they are superior in virtually every way to other children around the world. Our children will be raised in the finest schools. They have been pre-ordained for greatness, bred for greatness. Don't you see? When we win this war, our children will grow up to lead every other nation in the world! That is why it is important for them to learn other languages at an early age. They must be prepared for the day that they will be sent out to lead all of the other colonies of Germany."

Leigh was puzzled by his comments but decided to keep her reply neutral. "That is certainly a very interesting perspective, Colonel. I have to say that I have found the German children that I am teaching to be, for the most part, kind and considerate. And may I remind you that they are just children. I teach the six and seven year olds. They are excited to learn and are eager to please."

"Oh, but Leigh you are making my point for me. The children you teach are too young yet. Of course we want them this way when they are young. But look at the children who are finishing their high school years, as you call them. These German students are much, much different than the little children that you teach. After about their fourth year of school, that is when we begin to really shape them. We want them to feel good and trust their teachers – like you – when they are little, so that when we get them to the more formative years, the trust will have already been established. It makes for a much easier transition for them."

"What sort of transition?"

"The transition to them understanding that they are part of a very special race that has a very special destiny."

"I can see I the teacher have much to learn about Germany, Colonel."

"Yes. Yes you do, Leigh, but don't worry. "I will help you," beamed von Greim.

After their dance, von Greim led Leigh back to her father's table. "Thank you, Leigh, for a wonderful waltz," said von Greim, bowing.

"Why, thank you, Colonel," said Leigh, doing her best to smile.

After they had made their way back to the table, von Greim declared, "Edwin, this young woman you've raised is charming in every way."

To Leigh: "I would consider it an honor to have another dance with you the next time we are together." With that, he reached for her hand and kissed it. Before Leigh could pull her hand back, it was over.

"It would be my pleasure, Colonel."

Later that evening, as Leigh and her father rode the short distance to their home, father asked daughter about her conversation with von Greim. Leigh told him of von Greim's odd comments, including his thoughts about the children that she and the other teachers taught.

"Sounds like pretty standard Nazi philosophy," said Edwin.

Leigh looked skeptical. "Maybe he was just confused," she said.

"How so?"

"Well, he mentioned another teacher at my school. Her name was "Fraulein Eggold, I think. But the thing is, there is no Fraulein Eggold at my school. He must have been thinking of some other school."

They were at the top of the steps and ready to enter their home. Edwin stopped in his tracks. "What is it, Dad?" Asked Leigh.

"Leigh," said, Edwin, "I really don't want you to spend any more time with Colonel von Greim."

"Dad, I don't think you have anything to really worry about," said Leigh.

"Please, Leigh. Just stay away from him."

Leigh looked at her father, and said, "He asked me to lunch tomorrow, and I said yes."

"Yes," said Edwin, wearily. "I thought he might do that. Just don't let on about Fraulein Eggold, or whatever her name is."

"Why?" asked Leigh. "Just please, do as I say. And stay away from him. He has to be almost double your age." Leigh took her father's arm in hers. "Dad, please don't worry. I can handle myself."

After forcing himself to remain calm, Edwin said, "Let's talk about it tomorrow. We both need to get some sleep."

CHAPTER 16

Frank made his way up to room 301. He was exhausted but on edge, mainly because he had no idea why he had been brought here. He ordered some coffee and scones and sat on his bed, fighting the yawns. Within ten minutes his breakfast arrived and he kicked himself for not ordering eggs or something more filling. On the other hand, he reminded himself, there was a war on, so eggs were being rationed anyway.

The anticipated knock came about an hour later. As he made his way over to answer the door, it flung open. He was not anticipating seeing the face that was smiling at him.

"Uncle George! What? What are you doing here?" The space between them closed quickly and both men shook hands vigorously.

"Hello, Frank! How are you? You look great!"

"Uncle George! I just can't believe it! Never in a million years did I expect to see you here!"

"Well, lad, in war there are a lot of things that we don't expect to see. Speaking of which, I just saw your Dad the other day, if you can believe it."

"You did?" cried Frank. "How is he? Did you see Mom, too? And Katherine? And Evvie?" "No, unfortunately. I was there on business and wanted to just stop by quickly and say hello."

"How is Dad? Is he doing all right? I worry about him. He's worked so hard at the detective bureau. He never takes a day off. I just want him to be able to enjoy things now."

On the outside, George smiled at him. On the inside, he wanted to cry. "Here is this fine young man in a war and about to put his life on the line, and he is worried about his father. Where do we find such young men?" he wondered.

"I'm telling you, Frank, he looked as healthy as a horse to me," said George. He hesitated. "I told him that I was on my way over to Europe to see you."

"Now that's what I mean, Uncle George. What's an F.B.I. man want with me? I know that I didn't bootleg any liquor, and I promise you that I cut all ties to the Irish gangs in St. Paul. All right, I confess. I did take a coke from the ice box when I was eight and didn't tell my folks," laughed Frank.

"Unfortunately, Frank, it's nothing like that." He shifted gears and they talked about pleasantries for the next several minutes, sharing memories and laughs.

"You know, it was ten years ago the other day, Uncle George."

"Yes, I know. I never forget the anniversary. And I will never forget that day," he said quietly. "Your brother died a hero, and I know that you are very proud of him."

They sat in silence for several seconds, both lost in their own thoughts. One thinking about the past, and the other thinking about the immediate future. With that, George slapped his hands on his knees and stood.

"You get a few hours of shuteye. That ride all night couldn't have been pleasant. I have someone that I want you to meet over lunch. I've got some meetings here this morning, and I'll stop back in right at 1:00PM, OK?"

"That'd be swell, Uncle George. To be honest, I'm exhausted and could use the sleep."

With another firm handshake, the two men said goodbye, both knowing that in a few hours the conversation would be short of pleasantries.

CHAPTER 17

It was a glorious Sunday afternoon and after church, Leigh and her father decided to walk to town for a late lunch.

Finding a solid church was extremely difficult these days. Too many had been taken over by the Party. And too many of the others had compromised the message of the gospel just so they could stay in the good graces of the Nazis.

"Dad, I'm so glad that Colonel von Greim insisted that I come with you to Germany. It would have been so difficult being apart, especially after Mom and Jimmy…"

"Yes, my dear, I wouldn't have it any other way," said a distracted Edwin.

"What's the matter, Dad?"

"Things are getting complicated." "Between von Greim making passes at you and this project that I'm on, I'm not sure where things will end up," said Edwin.

"What about the project?" asked Leigh

"I'm struggling with it, lassie. I love working with Herr Lippisch. He is brilliant and we collaborate very well together. But I just don't know if I can trust him anymore. I am concerned that we are working on something that can certainly be used for good, but it could also be used to change the outcome of the war. And I concluded a long time ago that Germany winning this war would be the end of freedom everywhere."

"Dad, you mustn't talk that way!"

"You're right. But I can talk this way with my daughter."

He paused as he considered his next words carefully. "Leigh, I think it best that we not discuss anything of any substance while we are in our home. And please don't discuss anything on the phone. The phones are probably tapped. I've tested this theory on a couple of occasions and the Nazis have slipped up recently, thereby confirming my suspicions."

Leigh's eyes betrayed her surprise. "How, Dad? What makes you think that?"

"The other night you mentioned a Fraulein Eggold that is a teacher. You said that von Greim must have been confused. He wasn't confused. I was at home the other night and the phone rang. It was Pastor Hanke from church. He asked how you were doing and I told him that you were out with another teacher from your school whose name was Fraulein Eggold. Von Greim or one of his goons must have been listening in on our conversation. Do you see now, Leigh?"

"Yes, I do. You made up the name as a test to see if anyone was listening in on our calls, and they obviously were..." Leigh's voice trailed off.

"Actually, we don't know if our phone line is tapped or if they have hidden microphones in our home. Or both! I also think someone went through my briefcase at home the other night. Things seemed a bit out of place. At the very least, they would have at least heard my end of the phone conversation, so from now on we should assume that they have done both," said Edwin.

"Dad, what is going on? This is crazy! I've never heard of such a thing!"

"Unfortunately, this tells you how important this project is to the Nazis. For now, we will continue to play their game their way. But we must be very, very careful. Trust no one, Leigh! You will be tested in every social and professional circle. This is why it is imperative that you not know anything more about this project. You can't divulge what you don't know."

"My dear father, I am not worried about me. But I am worried about you! What will happen to you if the war efforts are not successful for Germany?"

Edwin didn't hesitate in his response. It was evident to Leigh that he had really taken time to think all of this through.

He looked at his daughter and said in a matter of fact tone: "There will be more pressure to get this project completed sooner. And I will need to figure out ways to ensure its failure or at least delay it. But Leigh, there's something...."

He stopped in mid-sentence as he spotted von Greim walking toward them.

"Good afternoon, Herr Conway! And good afternoon to you, Leigh!" von Greim was his usual plastic self.

"Good afternoon, Colonel von Greim," said Edwin evenly.

Von Greim ignored him and was staring at Leigh.

"What a splendid lunch we had the other day, did we not?" he cried.

"It was lovely, Colonel," answered Leigh. "I had a wonderful time."

"I'm so glad," replied von Greim. "I would love to finish our conversation about education in the Fatherland sometime, Frauler...Leigh."

"I would enjoy that as well."

"Perhaps at our next party?" asked von Greim.

"I look forward to it, Colonel."

"Well then. I hope it will be soon. Good day to you both!" Von Greim tipped his cap (no Heil Hitler today?) and continued by them.

When he was out of earshot, Edwin looked at Leigh and asked, "Why did you respond to him in that way?"

Leigh smiled at her father. "There's an old saying, Father. Keep your friends close and your enemies closer."

"Leigh," Edwin intoned, "This is no trite matter. These Nazis are ruthless thugs. Please do not do anything to encourage them!"

"Dad, I promise that I won't do anything foolish. But I think it would be foolish not to try to get information out of von Greim. It can only help you."

Edwin reluctantly nodded. "Just be very, very careful. Don't ever get caught alone with him out of my sight."

"Yes sir," she smiled.

CHAPTER 18

At exactly 1:00PM George Parker knocked on Frank's door. Frank asked who it was and, upon recognizing his uncle's voice, opened the door. Gone was the smile that Parker wore only a few hours earlier.

"Come down to room 305 in five minutes, lad."

"OK, Uncle George," replied Frank.

Five minutes later Frank approached room 305. As he was about to knock, the door opened and his uncle ushered him into the suite. It was a well-appointed chamber, with a full dining room, complete with fireplace and couches. Seated in the corner of the suite in an overstuffed leather chair was a distinguished looking gentleman with silver hair and a relaxed smile on his face. His broad shoulders reflected a man who had kept himself in shape over the years. He was smoking a cigar and had a drink in his other hand. Before Frank could say anything, Parker told him to have a seat.

"Hello, Captain," said the older gentleman.

"Good afternoon, sir," Frank responded. He knew the face but couldn't place him. He knew that this man was somewhat famous...

"We're sorry to make you travel all night. But this is something that really couldn't wait."

"Yes sir," said Frank, absently. He continued to stare at the man in order to place him.

"Frank," interrupted Parker, "I don't believe you have met Mr. Donovan. Mr. William Donovan."

"Donovan? The decorated war hero and attorney?" asked Frank, as he came to his feet.

"I'm afraid that you are correct," said Donovan. "Although the war hero stuff is a bit overstated, if you ask me."

Frank walked over to him and extended his hand. "It's an honor, sir."

"The honor is all mine, son," said Donovan. "Sit back down, Frank."

"Thank you, sir."

Donovan nodded to Parker, and the newly appointed O.S.S. man began by telling Frank that everything that they were going to discuss was top secret.

"There are questions that you may have that we will choose not to answer, Frank. You're just going to have to trust us, that we know what is best."

Frank nodded.

"Frank, the code name for this mission is "Operation Grab Bag." This assignment is so sensitive that there are only three people who know about it, and you are looking at two of them."

Frank took a breath as his eyes moved from Parker to Donovan, and then back to Parker again. "All right," he said.

Parker looked at his godson and smiled, albeit nervously.

He then continued, "It's come to our attention that the Germans are developing some sort of new technology to give them a significant advantage over our Army Air Force. We have almost no details. We don't know how far along their process is, or the number of resources that they have dedicated to it. We don't know what exactly they are doing with whatever technology that they have developed. We do know that they have two brilliant minds working full time on it."

Parker removed a picture from a manila folder and handed it to Frank.

"We know that one of them is Alexander Lippisch, a world renowned aircraft designer. He is German and is working for the Nazis very close to a Messerschmitt factory and airfield near Augsburg. In fact, this project is being conducted on the other side of the airfield, across the runways from the Messerschmitt factory. So on one side of the airport you have the inventory and assembly facility for Messerschmitt, and on the other side you have this secret facility that we know so little about. The building and grounds are not particularly well protected and it certainly isn't a high visibility research facility. Apparently they have subscribed to the idea that keeping it low key will not attract a lot of attention. Or bombs."

"But we haven't even begun bombing in the southern cities," observed Frank.

Donovan: "That's right. We haven't been able to put together consistently successful bombing raids anywhere in Germany. Yet. But Curtis LeMay is going to figure that out. He is one tough guy for someone who isn't Irish," smiled Donovan.

"Yes Sir, General LeMay is someone that we all believe in. If anyone will figure it out, it's him," said Frank. LeMay was a first rate General and aviator. He was in the process of overseeing the command of America's air efforts in the European theatre.

George gave him a minute to process all of this, and then proceeded. "We don't know if Lippisch is a Nazi or if he is being forced to work for them. He appears to be a purist in the sense that he just loves aviation."

Donovan jumped in: "Messerschmitt himself is very close to the Nazis. As a matter of fact, Göring saved him. Basically resurrected his career back in the early to mid '30's. What really saved him was the successful production of the BF109, the" –

"The best fighter plane in the war." Frank finished. Then: "Sorry, sir."

Donovan didn't even notice. "Yes, unfortunately that is an accurate statement, lad," replied Donovan. "He not only created it, but managed to figure out production on a mass scale. We are fairly confident that they are using slave labor in some of the concentration camps not far from Augsburg."

"Concentration camps?" asked Frank.

"Son, this is also confidential. Although why our government is choosing to keep this quiet is beyond me," said Donovan, angrily. "The Germans are systematically removing the Jews from their society."

"'Removing?' What do you mean by 'removing,' sir?"

Now it was Parker's turn. "It means that they are shipping them to these camps to work in slave labor. The Jews are being put to work building ammunition, guns, planes, tanks, and anything else the Germans need. Those that are too weak to work or are mentally incapable are killed. Lined up and shot, or even worse. Frank, it is absolute madness. It's barbaric!"

Parker had to regain his composure quickly. The look on Frank's face was complete shock. Not only was none of this known back home, no one in the military even knew about it.

"Why are we not telling our citizens about this?" he asked.

Donovan, now: "There is a concern that the German citizenry in America will be targeted or attacked by their fellow Americans. We can't afford any civil unrest. At least that's what those worthless bureaucrats are spouting in Washington," he said bitterly.

It was very clear to Frank that Donovan was not supportive of this policy. "No wonder his men followed him into battle so enthusiastically," thought Frank. "This guy is a man's man. I bet all of the pencil pushers back there drive him batty."

Donovan made a concerted effort to move on. "But enough on Messerschmitt. The guy is brilliant and clearly is owned by the Nazis. George, tell him about our target."

Parker slid Frank the envelope. He opened it to see several pictures of a middle aged man. George waited for Frank to study the photographs.

He then continued, "The other gentleman is of more interest to us. His name is Edwin Conway, and, as his name implies, he is Irish. He is originally from a small town in south central Ireland, in an area called Cork. He is a widower, having lost his wife several years ago. They had two children – Jimmy, their son, disappeared a few years ago and is presumed dead. Edwin has a daughter who lives with him in Germany. There is a picture of her in the envelope somewhere."

Frank found the photo and realized that he was looking at the most beautiful girl that he had ever seen. It must have been taken secretly, because she was looking well off the camera in it.

He made himself focus back on what George Parker was saying: "Conway and Lippisch go back many years, having met at a consortium that featured one of the Wright brothers as the main speaker. Both men share a love of aviation and have wanted to work together for years. There is a tremendous amount of mutual respect between the two men. Lippisch is the design expert and Conway is the engine expert. We have comparable design capabilities in the states but we are woefully behind in engine performance and technology."

Frank studied the pictures carefully, because he knew that he would not be taking the pictures out of the room.

OPERATION GRAB BAG: A FRANK SWEENEY ADVENTURE

"We need to find out everything we can about this project. The war's outcome may ride on this, Frank. We want you to work undercover as a journalist. As you know, Ireland is officially neutral as far as the war goes, but we know that behind the scenes, they are very supportive of the Allies."

Donovan jumped in. "We have established a cover for you with the Irish Independent, one of the oldest newspapers in Ireland. I know the editor personally. The Nazis are desperate for some positive press and will likely see this as a chance to spread more propaganda to Ireland, Scotland and even England. One of their goals is to turn the Irish against the English. Lord knows that such a goal is well within the realm of possibilities."

Frank couldn't help himself. He snuck another look at the Conway girl.

Parker continued, "Your name will be Frank McGuire, and you will get paid to cover the local and international news."

"How much can I tell you through writing an article?" asked Frank.

"You'd be surprised, lad," smiled Donovan.

"We will establish certain trigger words," explained Parker. "The first letter of every second word at the start of the paragraph will be the code. We will then accumulate the letters in each of the words in each of the paragraphs to see what words you are communicating to us. This code is simple but it will work. You'll be writing a few times a week, with a feature on Sundays. Obviously, shorter is better. You can't write full sentences. That will have to suffice for now. There will be days when you might not have anything new to say, so if the message is jumbled, then we'll know that you are taking a day off. But don't waste time, Frank. This is a very pressing matter. At a minimum, we want to know what this special project is. That's job one. Job two is to get Edwin Conway out of the country and either back to Ireland or directly here to London. We will be content with either. We want to debrief him and get all of the information that we can from him about this special project and any future developments in aviation. And we want him to come and work for us. We need him desperately on our side."

"Uncle George, no disrespect here, but you expect me to just waltz into Germany on my own and do this?"

"Yes, Frank, we do. Look, you were handpicked. We need someone who is not only Irish but looks Irish and acts Irish. Since Ireland is sitting the war out, this is the perfect cover. We need someone who could pass as a writer. Your writing skills are exceptional. And we wanted a pilot, because we needed someone who would understand the technical jargon of what the Jerrys are working on. There just aren't a lot of young men that fit all three of these qualifications. I've known you since the day you were born, lad. Believe me, if there was someone else – anyone else – I would have picked him rather than you." Parker choked up as he said this last sentence.

There was silence in the room for a full minute. Frank's mind raced. Donovan and Parker let him process all of it.

"Do you want me to try to sabotage whatever it is that they are working on?"

"Yes, of course. But if you have to choose between the two, Conway is the bigger mission. Getting him off of the project will serve as a big enough delay. Do not jeopardize the bigger mission. The main mission is critical. If we get Conway, we can get a full debriefing from him as to what the technology is. Once we know what the technology is and how and when they plan to use it, we can develop a plan to blow it up. That can come later. But mission one is to get him out of there. And mission two is to slow down whatever they are working on. In that order."

After another prolonged silence, Frank finally asked the question that no one wanted to hear: "What if I can't get Conway out of the country? What if he refuses to go, or I can't figure out a good escape route?"

It was Donovan who answered. "Edwin Conway will either come with you willingly or by force. We desperately need his knowledge and expertise on our side." Donovan now moved toward the end of his chair. His next words were spoken slowly but forcefully, with no room for misinterpretation: "But if you cannot get him out with you, then he must not leave Germany alive. Get as much information as you can from him first. Am I clear, Captain?"

Frank tried to hide his shock but he did a poor job of it. Slowly his eyes met Donovan's. "Yes, sir" he replied quietly.

Parker looked at Donovan, and the older man gave the slightest nod. Parker said, "Frank, I am going to tell you one more thing. We do have an asset on the ground in Germany. But I am not going to tell you who it is. If you are caught, then you won't be able to give the Nazis a name."

"How will I contact this fellow?" asked Frank. Parker and Donovan looked at each other awkwardly. Frank wasn't sure, but he thought that he picked up on a very subtle shake of Donovan's head. After a moment's hesitation, Parker decided to plow forward. "Honestly? We aren't completely sure. We have not heard from this individual for a while. We do have a way to communicate back and forth, but we will do so only with this particular individual. We cannot open up this same capability to you because then if either one of you are caught, we risk blowing the whole thing. After a while, if we think it is safe, we will open up this channel to both of you. But for now, our communication with you is one way – you to us. Is that understood?"

"Yes, sir."

"Several weeks ago we had communicated the contact method for you two to connect. Look for someone who asks you if you are related to Jack McGuire."

"Who's Jack McGuire?," asked Frank.

"Exactly," said Parker. "Your answer will be, "No, but I have a cousin named Thomas McGuire." Your code name will be Lion. Your contact's code name is Owl. When you have found Owl, you can let us know through one of your articles. Tell Owl to contact us through the normal means so we have confirmation from both of you. Owl knows that someone will be coming into Augsburg, but that's it as far as details. So you two will have to work to determine who's who. Sorry, but this is the best that we can do to protect both of you," concluded Parker. "But know one more thing: The only people who know the name of this mission – Operation Grab Bag – are you, Owl, and the two of us. That will ensure that we have no leakage in our information."

Another pause. "We have a ticket for you on a train to Dublin. It's in this briefcase, along with all of your papers, enough money for you, and an Irish passport. Colonel Donovan's friend at the Irish Independent is a man that the Colonel saved in the Great War. This man was raised here in London for the first 15 years of his life and fought for the Irish before settling in Dublin in the early 1920's. He has a great reputation there and only knows that you are on assignment for the Colonel. He is completely trustworthy and has his story down should any of the Germans ask any questions. Which is likely. There are German spies in Ireland who will likely be contacted to check you out. Anyway, he has arranged everything for you and will ensure that you get on a plane for Augsburg shortly after your arrival in Dublin. And, at the risk of stating the obvious, there are S.S. and Gestapo spies all over Augsburg. Trust no one."

Frank thought some more about the entire situation. 24 hours ago he was a pilot in the Army Air Force. Now he was a spy going in undercover to Hitler's Germany. Virtually no contact information. A cover story that he was a newspaperman. And orders to kill a man, if necessary. He was a long way from St. Paul. He wondered how his parents would react if they knew about this.

After a few moments of reflection, he looked somberly at the two men. "Gentlemen, it will be my honor to serve my country in this mission." He handed the envelope back to Parker and stood to shake the men's hands. Donovan rose and came to him. He shook Frank's hand and patted him on the arm, then moved away. Parker came next, holding his hand a moment longer than normal. He looked at Frank with tears beginning to load up his eyes, and said, "I'll be here when you get back."

Frank felt a giant lump in his throat. He swallowed hard. "Uncle George, if I don't make it back, please tell Mom and Dad and the girls that I love them all. It's best that they not know how I…well, you'll figure something out."

Now a tear dropped from Parker's eye and he hugged Frank. His voice cracked as he whispered in his ear, "God be with you, son."

Frank took a deep breath, gave his godfather a pat, stepped back, and faced both men. He came to full attention and saluted. They both returned the salute. Frank turned and walked out of the room, never looking back.

CHAPTER 19

Von Greim sat pensively in his limo as his driver navigated the traffic. Augsburg is the third oldest city in southern Germany. Named after the Roman emperor Augustus, the city is sandwiched by the Lech and Wertach rivers, and actually sits on the Singold River. It is most known for the Augsburg Confession, a declaration of the Lutheran faith by Martin Luther himself that took place in the 1500s. "It is truly a picturesque city," thought von Greim. "It offers the very best of Germany to its inhabitants. Perhaps the Fuhrer will reward me with a vice chancellor role here after the war." But then he came back to reality.

Things weren't going quite so well in Augsburg these days. Even von Greim had to admit this, but only to himself. To actually say it would be construed as disloyal to the Party and therefore to the Fuhrer himself, and von Greim would never say anything against his Fuhrer! Still, things were difficult. The good news was that the production of the BF109s was going quite well. The plane had emerged as the best fighter plane in the war for either side. One had to applaud Willy Messerschmitt for developing such a fast but reliable aerial weapon. The pilots loved flying it because it was lightweight and very maneuverable. But von Greim had nothing to do with the BF109. He could hardly garner any credit for that, other than the fact that the production teams were cranking out hundreds a year. That was because they had slave labor in the concentration camps outside of Augsburg producing many of the parts. No, the secret project was the real prize. Göring kept pressuring him to complete it. "That idiot," he said to himself. Göring knew nothing about aviation. Or almost nothing. Well, certainly less than von Greim. Yet he held the top position in the Luftwaffe, simply because of his long relationship with Hitler himself.

Wouldn't it be wonderful to strap the old fool onto the first prototype of the project and watch him plummet to the ground? "That would certainly guarantee a promotion for me," mused von Greim, not entirely dismissing the idea.

He turned his thoughts to a more pleasant subject: The Conway girl. "She is a beautiful young woman," thought von Greim. "Yes, she's probably over 20 years younger than me, but there is a war on and she will not meet any eligible men by being in a school all day, teaching young children." Her father would definitely be a problem, but he really didn't care. Edwin Conway would stay in line. "Yes," he thought, "Perhaps I shall call on her soon."

CHAPTER 20

Parker and Donovan walked through the hotel lobby and waited for their security men to pull up the car.

Donovan, ever the professional, waited until they were both in the car with the glass divider in place before he spoke. "George, that went about as well as we could have hoped."

Parker looked out the window and merely nodded. His thoughts were back to his godson. He was there in the hospital when Frank was born. He had seen him from infancy through his grade school years, before he started to work for the F.B.I. Still, he and his family would visit the Sweeneys every year. He even got to catch a few of Frank's ballgames in high school. And now here he was, hand picking this wonderful young man for the most important mission to date in this awful war. What had he been thinking?

Donovan sensed the seriousness of his friend's mood and leaned over to him. "This really is for the best. We simply have to know what the Germans are up to. If we hadn't come up with this plan, hundreds – probably thousands of our boys could be killed. And if the technology has the potential that it is rumored to have, we will lose the battle for the skies, and we both know what that would mean for our chances of stopping that mad man."

Parker never stopped staring out the window. Part of it was from being inconsolable and part of it was that he didn't want his boss to see the tears that had formed in his eyes. Finally, when he could speak clearly, he said, "Bill, this one is personal. That boy is my godson. I was there with his father the night that he was born. I watched him grow up. I was at the hospital when his older brother died after thwarting that bank robbery. I was this boy's father's partner for the St. Paul Police department before I joined the Bureau. His father is an incredible man of integrity and character. Do you have any idea how many gangsters wanted him dead? Or how many tried to bribe him so they could get away with their crimes? Too many to count, because they tried to bribe me, too. Michael Sweeney just stared them down and told them to stay out of his city. Then he told them if they ever came after him or his family, he would hunt them down and kill every single one of them. And do you know what? None of them – not a single one – ever messed with him." Parker paused. "And the apple didn't fall far from the tree with Frank. This kid is the real McCoy, Bill. My best friend has already lost one son. I don't want to be responsible for his only other one not coming home. But now it's too late for that. We are sending him into Nazi Germany without even a gun to defend himself. What have I done?"

Donovan put his hand on his friend's arm and said, "Don't forget. We do have Owl there to help him. And Owl will make sure that Frank makes it out."

"Owl is almost as inexperienced as Frank is, and you know it."

Donovan reflected on his man's comments and sighed. He had no answer for him.

CHAPTER 21

Frank's flight from Dublin to Augsburg was not crowded, but it was very bumpy. He admired the skill of the pilot, but he didn't compliment him upon deplaning. He was afraid that he would tip someone off as to his own pilot knowledge.

There were SS and military men all over the airport in Augsburg. No one spoke. There was no idle chit chat. He presented his papers to the authorities and passed through security with surprising ease. He took a cab to the Irish Independent, which was located in an old building just south of the city. He met his editor, a middle aged man named Michael O'Shea. O'Shea was all Irish. He stood about 5'10, was a bit stout, to put it nicely, and had red hair that he appeared to comb without...a comb. He also looked like he had managed to avoid the sun for all of his life.

"I'll bet he only has to shave a couple of times a week," thought Frank.

He shook Frank's hand, as his brown eyes looked over Frank for only a moment. "McGuire...McGuire... I knew a McGuire once back in Ireland. You don't know a Sean McGuire, do you?"

Frank stared at him for a second. "Um, pardon me, Mr. O'Shea?" Frank looked at him a bit more closely and said, "Can you please repeat that?"

"I said, I knew a McGuire once when I was still living in Ireland. His name was Sean. Do you know him?" Frank stared at him some more.

Finally, O'Shea looked at him and said, "You can speak, can't you, lad?"

"What? Oh, yes sir. And no, I don't know..." O'Shea had already turned his back and muttered something about "today's youth."

"False alarm," Frank speculated.

O'Shea started walking and explained how things worked in the office. He walked Frank through the deadline schedule per day, the expectations for his columns, and gave him an update on what was happening with the war. Frank was surprised at how neutral O'Shea was about the war. But then Ireland itself was neutral, he reminded himself. O'Shea then took him around the small office and introduced him to the eight other employees. There were two other reporters, and they were both German. Or at least they had German names. Hans Ungrodt stood up from his desk and walked over to greet Frank enthusiastically. Ungrodt was a bit shorter than Frank and looked to be in solid shape. A couple of strands of his brown wavy hair had decided to park on his forehead and almost touched the round glasses that sat on his nose. "Welcome, Herr McGuire. I look forward to working with you."

Frank nodded to him and smiled. "Can't ask for more than that," thought Frank, as he sized up Ungrodt. The German looked to be about Frank's age, and his English was surprisingly good.

Hans continued, "If I can be of any help to you, just ask me. After all, we are working for the same team. I grew up here in the city, at least mostly. In a lower voice, he said, "I studied over in America for four years in Milwaukee. That's where I learned my English. I felt right at home. There are a lot of Germans over there." Out of habit, Frank almost mentioned his home state of Minnesota, but said nothing. In his best Irish brogue, he finally said, "I've heard a lot about America. I would like to learn more from you about it at some point." Hans smiled and said, "We will have plenty of time for that."

The other reporter was more reserved. Otto Kruger nodded tightly to Frank as he was introduced. Frank noticed that, unlike Ungrodt, Kruger stayed seated when O'Shea introduced him to Frank. Kruger was a little heavy set with thick eyebrows. His English wasn't nearly as good as Hans,' but it was passable. There was no offer from him to help Frank, but he was also polite in welcoming the newcomer. Kruger had been at the paper for almost five years. "A study in contrasts," noted Frank.

After exchanging pleasantries with most of the rest of the staff, O'Shea nodded to Frank to follow him outside. When they reached the alley behind their building, O'Shea turned to Frank and said, "Our office probably has listening devices hidden somewhere. Our phone calls are almost certainly being listened in on. In addition, I think we have a mole in our office. I can't tell you for certain. I can't tell you who it is. But there are just too many coincidences. So far, we haven't been threatened by the Nazis for what we are writing. We've tried to remain balanced. I have to think that, because our country is neutral, they leave us alone. But they are everywhere. It is impossible to determine who is a Nazi versus who is just trying to stay alive versus who is against the Party. So my advice to you, Lad, is to trust no one. Just do your job and find interesting things to write about." Frank nodded. "And please, if you are going to write anything that is, shall we say, "Controversial," run it by me first. Ya follow?"

Frank said, "Yes, sir," and then got chastised for the "sir" thing.

"Just call me "O'Shea" or "Michael," All right?"

"Yes, sir... Um...Sure...ah....Michael."

After some more introductions and getting assigned a desk, Frank headed to the apartment that was arranged for him. It was conveniently located directly in front of the train station. Once on the train it was a 10 minute ride to the station nearest the newspaper. The entire commute was less than 12 minutes door to door. His apartment, if you could call it that, was located above a small flower shop. A middle aged couple named Peter and Wilhelmina Stoffel ran the business. They lived in the two story home that was attached to the back of the shop. Wilhelmina, who everyone called Minnie for obvious reasons, was a kindly woman with no shortage of energy. She was one of those people who smiled with her eyes almost as much as with her teeth. She was of medium height with dark hair that was just starting to turn gray. She greeted Frank warmly when he arrived.

"Herr McGuire, we have been expecting you! Welcome!" she cried. "I am Mrs. Minnie Stoffel. Are you hungry? I have made some fresh strudel for you!"

Frank shook her outstretched hand and said, "I would love some strudel. That is very kind of you, Mrs. Stoffel."

"Please. My name is Minnie, and my husband's name is Peter. We are so excited to meet you! It is not often that we get visitors from other countries. I have never been to Ireland, but I hope to go there one day. I am told it is quite beautiful."

"It certainly is," replied Frank, based on his one night spent near the Dublin airport. Peter came in from the flower shop and ate some of the strudel with him. He was a tall man with a bald spot on the back of his head that seemed to be getting more prominent. He held his wife's hand at the table as they conversed with their new tenant. Frank learned that the flower shop had been there for 30 years. It was started by Peter's father, who had passed away several years earlier. People came from all over the city to shop there, and it didn't hurt that the train stopped at the shop's front door. "The only inconvenient thing about living where we do is the noise from the train. It's rather loud, but after a while, you don't notice it very much," said Minnie.

Frank smiled and nodded. "I don't have much trouble sleeping through anything," he replied.

After a few minutes, the back door opened and in walked their daughter, Esther. Esther was an attractive young woman of 23 with sparkling blue eyes. She was coming home from her job teaching young children at one of the public schools. She greeted Frank enthusiastically in almost perfect English.

"Herr McGuire, you will love living here. The train can be loud when it comes in and out of the station, but you will get used to it. The convenience far outweighs the noise."

"Please, all of you, call me Frank."

They all nodded and smiled.

After another helping of strudel, Minnie walked Frank upstairs to his room. "This used to be where we kept all of our extra inventory before we expanded the shop a few years ago. It's basic, but you will at least have some privacy." The door opened to a standard, one bedroom apartment. There was a small kitchen and living area blended into a 12x12 room. Off to the side was a small bedroom with a single bed. Connected to the bedroom was an even smaller bathroom. "We are almost always home if you need anything. We tend to get a lot of visitors, because we have lived here for so long," said Minnie. "There is another room down the hall that is rented by a woman who works at a department store in the city. We don't see much of her. She keeps to herself and isn't here on the weekends. She stays with her family on Friday night and returns on Monday evenings."

As he was about to say good bye to the kind woman, there was a knock on his door. They turned to see Esther, with extra blankets in her arms. As she handed them to Frank, she said "I should mention that I am friends with Hans – Mr. Ungrodt," she said.

"I only met him briefly," said Frank, "But he was extremely kind to me." That brought a slight blush from Esther, and her Mom looked at Frank and winked. "They've known each other since elementary school," she said. "Hans comes by to help us with our garden, although he seems to be more interested in other things than our garden." Her eyes twinkled.

"Oh, Mother!" exclaimed Esther. Now they were competing with one another to get Frank to see what turned out to be nearly identical eye rolls. "Well, we certainly will have lots to talk about at dinner!" exclaimed Frank. They all laughed as the two Stoffel women made their way downstairs. "I certainly can't ask for a nicer reception," he thought. He reminded himself of his uncle's counsel about not trusting anyone. At this point, it was best to be suspicious of everyone, at least for now.

CHAPTER 22

Donovan and Parker were on their way to meet with MI6, England's spy organization that had been so helpful to Wild Bill's formation of the O.S.S. It would not become known for years, but Donovan had worked very closely with MI6 to build the foundation for the O.S.S. As a matter of fact, the O.S.S. was modeled very heavily on MI6's structure.

The MI6 headquarters were located in the heart of London. While this was its official home, MI6 had many other less visible sites where most of its business was done. The origins of Britain's original foreign intelligence organization dated back to the 1500's when it was given the name Special Intelligence Services. It was established by Sir Francis Walsingham, the Secretary to Queen Elizabeth. His goal was to gain intelligence about potential threats to the British Empire from external entities. The organization evolved through the centuries, and it really took hold around 1912, when Sir Mansfield Cumming saw the inevitable coming of the First World War. Cumming's visionary leadership laid the groundwork for England's significant advantage in intelligence gathering. In fact, over the next two decades the organization was acknowledged to be the greatest intelligence force in the world. Its name changed to MI6 in the 1930's. MI6 stands for "Military Intelligence, Section 6." MI5, its sister department, focuses only on domestic intelligence gathering. MI6's mission is to gather foreign intelligence and thwart any external enemy that would do harm to England and its colonies.

Donovan, who had been given private access to MI6 well before the war had even begun, had marveled at its capabilities. But as impressed as he was with what the British had built, he was even more concerned –

OPERATION GRAB BAG: A FRANK SWEENEY ADVENTURE

maybe even panicked – over how far behind the U.S. was in these efforts. He had lobbied F.D.R. incessantly for such an organization. The challenge was political, as everything was with the President. There were turf wars with each branch of the military, arguments about how to fund the department, reporting structure...all of which Donovan viewed as bureaucratic nonsense. Wild Bill was a man of action and he despised anything and anyone who got in the way of him building what he envisioned would be the finest intelligence agency in the world. At least the President had finally decided correctly. And for that Donovan was grateful.

Donovan and Parker greeted Felix Cowgill, MI6's top man, at the Englishman's office in London. This particular makeshift office was actually under the city. The London bombings had been going on since September of 1940 and there was no end in sight. Churchill opted for meeting below the city and would operate England's war from there.

Cowgill had been meeting with one of his underlings and rising stars, a man by the name of Kim Philby. Cowgill introduced Philby to the two Americans, and then Philby excused himself. Donovan, who had known Philby when he was stationed in Washington a few years ago, politely engaged him. But Donovan didn't care for him. That was unusual for Wild Bill. He liked almost everyone – to a point. But there was something about Philby that seemed...insincere and opportunistic. He had not shared his thoughts with Felix, but he might over a couple of drinks at some point. The strain of the war was showing on Cowgill, thought Donovan. He tried hard to be cheerful and engaging, but the outcome of the war at this point was anything but certain. A tall and thin man with a thin mustache and a bald spot on the back of his head that seemed to grow every time they got together, Felix put his best foot forward and smiled broadly when the three men sat down.

"Can I get you some tea, Old Boy?" He asked Donovan. "No, thanks, Felix. I'm fine for now."

"And you, George?"

Parker smiled and said, "How can I turn tea down when it's offered to me by an Englishman?"

Felix rotated his chair and had two cups of tea in front of them in no time.

"Well, all right, thank you, Felix," said Wild Bill.

Donovan's main mission for this meeting was to get Parker better acquainted with Cowgill. The O.S.S. commander laid out in very general terms that the U.S. was now employing assets inside of Germany to gain information that could help the Allies.

When Cowgill pressed him for details, Donovan just smiled and shook his head. "Too early for that, Felix. We hope to update you on a regular basis as things develop."

Cowgill, a laconic man on the surface but with a razor sharp mind, retorted, "So, my dear William, what you are telling me is that your latest "asset" has just landed in Germany within the last few days."

Donovan looked at his old friend and said, "Something like that."

"Why are you telling me this, William?"

"I'm telling you this because we are partners and because at some point we may need to share resources so that we can get our asset out."

"Can you at least tell me where this latest contact of yours is located?"

Donovan hesitated. "Southern Germany is all that I can tell you for now."

Cowgill raised his eyebrows. "Well, since you have been somewhat forthright, I will be somewhat forthright with you. We also have an asset in southern Germany."

Donovan said, "Thanks, Felix. That is good to know. Our operation could be termed, "High Risk." He paused for a moment, then went on. "But it is essential to the war. No big surprise, I know. But if it looks like we have a shot at success, I will pull you into this and tell you everything. Since we now have knowledge that we both have assets in the country, maybe at some point we could combine our resources." Wild Bill paused again. "There is one more thing, though."

Felix looked at his old friend. "What is it, Old Boy?"

The older American said, "This case is top secret. That means that you do NOT have my permission to share this with anyone except the Prime Minister himself, and only him if I give you the OK. More specifically, I don't want any paperwork on this in any way. I don't want you mentioning this to any of your people in your department, no matter how high they are cleared for this sort of thing."

Cowgill stared at Donovan for a moment. "If that is how it must be, then so be it. But I shall require the same of you when it comes to me sharing our information."

"You have my word, Felix."

"Well, that's good enough for me," replied Cowgill.

"OK, now that we are clear on that, let's talk about what's going on in Italy."

Back in their hotel, Donovan reviewed their meeting with Cowgill. "He is a trustworthy man, George. In this crazy war, we have to trust someone if we are to achieve our goals. And Felix has earned that with me. However," he continued, "Philby has not."

"Philby?" Asked George. "He is their rising star, from what everyone tells me."

Donovan looked away for a moment. He then turned and faced George directly. "I don't like him and I certainly don't trust him. I spent enough time with him when he was stationed in D.C. He drinks like a fish and something about him just strikes me as off. I was subtly trying to tell Felix that today. I'm not sure he picked up on it. In any case, don't confide in Philby or anyone else."

"Thanks, Chief. I won't."

CHAPTER 23

Frank arrived at the newspaper at 8:00AM along with the rest of the people who made up the relatively small staff. He was now starting his second week on the job. He had ridden with Hans Ungrodt for a couple of days last week and found him to be a delightful man. Otto Kruger was warming up a bit, but was still somewhat standoffish. Before he could sit down, Michael O'Shea called him into his office. Frank hurried in and took a seat.

O'Shea looked at him for a moment and said, "OK, lad, you've had as much time as we can afford for training. I'm looking for a feature story soon. Don't ask me about what because I don't know. For much of the war we have just been reporting back to Ireland as to what is going on here as we see it. Anyone can do that. I want to put something more personal in our paper. Find someone to write about. Do a feature on one of the families here whose husband or father is off at war. What did they do before the war? How is his family coping? Find something. Find someone. Maybe there is some Irish family here that is worth writing about. But be prepared. The Nazis will want to censor it, if it will even get printed. Don't ask me any questions because like I said, I don't even know what I want. Take Ungrodt or Kruger to lunch and ask them what they think. Ask them who you could talk to. That's all."

Frank had wanted to ask him several questions as the editor vomited up his ideas. But by the time O'Shea finished, he had already turned his back on Frank and begun dialing a number on the phone. Frank walked out of the office and wandered around for a couple of minutes to think about the assignment. He decided to ask his new friend Hans Ungrodt for some help. "Herr McGuire," said Ungrodt, "What sort of things interest you?" What are you curious about?"

"Call me, Frank, Herr Ungrodt," smiled Frank.

"If you call me Hans."

"Deal." Frank extended his hand and Hans shook it. They were sitting on a park bench a block from the newspapers' office. Frank had purposely wanted to get Hans out of the office so they could talk more freely.

"Tell me, Frank," began Hans, "Why did you want to talk to me here? Why not just talk in the office?" Ungrodt asked the question in an innocent voice, but Frank caught an intensely curious look on Ungrodt's face. "No reason, other than to enjoy the outdoors for a few minutes," replied Frank.

"Really? I thought it was because our office has so many listening devices in it," replied Hans matter of factly. Hans continued to eat his sandwich and made no eye contact with Frank. The Irishman didn't know what to say at first. Given his blunt answer, Frank waited for Hans to ask him the question. It did not come. Finally, Frank thought it was time that he took a chance. "Do you want to ask me a question, Hans?"

Hans thought for several moments as he chewed his sandwich. Frank waited anxiously for Hans to answer.

"Well Frank, I'm a reporter. Of course I have lots of questions for you, but they will have to wait for another time. We should focus on what or who you should write about."

Frank stared at Hans for a moment, looking for anything in his face that would give him any indication of...something. He looked around the park area to see if they were being watched.

Seeing nothing, Frank opted to try to answer Han's question. "I'd like to do a story about the military here. Maybe a feature on one of the prominent Luftwaffe leaders. I know that there is a large airbase here. Maybe do something with one of the leaders who are stationed at the base."

Hans thought about that for a moment. "The air base is a very interesting subject, but one that you will have a hard time writing about."

"Why is that?"

Hans hesitated for a moment. "Frank, do you find anything about the air base unusual?"

"I don't know, Hans. I've only been here a couple of weeks."

Hans looked around casually before he spoke. "Don't you find it odd that there are hardly any planes that are arriving and taking off from the east side of the base?"

A chill ran down Frank's spine as his heart skipped a beat. "Well, come to think of it, I guess I haven't seen any planes come and go from there. I've seen plenty take off from the west side of the base."

"Those are the BF109s that are being put in production. They are excellent planes. But they all take off from only the west end of the airport. Odd." Then Hans shrugged his shoulders.

The two young men sat quietly for a full minute. Finally Hans broke the silence as he pretended to look up at a bird in a nearby tree. "There is an interesting military man that I could introduce you to. He was a hero in the first war. He would love some publicity. And he is doing something of significance, although no one knows what."

"What is his name?" asked Frank.

"Colonel Robert Ritter von Greim."

"Von Greim, von Greim," repeated Frank, as he racked his brain. "Wasn't he a famous pilot in the Great War?"

"Yes, that's him," replied Hans. "He was a national hero of sorts. His big break came after he began piloting the Fuhrer all over Germany back in the last decade. Now the only person standing between him and Hitler is Göring, whom he also reports to."

"Wow. He *is* pretty prominent, then," said Frank.

Hans looked at him as if to say, "Gee, way to put that together, Genius."

After another pause, Frank asked another question: "Why do you say that he wants publicity if he is working on something secret?" asked Frank.

"The word is that von Greim has no use for Göring and sees him as a road block – is that the right word? - To gaining direct access into Hitler's inner circle. Göring is certainly more feared than revered. Von Greim is admired for his performance in the first war, so he is trying to leverage that into favor with Hitler. Unfortunately for him, his agenda is so obvious that it makes him even more unlikable than Göring, at least in some people's eyes."

Another pause. Then Hans offered, "There is an Irishman who you might want to meet. He is also part of whatever they are working on."

Frank, trying to remain nonchalant, asked, "What's the Irishman's name?"

"Edwin Conway? Edward Conway? Something like that," said Hans.

"How can I go wrong with an Irishman?" smiled Frank.

"It won't be that easy," cautioned Hans. "They are working on some special project undoubtedly related to the war. They won't want to talk about that. Even if they did want to, they probably can't."

"Easy, Hans. At this point, we just want to talk to them. I wonder where we can meet them."

"You can forget meeting them on the air base," said Hans. "The public is not allowed on the base. They often gather on the weekends at Berghoffs, a high end social club here in the city," offered Hans. "It's mostly reserved for the well to do in Augsburg, as well as high ranking military members and their families. They have wonderful bands and a large dance floor."

"Well, Hans, I guess I better work on my dancing," announced Frank.

CHAPTER 24

Several Days Later

Felix Cowgill stared at the report. His assistant, a loyal man named Henry Block, waited patiently for his superior to digest this latest information. "This data…is it trustworthy, Henry?" asked the little man as he tugged on his mustache.

"Sir, I can't answer that, at least right now. The best thing that we can do is take it at face value as if it is real and try somehow to confirm it."

"But if this is real, Henry, it is…this could be the final blow for us," Felix said quietly.

"Yes, sir, but, assuming it is real, at least we finally know what they are up to. And, more important, we know where they are working on it."

Felix let the comments from his assistant settle in. "Yes, of course, Henry. Of course you are right. We need to formulate a plan. Get back to Badger and ask for confirmation on this. And Henry? Not a word to anyone about this. No one."

"Yes, Sir. Of course."

Henry waited. After working such long hours in the same quarters for what seemed an eternity, he could sense his boss's rhythm of thought, so he knew Cowgill wasn't finished yet. After a full minute, Cowgill reflected, "Badger's reports are getting more frequent and certainly have greater content. Can you track how often we have heard from our friend?"

"I thought you might want that, Sir," answered Henry. "I took the liberty of putting that together. Badger's correspondence has increased from once a month to approximately once a week over the last 6 weeks. And, obviously the reports that are coming in are much more in depth of late."

"Yes, but this is the biggest news that we could have hoped for – or wished against," Felix corrected himself.

"Yes sir," said Henry.

After Henry left, Felix found himself deep in thought for the second time in less than an hour. He was wrestling with who to tell. And when. Clearly the Prime Minister needed to know this information. But who else in the government? He was concerned about leaks. It seemed that some of the things they worked on the Germans had anticipated. Or worse. Yes, he would need to be very thoughtful about whom to share this with. Then he thought about his old friend Donovan. It might be time to bring him into what they knew. But then caution took hold.

"We must get confirmation of this before we get too far ahead of ourselves. Making the wrong move with wrong information would have consequences of its own," he decided. "What if Badger was fed bad information? That would send us down a wrong trail and away from the real secret, which would mean more time lost. And more time for the Germans to perfect whatever they are up to." He would wait for Badger's next report.

CHAPTER 25

Von Greim waited for Leigh to come out of school. He had been thinking a great deal about her lately, and his attraction to her was growing stronger. He had already rationalized the whole affair issue. After all, it wasn't his first. "Every important man in the Party has a mistress," he reasoned. "Why not have a couple?" Even that idiot Göring had one. "I wonder how much he has to pay her to even be seen with him?" he snorted. "Who in their right mind could even stand to be around such a bore? How such an imbecile has gotten between me and the Fuhrer is mind boggling," he ranted. "I have proven my devotion to The Fuhrer, and have delivered real results! What has this little madman ever done?"

The truth was that Herman Göring had done a lot. He was in fact a very bright man, and von Greim knew it. Like von Greim, Göring was an ace pilot ("but certainly NOT in my class," von Greim reminded himself). And yes, Göring did form the Gestapo, but von Greim told himself that anyone could have banded together a bunch of ruthless vigilantes. After all, isn't that what made up the whole Party?

His relationship with Göring had started out well. Since they were both pilots, they had a few things in common. More important, Göring showed much respect for von Greim's war record. But over the years, Göring was given more and more responsibility. He had become Hitler's trusted confidante and right hand man. Von Greim was content to ride his boss's coattails for as long as it was helpful. Being assigned to this key and top secret project was the culmination of much work and sacrifice. But it seemed that the higher in rank and responsibilities that he gained, the more isolated he became from the inner circle.

Surely there was much happening that he wasn't privy to. There was a rumor about what was really going on with all of the Jews in Germany. The official line was that they were being moved to camps to help build ammunition and supplies for the war. He knew firsthand that that was true, for without the camps near Augsburg there would be no 109s. But when he asked his boss directly about it, Göring merely smiled and said nothing. Despite being an outgoing man with a hearty laugh, Göring's eyes were…dead. Especially when he talked about the Jews, or anything that he believed got in the way of the Third Reich's mission. Von Greim would never admit this, but Göring's cold eyes frightened even him.

Another rumor – one had to very careful with rumors, especially as they related to Göring – was that he was addicted to morphine, the result of a hip injury that he sustained during aerial combat during the Great War. Or maybe it was a result of the Beer Hall Putsch in 1923. Either way, the rumors were strong. Maybe that was something to be used against the little fool at some point in the future, mused von Greim. Having achieved as much as he could through Göring, von Greim now saw his boss as a road block to direct and daily contact with the Fuhrer.

His thoughts drifted back to Leigh Conway. He congratulated himself on the brilliant plan that he conceived to ensure that Edwin would come to Germany. If Edwin knew what was good for him, he wouldn't interfere with any relationship that von Greim was trying to form with his daughter. Besides, neither Dr. Conway nor his daughter had any idea that he was even married. His wife was back in Dusseldorf teaching at the university there. They had no children. This assignment in Augsburg was secretive. His wife didn't even know where he was stationed or what he was doing. That was very convenient for him. And Elsa was very low profile, virtually unknown in Augsburg. Sometimes war had its benefits.

Leigh wrapped up her day by waiting for a couple of little girls to finish in the bathroom. She loved her work teaching, but she missed home more. She found the children to be no different in Germany than she knew in Ireland. At least at this age, anyway. They all required attention and discipline and encouragement. And they needed kind and loving parents. But even if a child had all of these things, there were no guarantees. Indeed, one only had to look at the mess that the world was in to come to that conclusion. "I wonder what Hitler's parents were like?" she asked herself.

The other thing that was happening in the older grades was the indoctrination into the Nazi way. The older children were being eased into placing their faith in the Party before all else, including God and their parents. Leigh was getting a firsthand look at how the Third Reich operated, and it was frightening. The teachers in the older grades were under strict orders to implement the Party's philosophy and, just as important its agenda. The teachers were polite to Leigh but generally distant. Leigh was one of two non – Germans at the school.

She felt the principal, Herr Martin, was watching her closely. Any doubt that she had was eliminated by a conversation she had with him the other day. The short, bespectacled man was always running between each of the classrooms and inserting himself into the process. Worse, Leigh thought that some of her notes were missing from her classroom. She couldn't be sure, but her first thought was her boss.

Their weekly staff meetings consisted of about ten minutes of informational content about the overall schedule for the school, and twenty minutes about implementing and following up on the Party's philosophy.

Herr Martin had made it clear to her that she needed to do nothing to compromise or undermine what the children would be taught after they moved on from her class, so there was no doubt as to where he stood. "After all, Fraulein, they are the future of the Party."

"If they take after you, your Party is doomed," thought Leigh.

She wondered at what point things had turned the corner and gotten so out of hand in Germany. She had read about the "Night of the Long Knives," a three day period in 1934 that resulted in all of Hitler's major detractors either being killed or exiled. It was the end of the rule of law in Germany. The propaganda machine was in overdrive during that period of time. Anyone who disagreed with Hitler was made to look like they were part of a plot to overthrow the government and drive the country into chaos and bedlam.

That was really the beginning of the end for the nation, for at that point people lived in fear of their government and few were willing to speak up and challenge the Nazis. And of course, the "enemies" in Germany moved from anyone questioning the Party to the Jewish people. Leigh had heard awful rumors about what was taking place in other cities, but the oppression of the Jewish people in Augsburg hadn't reached anything close to those levels, at least not that she could see. Of course, she lived a rather isolated life right now, going from home to school and home again. She wondered if there was more going on in Augsburg than she knew about.

Certainly not all of the German people were Nazis. But there was such an intimidation factor. She noticed it almost everywhere, including the church, and more disturbing, the church leadership. There were exceptions, but there were fewer and fewer of those lately. After they had first arrived in Germany, she and her father heard a sermon delivered by a man named Dietrich Bonhoeffer, and it was excellent. Bonhoeffer had no fear. He simply preached the gospel and his inferences to the Third Reich's evil intentions could not be misunderstood. Bonhoeffer had travelled around Germany to deliver these messages, and soon after he preached in Augsburg, he was censored from all communication, written and spoken, as it related to the Party and the war.

As Leigh made her way out of the school, she saw von Greim waiting in the backseat of his car. The window was down and he was waving to her. "Here we go," said Leigh to herself.

"Leigh!" "Leigh!" called von Greim. He got out of the car and stood at the sidewalk, motioning her over to him. "Hello Robert," said Leigh. She had a smile pasted on her face, but her eyes betrayed no emotion. Von Greim, too engrossed in the moment (and himself) didn't seem to notice.

"It's so good to see you again!" he cried.

"This is a surprise," said Leigh.

"I was just on my way to an early dinner. Would you care to join me?" asked von Greim.

"Unfortunately, I need to get home to cook dinner for my father."

"Well, I have some bad news and some good news there. The bad news is that your father is going to be working late tonight. They are behind on a certain project, and he said that he was going to stay late to work on it."

"Oh, no. Not again!" said Leigh, genuinely disappointed.

"And now the good news," beamed von Greim. "Since he won't be home for dinner, I can take you to have a meal with me!"

"Robert, I don't want to impose…"

"Nonsense! I am inviting you to dinner!"

"Only if you're sure that it's no trouble?"

"On the contrary, I would be delighted!" cried von Greim.

"Well, I guess that it's a date," said Leigh, instantly regretting her choice of words.

CHAPTER 26

Frank went home that night and thought about what he had learned. As he lay in bed mulling over the last few days, he began to try to assess everything. All he had so far was that there was a Luftwaffe base near Augsburg and that the Nazis were working on some sort of secret project. Edwin Conway was a critical component in this project, and he had to get information one way or the other from this man. Of course, he knew all of this already, because the very people who sent him here told him. "A fine spy you are making so far, Frank," he thought. "I need to report something back. All I've done so far is to tell them that I made it here. I'll write a short article about something or other and just use the code to tell them that I am working on some things. This whole thing is taking too long. Plus, I still have no idea who my contact is. Other than that, things are going perfectly."

He was short on sleep and long on questions. Frank was naturally a bit more reserved. Than who? Funny how he still thought of Jack that way. After ten years, he still found himself comparing himself to Jack. He missed his brother and the ten year anniversary just made him think of Jack more. "Jack would be...37 now?" He would have undoubtedly had children by this time. Frank would likely be an uncle a few times over. He knew that Kathleen Geraghty had not married, and she was still close with the Sweeney family. Maggie loved her like another daughter. Even Michael looked upon her with affection.

"I wonder if I'll ever get married," Frank asked himself. He certainly had no one at home waiting for him. "It was better that way," he thought.

OPERATION GRAB BAG: A FRANK SWEENEY ADVENTURE

"After all, who knows how long this war will last? Who knows how it will end?" The war. That put his mind back to the task at hand.

Hitler was evil, there was no doubt about that. He had broken virtually every promise that he had made prior to the war. Neville Chamberlain - England's previous Prime Minister - was a fool to believe anything that Hitler told him. Chamberlain was almost in hiding, given how badly he had been played by the madman.

Churchill certainly had some guts. At least he talked tough. His radio messages to the English people inspired them and calmed them at the same time. Churchill was completely committed to driving the country to victory. But he couldn't do it without the U.S. No way. FDR was a good compliment to Churchill. Like the Prime Minister, FDR spoke of victory and put the nation's money and resources behind the rhetoric. "Fighting two wars on two different continents against two different enemies…only a country such as ours could do it," thought Frank. The one question that he hadn't asked himself that was below the surface was just how in the world was he going to get out of Germany alive?

CHAPTER 27

Peg McFarlane was a dedicated and trustworthy public servant. She would need to be. After all, she worked for the number one spy in the country. Wild Bill Donovan walked into the outer office as Peg picked up the phone. Her eyebrows raised a notch as she caught Donovan's eye. On the other end of the phone was Jane Patterson, FDR's secretary. Donovan didn't even bother to take off his coat. He waited until Peg finished her conversation. As she got off the phone, she merely said "11:30 lunch with the Man." Donovan sighed and nodded, then proceeded into his office. He knew what questions the President would be asking. After he got settled, he called Peg and asked her to find George Parker and get him in. "Should I ask him to call you?"

"No, I need to talk to him personally," he replied.

"Yes Sir," and she rang off.

15 minutes later, Donovan's phone rang again. "He's here," said Peg.

"Thank you, Peg. Please send him in."

Parker entered. "George, you look…terrible."

The other man smiled softly. "Thanks, Chief. Nice to see you, too."

As Parker sat down, Donovan assessed the man who had become invaluable to him.

Before Donovan could ask, Parker said, "We've only got one message from the lad, and that is that he is in Augsburg. He wrote some fluff piece on German art and used our code. All he said was, 'Here safe'."

"When did that come in?" asked Donovan.

"Just the other day…what's today? Friday? So our people saw it three days ago, which meant that he probably wrote it the day before, on Monday."

"Well, my lunch today with the President will be a short conversation, at least as far as how it relates to our actions over there. Nothing about him getting in touch with Owl, or vice versa?"

"Not yet."

Donovan sighed. "OK, George. Patience is the word of the day, but we really need to start hearing something."

"We've dropped the kid into the middle of an enemy country with no contacts and an assignment with no details, and no support."

"Yes, I know. But he is capable. The most capable guy for the job. We both said that. We'll give it a little more time. I'll just have to get the President's mind on something else, and that won't be hard, seeing how the war is going in the Pacific theatre," said Donovan ruefully.

CHAPTER 28

Von Greim was enjoying his dinner with Leigh. Being an officer in the Luftwaffe had its privileges, and this was one of them. The wine was flowing freely, and he was relaxing after another long day. For her part, Leigh could barely hide her disgust from the man, as she knew his intentions with her were less than honorable. But she had to play along.

Leigh said, "Robert, your future within the Party must be very bright. After all, for a man of your age to be so far along in his career must be very unusual."

Von Greim bit hard as his eyes lit up. The wine was certainly working. "Thank you, Leigh. I have high aspirations."

"Tell me more, Robert. I don't know much about these military things. After all, my country is neutral in all of this."

"Yes, it is, isn't it?" replied von Greim. "How very unusual for England's cousin to not be involved in the effort."

"I'm not sure my country would really add much anyway," said Leigh. "We've never really recovered from the famine all of those years ago. The Irish are a very proud and independent people, but we have enough problems of our own with our economy. Anyway, tell me, Robert, what would be your next role?"

"I shouldn't really talk about these things," said von Greim.

"Oh. Well. I understand," said Leigh, feigning hurt.

Von Greim chuckled. "Please, Leigh. We are having such a nice dinner. Let's not spoil it by talking about things that shouldn't be discussed."

Leigh looked at her plate and said, "Of course."

There was more than a moment of awkward silence.

Finally, von Greim said, "Oh why not? I will tell you just a little of my dreams. But this must not go any further."

Leigh's face lit up. "Oh good! I mean, of course I won't say anything, Robert. I am just interested in learning more about you, that's all."

Von Greim drank more of his wine. "Keep guzzling," she thought. She herself had managed to merely sip on her wine and take micro swallows. Von Greim was too engrossed in his own self-aggrandizing thoughts to notice. Leigh poured more wine into his glass and pretended to fill hers as well.

Von Greim thought for a moment. "You realize, of course, that I know the Fuhrer personally." Leigh's eyes widened. "Robert! No! You actually know him? How?"

"We met years ago. When he was secretary of Morale, I flew him around the Fatherland. We got to know each other quite well. And my war record impressed him. When he came into power, he remembered me and contacted me directly to ask me to serve in a critical role in the Luftwaffe."

"Really? How exciting!"

Not all of this was entirely true, of course. That incompetent Göring actually told Hitler about von Greim. Hitler did remember von Greim from the Great War and after the war, when Hitler was in charge of propaganda, von Greim did fly Hitler around the country.

"Tell me, Robert, what is the Fuhrer really like?"

"He is a great man! The greatest man on earth!" Von Greim fairly shouted. "He will make sure that the world never forgets Germany. He will make sure that the German way is spread all over the world."

Leigh said, more quietly, "He is fortunate to have men like you supporting him."

"Yes, but some men are more competent than others," said von Greim.

"What do you mean, Robert?"

"I've said enough for one night, Leigh."

"Please, Robert." "This is so very interesting!"

"No. Maybe some other time we shall continue this discussion."

"At least tell me one of your dreams. After all, you said that you would."

Von Greim examined his glass of wine as he thought about his response. Finally, he said, "I will tell you this: if we are successful with one of our major projects, my career will...propel forward rapidly!" Then von Greim laughed. And laughed again, even harder for a full 30 seconds.

Leigh looked at him, bewildered.

Finally he looked at her and said, "I'm afraid that I have to depart now. I have many meetings tomorrow and I must be fresh for them."

"Yes, of course. Thank you for a lovely evening, Robert."

"The pleasure was all mine, Leigh. Perhaps we might have dinner together again sometime?"

"Perhaps," smiled Leigh.

Back home, as she waited for her father, she thought about what von Greim was referring to. She decided to not tell her father about her evening with the Colonel. At least for now.

CHAPTER 29

Edwin's office was a nondescript 12x12 room with extra thick walls to prevent anyone eavesdropping on his conversations. At least anyone who wasn't authorized to eavesdrop. While Lippisch's office walls were filled with his awards - fellowships, degrees, honorary degrees, and pictures with the infamous - Edwin's awards were nowhere to be seen. Indeed, his accomplishments actually exceeded those of his old friend. While Herr Lippisch was at home in Augsburg, Edwin was decidedly not. There was a picture of Hannah on his desk, and another one of Leigh. And off to the side of the desk was a picture of the family before Jimmy had disappeared. Beyond these two pictures and another one of Leigh, the plaster would have to do. He stared at his son's picture for a full minute before turning back to his work.

After spending several minutes pouring over the latest test results, he found his mind drifting back to Hannah, and to better, simpler days. He missed her terribly. His eyes found their way back to the picture of his wife. Theirs was a happy marriage, even with his long hours that were required with his work. He travelled frequently. And, ironically, almost always by train. The rides were long and unglamorous. Despite his schedule, Hannah never complained. She took as much joy and pride in Edwin's work as he did. They were a true team. Add to that two wonderful children and they had a terrific life together.

The arduous trips by train actually served to drive him forward in his dream: to launch a commercial airline that would serve as a more efficient, comfortable and reliable method for travel than trains and buses. He envisioned "highways in the sky" that would allow for safe air travel and effective air traffic management. All the more reason for his interest in pursuing this new technology that he and Herr Lippisch were working on. But he also understood man's temptation to use something that was designed for good to be used for evil. As he pondered this paradox, Alexander Lippisch knocked and entered his office.

Lippisch was a small man of stature but made up for it with a huge personality. "Good morning, my friend. We need to go over the latest tests on the engine parts."

"Yes, we must do that," replied Edwin. "Perhaps we can discuss the results as we walk."

"Certainly. We can walk and talk for a few minutes." Since Edwin's realization that his home had listening devices, he naturally assumed that his office was bugged as well. Lippisch had reached the same conclusion months earlier.

Alexander Lippisch was a purist in terms of his learning, but apolitical when it came to politics. His passion was aeronautical design and nothing else. He cared about the war only from the perspective that he wanted his family protected and his work to go on without any interference. He played to the Nazis as necessary, but had little regard for von Greim and even less for Göring. He shared the same passion as his peer Conway: to change the way people travelled all over the world. He and his Irish friend would talk for hours about their dreams of utilizing the technology that they were perfecting for commercial applications. So sure were they of what they were doing that they had already discussed how to take a company public to ensure the necessary funding.

"Edwin, hopefully the air tunnel testing on the prototype fuselage will come back within our specifications. That means that we should be ready for our first overall prototype test within three weeks, maybe four. We know the engine works beautifully, at least when we run it in a stationary position. Did you ever think when we first met all of those years ago that we would work together and achieve this? Who would have thought it possible?"

"Yes, my friend, we have accomplished a lot. But for whom and for what purpose?" asked Edwin.

Lippisch looked at Edwin and rolled his eyes. "We have been through this many times, Edwin. We are not here to be judge to what is taking place. We are being given a chance to experiment and perfect technology that will be used for generations! And we have our own private lab paid for by someone else to do it in!"

"Alex, do you not feel any sense of responsibility here? Your countrymen will use this technology to try to win the war. Does that not bother you?"

"Not really," shrugged Lippisch. "Honestly, I doubt that we will be able to get these into production fast enough to produce the number of machines that it would take to shift the war in the Fatherland's favor."

Edwin countered: "But you also fail to recognize that this facility is very much kept secret…no one knows what we are doing here."

"No one?" smiled Alex. "My dear Irishman, I suspect more people know what we are doing here than you might think."

"How is that possible?" asked Edwin.

"You'd be surprised, my friend," said Alex.

Just as Edwin was about to ask further about this, von Greim appeared, seemingly out of nowhere.

"Ah! The two men that I was looking for! I was just on my way to see you. I believe the fuselage tests are ready, yes?"

"Yes they are, Colonel," said Alex. "Barring anything unforeseen, I should think that you will be quite pleased with the results."

"Excellent! Let's review them as soon as possible!"

The three men walked back to the testing area. Two of them were excited, and one was decidedly not.

CHAPTER 30

The results of the testing did come in and were indeed impressive. Edwin was understandably torn. He was very proud of the work that he and Alex had done together. They were in the very infancy of changing travel...certainly for Europe but eventually the entire world!

But he also knew what Germany would do with this new technology, and that troubled him deeply. On top of that, he had to deal with von Greim, that despicable man who knew what buttons to push with him. Edwin hated the fact that von Greim was holding all of the cards. Despite being warned – well, threatened would be the more accurate word for it - he had tried to tell Leigh one night about his dilemma but he was interrupted by von Greim himself. On top of all of this, he also knew that von Greim had wormed his way into Leigh's life for a variety of reasons. First, his daughter was beautiful. Knowing that this man almost his age had his eye on his only daughter made Edwin's skin crawl. But von Greim had other motives for trying to endear himself to Leigh, not the least of which was to send a not so subtle message to Edwin that von Greim had complete control over the Conways. In the quietness of his office, and in the middle of all of this chaos, Edwin Conway did the only thing that he could do in such a situation. He bowed his head and prayed.

CHAPTER 31

Hans Ungrodt put his sandwich down for a moment to listen again to his Irish friend. "Frank," he said patiently, "They simply will not let you onto that base. No civilian is allowed. No one!"

Frank looked at Hans for a long moment. "OK, Hans, you have been very clear about that. But I see a story here. How can we find out what is really going on over there?"

"I told you," said Hans. "Put on your dancing shoes and get over to Burghoffs this Saturday night."

Three nights later, Frank walked into Burghoffs with Hans. What Hans had failed to tell Frank was that in addition to the Conways being there tonight, some of the local Nazi Party leadership would likely be in attendance as well. Hans knew his new friend well enough by now to know that Frank would come to the same conclusion that he had about some of the characters in this play. Off in the corner of the dance hall he spotted Otto Kruger, their colleague at the newspaper. He was sitting with two other young men. Kruger pretended not to see them.

As they took their seat at a table, Hans ordered a couple of drinks for Frank and him. Frank looked around the establishment for a while and asked Hans where von Greim was. "Patience, Frank," smiled Hans. "He will be here. His wife lives in Dusseldorf. He is either at the airbase or here virtually all the time."

Frank scolded himself for coming across as anxious. "Relax, relax. Let this whole thing come to you. Don't force it!"

As he nursed his drink, he watched as Hans began tapping his hand on the table to the music. Just as he was about to ask Hans what von Greim looked like, he watched Hans' eyes move behind him toward the other side of the hall. Hans quietly said, "Herr Conway is coming our way, but I don't know who that is with him."

That last part was said with a certain amount of curiosity. Frank made himself not turn around. The hostess led Conway and his companion to the table right next to Frank and Hans. There was another couple seated at the large table across from the two Conways. They did not appear to know one another.

"Well, Frank, you couldn't have asked for a better set up," said Hans. Frank, still not moving his eyes from Hans, asked, "How should we do this?"

Hans looked back at his friend and said, "What more do you want me to do? Deliver him gift wrapped to you?"

Frank implored his friend. "Hans, please?" Hans gave an exaggerated eye roll, and said, "Oh, all right. I'll make the introduction, but after that you're on your own."

"Thank you," mouthed Frank.

After letting Herr Conway get settled, Hans rose and walked the short distance to the other table. "Herr Conway! What a delightful surprise!" Conway looked at the other man, not sure as to who he was. "I'm Hans Ungrodt from the Irish Independent newspaper. We met here several weeks ago. Do you recall?" Edwin looked at him for a moment and then said, "Yes, I think I remember that."

Hans smiled warmly and said, "Let me introduce you to a fellow countryman of yours: Frank McGuire." Frank had turned around and started to say hello to Conway when he looked at Conway's guest. He got to "Hell" and stopped. Seated next to Edwin Conway was a stunningly beautiful young woman with brown hair and beautifully bright brown eyes. He had extended his hand to the older gentleman, who took it and said, "Nice to meet you, Mr. McGuire." Frank stared at the young woman for another second and then caught himself.

"Dr. Conway, it is nice to meet you. I've read quite a bit about you."

Edwin, seeing the obvious way that the young man had looked at his daughter, was confused for a second. But then, he thought, "The lad is Irish and he is not twice her age and he's not a Nazi. It could be worse."

"Mr. McGuire and Mr. Ungrodt, may I present my daughter, Leigh?"

OPERATION GRAB BAG: A FRANK SWEENEY ADVENTURE

Frank dropped Edwin's hand and immediately placed it within Leigh's outstretched hand before Edwin had even finished his introduction. "Very nice to meet you, Miss Conway. It is Miss Conway, isn't it?"

Leigh returned his stare for a second and caught herself. "Um, pardon? Oh, yes. It's Miss Con...Leigh Con- please, call me Miss. Please call me Leigh."

Edwin was smiling with his eyes and nothing more. But he was definitely smiling. He had never seen his poised, calm daughter rattled. "Please, won't you both join us?" Frank had already sat before the words were out of Edwin's mouth.

He was awestruck by Leigh's beauty. He had been totally focused on Edwin Conway and establishing a relationship with him. He was not expecting someone like Leigh. His uncle had merely mentioned a daughter. Frank thought back to the picture that he saw of her. Though she looked beautiful in the picture, she was stunning in person. He kicked himself into gear and tried to recover.

"Where are you from, lad?" asked Edwin.

"Just south of Cork," replied Frank.

"We know some McGuires. Are you related to James McGuire?" Frank's face froze for a moment. "Did you say James McGuire?"

"Yes, James. He owns a print shop over there."

"James McGuire," repeated Frank. "Are you sure that it's not-"

"Well, what have we here?" All eyes at the table turned to see von Greim, who seemed to appear out of nowhere. Again.

"Herr Conway, who are your friends?" Before Edwin could reply, von Greim said, "Hello, Leigh, it's so good to see you again!"

Leigh hesitated, and said, "Hello, Colonel."

Edwin recovered and said, "Colonel von Greim, these two gentlemen are from the Irish Independent Newspaper. This is Frank McGuire and his friend Herr....Hans...Hans, forgive me, but I forgot your last name."

"Ungrodt. Hans Ungrodt," replied Hans.

"Colonel," said Hans, jumping up to shake von Greim's hand. "I can't believe that I have finally gotten to meet you! I am so honored to do so!"

"Thank you." "Leigh, I-"

"You are a national hero!" exclaimed Hans. "May I at least buy you a drink?"

Von Greim paused for a moment. "Thank you. That would be very kind of you."

"I don't think we've met you," Hans said to the other couple at the table. Introductions were made all around. Von Greim turned to Leigh again. But before he could say anything, Hans set the hook: "I have followed your career since the Great War!"

Now Hans had von Greim's complete attention. The Colonel eyed him. "Really? What did you say your name was?"

"My name is Ungrodt. But that isn't important. Von Greim is the important name at this table! He turned to the couple on the other side of the table. This man was a war hero in the Great War and now he is playing a very important role in the Luftwaffe!"

"Well, thank you, my friend," the Colonel replied, in complete false humility. "But I am really at the service of the Fuhrer."

"Well then, the Fuhrer is very fortunate to have a man of your record serving him!" Hans was laying it on thick.

Frank quietly asked Edwin if he would mind if he asked his daughter to dance. Edwin quickly nodded his ascent, and von Greim, with his back to Leigh because he was so fascinated with Hans, didn't even notice. As Frank and Leigh made their way to the dance floor, Hans recited what he knew about von Greim's career, all the while filling him with more alcohol as von Greim corrected him or amplified on Hans' knowledge. The other couple, forced by Hans to be drawn into the conversation, tried to pretend to be interested. Edwin merely watched in a detached but amused way.

Out on the floor, Frank tried not to stare too overtly at Leigh as they danced. Neither one of them were concerned about the music, or keeping in step with it. If you asked either one what song that they were dancing to, they wouldn't have been able to even guess. They were in that rare air…totally ensconced with the other person and oblivious to their surroundings. As far as they were concerned, for just those precious moments, they were the only ones in the room. The room? Maybe in the whole world.

Neither Frank nor Leigh would normally be characterized as shy. But when it came to dating, both would be flattered if they could be upgraded to "shy." Neither one had had time to date. The war interrupted all of that, demanding that they and so many like them grow up, and fast.

Frank finally found his voice and asked, "What brings you to Germany?"

"My father's work. He is one of the foremost aeronautical engineers in the world, and he was asked to work with a colleague who happens to be an old friend of his. What about you? Why are you here?"

Frank continued to stare at her. After a moment, he said, "I'm sorry?" Leigh asked again, "What brought you from Ireland to Germany?"

"Oh, yes," replied Frank. "Well, I'm a reporter with the Irish newspaper here. As you know, we are neutral in this war, and our countrymen want to know what is going on over here. So, here I am."

Frank asked, "What do you do all day while your father is at work?"

Leigh smiled at the give and take. A sure sign of a well-adjusted individual is their ability to keep the conversation on the other person. People love to talk about themselves. She found it almost a game to continue to ask questions, but she found in Frank an equal competitor. He was doing the same thing back to her. But she actually enjoyed it...the give and take.

"Actually, I am a teacher. I teach the third grade in a school not too far from here. "Mostly German kids?" Asked Frank.

"Yes. They are all German, at least in my class," replied Leigh.

"How are the German kids compared to the children in Ireland?"

Leigh thought for a moment, and said, "Children are children no matter what country they're from. At least that's true in the third grade. I suspect that all of that changes when they grow older and get indoctrinated."

"How so?"

Leigh smiled at Frank. "You sure aren't shy about asking questions, Mr. McGuire."

Frank feigned wincing. "Well, after all, Miss Conway, I am a reporter."

Leigh kept grinning. "Are you really a reporter, Mr. McGuire?"

Frank blushed, caught off guard. "What do you mean, am I really a reporter?"

He recovered quickly and smiled back at her. He hoped that she hadn't noticed him getting flustered.

"Don't look so defensive. After all, I am a teacher and I give tests all day long. By the way, I do have a question for you. I was wondering…"

Before he could respond, there was a tap on his shoulder. Standing behind him was Colonel von Greim. The man's timing was impeccable. And annoying.

"Excuse me, young man, but may I?"

Frank blushed for the second time in less than a minute. He looked at von Greim and then back at Leigh, whose smile had vanished in an instant.

"Why, of course," managed Frank. He bowed to Leigh and made his way back to the table and joined Dr. Conway and Hans.

"Thank you, lad, for dancing with my daughter," said Edwin. "I'm sure that that was the most fun that she has had since she's been in Germany."

"She – she – she's a wonderful dancer," sputtered Frank, instantly regretting it. "What an idiot you are!" he said to himself. Edwin looked at him and saw right through him.

He smiled kindly at him. "You know, Frank…it is Frank, isn't it?" Out of nowhere came Hans' enthusiastic contribution: "Ja! Ja! His name is Frank!"

Frank and Edwin slowly turned to look at Hans. Hans, completely clueless as to what the problem was, just smiled and nodded.

"Anyway…Frank," he continued, with a slight look at Hans as he pronounced Frank's name with emphasis, "You should think about stopping in here more often. We are here almost every Saturday evening. It's a way for us to get out and away from our work for an evening."

Before Frank could respond, Hans jumped in again and said, "What a marvelous idea! Yes, yes, we will need to come here regularly now!"

Frank and Edwin's eyes connected for a moment and smiled, sharing the same thought.

Frank, never breaking eye contact with Edwin, said, "Yes, that is a marvelous idea, indeed."

CHAPTER 32

Henry Block was working late again at MI6. He stared at the latest report one more time. The effort in southern Germany was beginning to make progress. Unfortunately, they still could not confirm the initial report that indicated what the Germans might be working on. Conjecture and speculation would not be enough for the Prime Minister. But at least this particular report indicated solid contacts were being formed. "It would really be helpful if the Yanks would tell us who their contact was down there. You'd think that we could trust each other," he muttered.

"What's that, Old Boy?" Block turned to see Kim Philby standing behind him.

"What? Oh, nothing."

"Come on, do tell," pressed Philby, amiably. "I heard you mutter something about trusting one another."

"Really, Kim, it's nothing. Nothing worth talking about."

"Suit yourself, then." And with that, Philby sauntered away.

Henry carefully folded up the report and put it in his coat pocket. He would not take it out again until he met with Felix Cowgill.

CHAPTER 33

The days began to move more quickly. Frank found more and more stories to write. He covered everything from the architecture in the city to profiling prominent families in and around Augsburg. But while the days flew, the nights dragged. He showed up at the club most nights, hoping to see Leigh again. Saturday nights seemed to be the best night for success. She had come in with her father each Saturday night. They talked and danced, and then talked some more. He wrestled with how much to ask her about her father. Despite his feelings for Leigh – and the feelings for her were intensifying by the day - he had his orders. He tried to be as subtle as possible in his conversations with her. Thankfully, he didn't always have to do all of the work. Occasionally, Leigh would surprise him and talk about her father's work without any prompting. Unfortunately, it didn't appear that she knew much about the project that her father was working on.

After another day of work, Frank made his way to the dance hall once again. He was so deep in thought that he almost walked right by the club. He saw Hans making his way into the hall, and breathed a sigh of relief that at least he would have someone to talk to if Leigh and Edwin didn't show up. Just as he thought about this, his heart leapt as he noticed Leigh and her father walking in, almost directly behind Hans. As he made his way across the street, his mind drifted back to the situation at hand.

The strange part of all of this was that he had come to enjoy a personal relationship with Edwin. Frank not only liked the man, but had come to respect him as well. Frank had concluded that Edwin was clearly not a Nazi, or even a Nazi sympathizer. Edwin was a lover of discovery and innovation. Along with a deep love for his daughter, these were his passions.

Just as important, Edwin seemed to take a liking to Frank. Frank had learned about the disappearance of Edwin's only son, and the toll it had taken on Edwin and Leigh was evident. Occasionally, Frank noticed that Edwin would refer to Jimmy in the present tense, as if the older man thought that his son was still alive. At those moments, Frank would pause. He almost told Edwin about his own experience about losing a loved one, but caught himself. Seeing the pain in Edwin's eyes made Frank even more empathetic for his own father, who was living the same anguish half a world away.

Any questions that Frank brought up to Edwin about his work were quickly dismissed and the subject would be changed. Even when Hans was there and asked follow up questions to Edwin, the matter was dropped. Edwin became visibly uneasy when Frank and Hans asked about his work. His eyes would dart from the table to the rest of the dance hall, scanning the tables for...what? A spy? An onlooker? An eavesdropper? Occasionally Frank would follow Edwin's eyes as they moved from table to table. No one seemed out of place or even interested in their conversation. On top of that, the music was quite loud, so it would be difficult for anyone to really hear anything.

He needed to give his uncle George some information. But what? While there was value in getting to know Edwin, he still didn't know anything about the project. He really hadn't made much progress. He had a short story on the flowers around Augsburg and the agreed upon code had spelled "met EC." He wanted to get on the air base, but he was beginning to realize that that might impede his objective of getting Edwin Conway out of Germany. He tried not to think about the alternative objective to make sure, one way or the other, that Edwin Conway would no longer work for the Germans.

Von Greim had also shown up and invited himself to sit down at the table. Hans engaged him by being a good reporter: asking him a lot of open ended questions about his life between the wars, the many assignments that he had had, his interactions with the Fuhrer...anything to keep him talking and keep him drinking. Frank took this as another opportunity to quietly ask Leigh to dance. He looked into her sparkling brown eyes as he asked her. She turned to him and was caught a bit off guard and caught his look. She caught her breath, and both were momentarily lost in the moment. Recovering quickly, they rose from their seats and made their way to the dance floor.

Frank was not surprised – maybe relieved? To hear that she was a school teacher. There was no doubt that he had fallen hard for her. Their relationship – could you call it that? Was beginning to grow. During the waltz, he asked her again how they had come to live in Germany, and Leigh told him what little she knew about her father's job. Frank was careful not to ask too many questions about Edwin, so he asked about the rest of the family. Leigh grew very sober when discussing her mother and brother. Then she changed the subject back to Frank and his family. He had to think quickly about the cover that his uncle had given him. Before they knew it, the band had announced that they were taking a break. They stood on the dance floor together, awkwardly trying to figure out what to do. They both knew that they didn't want to go back to the table, but Frank, recalling his assignment, gamely said, "Your father is going to think I kidnapped you," and escorted her back to the group.

Hans caught Frank's eye as they sat back down. His eyes looked at him in disbelief, as in "Really?" "Really? You would do that to me?" Frank gave him a shrug and mouthed a quick "Thank you" as von Greim finally came up for air.

"So, Hans, you can see that my career has indeed taken off, so to speak, but I've been very lucky, too," he said, completely insincerely. He had taken in so much wine that he was beginning to slur his words and lean to one side of his chair.

Hans replied, "Colonel, a man of your experience and reputation doesn't climb the mountain by luck! What do you think your next assignment will be? Or, will you be here for the next several years?"

Von Greim noticed Leigh again, and, not wanting to be perceived as anyone other than a fast tracker, said, "Frankly Hans, I think if things go well here over the next several weeks, I will be on to the next promotion."

Edwin said, "I'll drink to that" and raised his glass of champagne. Von Greim, completely misreading Edwin's intent, said, "Why, thank you, Dr. Conway."

CHAPTER 34

Henry Block sat in his small office, which was located below old and unused train tracks somewhere under London. The location of this particular division of the MI6 branch was one of the best kept secrets of the war, and it was essential that it remained a secret. The lights in the corridors would often flicker when nearby trains ran overhead. They were a good five stories below ground, and an old freight elevator was the only way down to the offices. The ceilings were reinforced with concrete, in the hopes that a bomb dropped from one of the Luftwaffe planes would allow most of the facility to survive. No one there had any interest in testing that theory.

Block's hours were long. He hadn't had a day off in weeks. His wife had an idea as to what he did, but not because Henry had confided in her. She was no fool. War or no war, no one worked a regular government job every single day at a location that no one knew about for people that she had absolutely zero chance of meeting. Other than that, he had a perfect cover, he thought ruefully.

The stack of correspondence that he had to go through today looked like all of the other stacks that he went through every day. The process took hours and required his complete attention. There was one particular envelope that caught his eye. It held a 300 page product catalog from a home and farm repair company. He quickly turned to page 221, which had brief descriptions of various parts for a certain tractor model. Buried in the single spaced print was a cryptic message from their asset in Germany. He pulled out a magnifying glass to make it easier on his tired, sore eyes. The first line of the message made him immediately sit up in his chair. He read the material in full, and was struck by the sense of urgency in the coded letter. The more that the studious intelligence expert read and re-read, the more alarmed he became. It was apparent that the Germans were making a lot of progress on their top secret project. He needed to share this information with Felix Cowgill, his direct superior. This was the confirmation that they needed and had been waiting for. He was sure that Cowgill would have to get the Prime Minister involved.

As he made his way to his boss' office, he wondered about the implications of the material that he was carrying. He had many questions, but his priority was to deliver the package to Cowgill and give him time to process all of the information.

CHAPTER 35

Mary Holst's phone rang incessantly. A dark haired, blue eyed patriot and mother of two boys, Mary had volunteered to answer phones and do office work in various areas of the government. With her children in grade school and her husband having a predictable schedule, she felt it her duty to help in any way that she could in the war effort. Her efficiency and dependability got her noticed, and before she knew it, she was working for George Parker in an area of the government that she didn't fully understand, and she wasn't sure that she wanted to. She had seen enough to know that this particular office operated by a different set of rules. On the one hand she found it exciting, but on the other, she thought it a bit...terrifying. However, the country was at war on two different continents fighting two separate and distinct enemies, and Mary Holst was going to do everything in her part of the world to make sure that her young sons would not be called upon to fight either enemy when they came of age in a few years.

The hours tended to be longer than when she first started, but she felt obligated. Parker was a fine man, and she enjoyed working for him. The number of calls that came in had increased exponentially since that infamous day in December. The calls were rarely for her, and mostly for her boss or the other men that worked for Mr. Parker. As George made his way into the office after a meeting with a couple of Senators on "the hill," Mary told him of an important call that would take priority. She gave him the note from the call. "He seemed like he was trying to act calmly but was really anxious on the inside," said Mary. George glanced at the name and understood why his secretary would draw that conclusion. "Thank you, Mary. I will call him right away."

George sighed deeply as he made his way into his office. Michael Sweeney answered on the first ring.

CHAPTER 36

Colonel Felix Cowgill sat at his desk, slowly stroking his thin mustache. He read and re-read the coded message, and looked across at Henry Block. "Well, Henry, this certainly looks like the confirmation we needed."

"Yes, Sir," answered the bespectacled smaller man. "There appears to be no doubt about it."

"Right," said Cowgill. "I'll need to get this to the Prime Minister right away."

"What about the Americans?" asked Block.

Cowgill hesitated, but for only a moment. "We have no choice. We have to tell them, now that it is confirmed. I've known Bill Donovan for years, and I would trust him with my life. Besides, we are going to need all the help we can get right now."

"Yes Sir, that would be the right step to take at this point," replied Block, as his voice trailed off. He seemed to be fixated on a pigeon that was sitting perfectly still on a tree in the courtyard below.

Cowgill followed Henry's gaze and then studied his colleague for a moment. They had worked together for several years now, and each man understood the other's moods. It seemed to him that Block was either preoccupied or that he wasn't telling him everything.

After waiting him out and getting nothing from him, Felix quietly asked, "What is it, Henry?"

The smaller man looked at his boss for several moments, and then nearly knocked him over with his next statement: "I think it's entirely possible that we may have a spy in our office."

Cowgill sat there stunned, and said nothing. Finally, he asked Henry to explain himself.

"I can't really say for certain," stated Block. "You and I are in the spy game, and we get paid to notice little things. For example, I've noticed that whenever I leave papers on my desk, no matter how insignificant that they are, I would almost swear that someone had moved them ever so slightly when I went to lunch or to a meeting of some sort. More important, we have identified two suspected foreign spies living in London in the past two weeks, and when I gave the go ahead to bring them in for questioning, both eluded our people and were not caught. One of them had moved out the previous night before our people showed up to grab him. The other went to a concert here in the city and never returned."

Felix tried to remain calm on the outside but his mind was racing in several different directions as he processed Henry's bombshell statement.

"Henry, this particular information that you just brought me..." Henry interrupted before Cowgill could finish his sentence: "Oh no, of course not. There is no document or anything in writing, other than the coded message itself that you just read. I didn't make copies or anything. This is the original message taken directly from the catalog. You and I are the only ones who even know about our asset in Germany, and this form of communication."

"Right, well that's a relief," muttered Felix. Then: "Not a word of this to anyone. I mean, your suspicions. No one is to know or suspect anything."

"Yes, of course," replied Block. He waited for the obvious question. He didn't have to wait too long. "Who do you suspect?"

"No one that I am ready to identify," he answered. "You know how these things go. Your imagination gets active, and pretty soon you suspect everyone."

"All right,' said Felix. "But keep me in the loop. And I will be more vigilant as well."

"Can't hurt, now can it, Sir?" said Henry.

CHAPTER 37

"Mike, I know. I know. Yes. Yes. You know I can't tell you that."

George Parker was almost doubled over in pain, so great was his misery in not being able to share anything with his close friend.

Michael Sweeney...the quiet and unflappable cop who took on mobsters, crooked police chiefs and even more crooked politicians. Michael Sweeney, the man who single handedly designed the country's first armored car, and then built a company around that car to keep good people's money out of bad people's greedy pockets. This was not the Michael Sweeney that George Parker knew. The voice of the man that Parker found himself talking to on the other end of the phone belonged to a broken man on the verge of panic as he inquired and pleaded with his best friend for any news about his son who, like so many young men, had been sent off to a foreign land to fight a war for the very survival of his country.

Michael had heard nothing since that day when Parker showed up at his doorstep. He couldn't let Maggie see him like this, so he waited until she took the street car downtown to do some shopping.

"I know that you can't say much, but just give me something," pleaded Michael. There was a long silence. Parker finally spoke, quietly and painfully. "Mike, I can't tell you what I don't know. And the truth is, I haven't heard from him directly. I do know that he arrived safely at his destination. The fact that we haven't heard much from him is not bad news. If I can share more at a later date, you know that I will call you immediately."

Firmer: "Now buck up, Mike. Maggie and the girls need you! Stay strong and have faith. Our God is bigger than all of this, and he is holding Frank in the palm of His Hand."

Mike, more calmly: "Thanks, George. I guess I just needed to hear that."

George: "I promise that I will stay in touch. I need to go now."

Mike: "Please do all that you can, George, to get him back here in one piece." Both men knew that Mike's request was a statement of the obvious, and that it was pointless.

"I promise, Mike." Only one of the men knew that this response was baseless as well. George hung up the phone and began to sob. He knew that he had no control over fulfilling his promise to his friend. He looked at his desk and simply muttered, "I hate this war."

CHAPTER 38

William Joseph Donovan sat in his office, staring out the window at the traffic below. The Office of Strategic Services headquarters was located in a six story building three blocks from the White House. Unlike his counterpart in the F.B.I., Donovan hated notoriety of any kind, personal or public. He looked at it as an impediment to the organization's success, and his own personal effectiveness.

J. Edgar Hoover loved the notoriety and prestige of being in charge of the F.B.I. and he used the newspapers and radio to instill and promote the bureau as an unconquerable machine that "always got its man." Hoover, who had worked for Donovan in the Justice Department two decades earlier, craved recognition for himself and the bureau, in that order. Wild Bill Donovan hadn't liked Hoover from the beginning, and the ensuing years after Hoover's assignment to Donovan was finished hadn't changed that assessment.

Bill Donovan's priority was to work in the shadows and stay out of the newspapers. He often travelled in disguise, since he was well known, especially in the northeast. Being a hero in the Great War had made it difficult to keep a low profile. He was awarded the Medal of Honor for his heroism in the war, an award that he did not accept. The Medal of Honor was the most prestigious recognition a soldier could receive. He felt the medal belonged to those who never made it back from Europe, not the ones (like himself) who miraculously came home.

Over time he was awarded every major medal that there was in the U.S. military for exemplary bravery, being wounded in combat, and service. He was also decorated over a dozen times from several different countries.

All of his medals remained locked away in a couple of bureau drawers at home.

It wasn't just his military prowess that kept him in the limelight. His whole career had helped make his anonymity almost impossible. He worked in the justice department after the First World War, and he also had started his own law firm in New York. He had travelled the world on unofficial business, gathering intelligence so that he could determine where the next hot spots would be for America. He had met F.D.R. when the two of them were in law school at Columbia University. Despite their political differences, there was a kinship that had formed.

Roosevelt felt that, had Donovan been a democrat, he could have one day been elected President. The two stayed in touch over the years, since Wild Bill's law firm was based in Buffalo and F.D.R. was the Governor of New York.

Donovan also knew Churchill through his travels in Europe. It was Donovan who had told F.D.R. of Germany's coming resurgence in 1930's Europe. Against the objections and ridicule of Joseph Kennedy, the U.S.'s ambassador to England, Donovan predicted that Germany would start another war in Europe, and that Hitler would be a force to be reckoned with. This savvy and bold analysis had earned him a tremendous amount of credibility within Roosevelt's inner circle. To have a conservative Republican be given almost unlimited access to the President was unheard of. But it also helped that everyone knew that Donovan had no desire to enter politics at this point in his life, so he was not seen as a particularly serious threat to the President or the Democratic Party.

He was not a man who was terribly introspective, but today he found himself reflecting on his incredibly busy life. And the war. Always, the war. His disciplined mind made him come back to the present.

Donovan had a good idea why George Parker had urgently requested a meeting today. It was likely about Germany's secret project. Bill Stephenson, or "Little Bill," as he was known, was MI6's spymaster who was located in the U.S., at least part of the time. With Churchill's support, Stevenson was helping him build the O.S.S. He had met privately with Stevenson yesterday, and his English counterpart had shared the news about the top secret effort on Germany's part. No one save Churchill and Roosevelt knew that Stevenson and Donovan were permitted to share virtually everything with each other.

After his meeting with Parker, Bill would head over to the White House and brief the President, who had returned this afternoon after a few days at his residence in Hyde Park. Roosevelt would be anxious to get this information, and he would want to know in short order what Donovan and the allies could do about this.

His thoughts were interrupted with the inevitable knock on the door. There stood the ever reliable Peg McFarlane, the hardest working secretary around. Bill noticed that Peg never waited after she knocked to enter. Odd how that was. Even stranger, he never thought to even ask her to come in after the knock. They apparently just got used to each other's habits. It worked.

"Mr. Parker is here to see you," said Peg.

"Please send him in, Peg."

As she turned to get him, Parker blew right past her. Peg caught Bill's eye and gave him a small shrug.

"Come on in, George. This must be important."

"It is, Bill."

"Did we hear from Lion?"

"Huh? Um, well, yeah, a little. But the information I am sharing with you didn't come from Frank…I mean, Lion." Donovan made it very clear that real names were never to be used, not even between the two of them. The risk was just too great that something – or someone – could slip.

"This information came from Owl."

"Owl? Really?" said a surprised Donovan. "That's encouraging."

"Yes, it is," replied George somewhat absently.

"Well, George, it doesn't sound good."

"It actually sounds awful," stated George dejectedly.

"Let's have it, lad," said Bill.

Parker proceeded to outline what he knew. For the second time in less than 24 hours, Donovan listened to essentially the same story. His only conclusion was that the second time he heard it was as bad as the first.

CHAPTER 39

Washington National Airport was the product of two previous airports: Hoover Field and Washington Airport. Located near downtown D.C., it was finished in 1941 and offered the best facilities for the Washington mucky mucks. Felix Cowgill didn't even notice the new airport as he deplaned. His flight was supposed to arrive at 9:00AM local time, but due to delays in London and a strong headwind, he arrived three hours late, exhausted and hungry. Donovan had offered to have him picked up by an O.S.S. driver, but Cowgill demurred, choosing instead to have one of his embassy's people pick him up. He arrived at Great Britain's embassy a few minutes later and, after a quick sandwich with tea, promptly fell asleep in his room for two hours.

He awoke at 2:30PM to a ringing phone next to his bed. He let it ring three times, allowing him to clear his head for a moment.

"Hello?" he asked, trying hard to make it sound like he was fresh and been awaiting the call.

"Sir, there is a call for you from a Mr. Parker," said the voice on the other end of the phone.

"Yes, yes, put him through."

There was a five second pause before George Parker's voice came through. "Felix?"

"Yes, George, it's good to hear your voice."

After the usual pleasantries, Parker suggested dinner at the Donovan's home at 7:00PM that evening.

"We can have a car pick you up at 6:45PM," suggested George.

"Actually, we would prefer it if we did pick you up."

"Security," thought Felix. Then: "Yes, quite. That should be just fine. Cheerio."

Felix yawned, looked at his watch, and determined that he could sleep another hour before having to meet with anyone in the embassy. He did just that.

CHAPTER 40

Frank sat in his apartment. It was really just a studio with a bathroom in a nondescript part of Augsburg, but he wasn't real picky. It was a very convenient location for him. He had still not gotten used to the noise from the train, but that would come.

His room faced a square in the city where he could see sparrows and crows competing for limb space. The occasional squirrel would chase both violators off of his property. His room's hot water worked sporadically and he had no real control over how hot the stove would get. He really used it just as a place to sleep. And think. It had been several weeks since he had arrived in Germany. Once again, he took stock of what he had accomplished thus far. It was a short list, from his perspective. The good news was that he had made contact with Dr. Conway. He was building a solid relationship with him. And his daughter.

Frank was convinced that Conway was not a Nazi, and that he abhorred the Third Reich's philosophy. "Why? Why did he come here?" he asked himself. "Why would a bright man who is so well respected in the aeronautics community work for such evil people? It just doesn't make sense," mused Frank. On top of that, his repeated attempts to get anything out of the good doctor had been fruitless.

"Uncle George was obviously right. There's no doubt that Edwin Conway is working on something top secret. But why would a man work on something for a cause that he doesn't agree with? Is it the money? Dr. Conway doesn't appear to be very money motivated. Besides, his reputation alone would command top dollars all over Europe. Maybe since he had lost his son and then his wife, he figured he could just pour his life into his work to ease the pain. That theory has some merit," Frank reasoned.

He had seen his own father do that after Jack was killed. "Still, this is no picnic for Leigh," he ventured. "To drop everything and move to Germany couldn't have been easy. Yet, she seems content to be with her father. After all, it's just the two of them now, so what alternative did she really have? Still, even though he brought Leigh with him to Germany well before the war started, he had to know that Hitler was up to no good. Unless…"

CHAPTER 41

At his daughter's insistence, Edwin spent the afternoon with Leigh strolling through one of the parks that Augsburg was famous for. They found a place to sit that was far enough away from anyone else, which ensured that they could talk privately.

"We are fortunate that the war has not found its way to Augsburg," said Leigh.

"It will, lassie. It will," replied Edwin.

They sat quietly for several minutes, each lost in their own thoughts. Finally, Edwin said, rather firmly, "Leigh, I have something that I want to tell you."

She glanced at him, her brown eyes dancing in the sunlight. "What is it, Dad?"

He looked at her, and was suddenly struck by how much she resembled Hannah when Hannah was young. Just the image in his mind made the memories come flooding back.

"Do you know how much you look like your Mother?"

"That's one of the nicest things anyone could ever say to me," she smiled.

"We used to go to the park all the time back in our country. Even after you and Jimmy were born, we would try to bring you there, just to be outside in the fresh air. Things were so different back then…so…simple. There was no war to worry about. The Great War was over and people were excited about moving on with their lives. And here we are, not so many years later, at it again with no end in sight."

Edwin looked around to make sure no one was too close. Then he continued: "The people that we met when we first came here seem to have changed. They are much more guarded and less friendly. The rise of the Nazis has given way to all kinds of horrible violence. No one knows who to trust anymore. Everyone is afraid to speak up. You've seen the difference in the messages at Church. Even most of the clergy have compromised! Let's face it. We are living in a country run by a mad man who is trying to take over the world. I cannot contribute to that. I won't contribute to it!"

After a long pause, his voice choked as he said, "I so miss your Mother."

He began to sob quietly. Leigh held him close and hugged him. And she too began to cry.

CHAPTER 42

The knock on Frank's door wasn't expected. But on the other hand, since the train was nowhere near the station at the moment, he could hear someone coming up the steps. "Frank? Are you in?" It was Peter.

Frank called out, "One moment, please. I'm coming."

He opened the door to see Peter with a plain white envelope.

"Hello Peter! Come in!"

"Thank you, Frank. I just wanted to tell you that we will be having a late lunch today. We will eat in about an hour."

"Thank you, Peter. I'm sure that I'll be quite hungry by then." Frank looked down at the envelope that was still in Peter's hand.

"Oh, I almost forgot," said Peter, picking up on Frank's gaze. "This was left inside the door last night. It has your name on it, but there is no address, so it didn't come through the mail."

"That's strange," replied Frank. "Maybe it's a hot lead for a story from someone," he said with a laugh.

Peter just smiled and said, "I'll see you at lunch," and turned to walk back down the stairs.

Frank shut the door and opened the envelope. It was a brief, typewritten letter of three sentences:

"This is O. I think you might be L. If you are, meet me in the park down the street from the flower shop tomorrow at 7:00PM by the statues."

OPERATION GRAB BAG: A FRANK SWEENEY ADVENTURE

Frank got out his magnifying glass and spent the next several minutes examining both the letter and the envelope. He held both up to the light to see if there were any fingerprints or smudges. Nothing.

Felix Cowgill arrived at Wild Bill Donovan's home at exactly 7:00PM. He was greeted by Bill's wife Ruth. Ruth hailed from Buffalo, New York. She and Bill had met there many years ago. One of the many things that the Donovans had in common was their love of entertaining guests.

Unlike her husband, Ruth had grown up in privilege. She saw firsthand how to make guests feel welcome in an unpretentious way. She also knew how to throw a party. Not the raucous, out of control type of gathering, but a fun and relaxing event that made all want to be invited back. That upbringing, however, didn't make her any less a patriot than her husband. To the contrary, it was Ruth who would often be so engrossed in conversations about the war and the nation that Bill would have to quietly remind her to mingle more at her own party. Tonight would not be a party night at the Donovans. It would be a small gathering of three men who had much to discuss.

Ruth and Felix had met several times over the years. She greeted Felix warmly at the door and ushered him into the living room. As she was hanging Felix's coat in the front hall closet, the doorbell rang again. "That would be George," smiled Ruth. Sure enough, George Parker appeared at the door with flowers in hand. George kissed Ruth on the cheek and handed her the flowers. "They're gorgeous, George! Thank you!"

Felix looked a bit awkwardly at the two of them and was ready to apologize for not bringing anything. "Felix, we want you to relax as best as you can tonight and enjoy yourself. Having you here is a treat in itself," she said as she gave him a reassuring hug. As they embraced, Felix looked beyond Ruth to George, who gave him a "what can I say?" shrug.

Ruth continued, "Bill is in the study on your left. He is making the drinks and the food is all prepared buffet style. I am off to the movies with a couple of girlfriends, so I will hopefully see you a little later tonight."

With that the two men made their way to the study. The room itself was large – larger than Felix remembered it. Dark stained wood was featured throughout the room, giving it an inviting feel. Leather furniture was perfectly arranged in each corner, with a large mahogany desk facing the entry. To his left as he walked in was a bar, and standing behind said bar was Wild Bill himself, mixing a couple of highballs. Just to his right was a roaring fire in the fireplace. Next to the fireplace was a table full of food – steaks, baked potatoes, green beans, and chocolate cake. Delicious food, and unusual during wartime shortages. Donovan came over and greeted Felix warmly. "Thank you for coming all this way, my friend," said Donovan. Felix smiled and nodded, saying, "If the circumstances were reversed, I know that you would do the same for me." It was Donovan's turn to nod in agreement. "Yes. Yes I would."

With that, Donovan gestured to the food. He didn't need to do it twice. George watched as his English friend quickly made his way to the table full of food. He wasted no time in stacking his plate, and was completely unaware as George and his boss exchanged bemused glances with one another as Felix tore into his meal. Rationing in England had been much worse and had been going on much longer. Plus, "Let's be honest," George whispered to Wild Bill: "The words "English" and "food" don't exactly go well together."

After dinner they all enjoyed a couple of drinks and fine cigars from Donovan's stash.

The Americans waited patiently for their English cousin to tell them what they were fairly sure they already knew.

CHAPTER 43

After they had gathered their emotions, Edwin and his daughter walked around the park for a few more minutes. Both father and daughter had learned to look around casually to see if they were being followed. On this day, there was no one in sight. They stopped at another bench and sat again. Edwin had weighed the risk and decided to tell Leigh. He had decided that she deserved to know. Plus, he was exhausted from carrying this heavy load by himself. He told her…enough. Not everything. After all, should the worst happen, she would be protected to some extent, since she didn't know some of the major elements to the overall plan.

He told her about the technology that he was working on, and the ramifications of such technology. The positives and potential world altering effects of it, and the potential damage it could bring if misused. He spoke of the world that he envisioned with the technology. And he spoke of the deadly consequences of it being in the hands of the wrong people. Leigh listened, not commenting at all. She would occasionally hold her father's hand as he became more emotional or frustrated. As he told her, he would casually look over her shoulder as she looked over his, always watching for someone to come out of nowhere to arrest them. After he was finished, he looked around the park one more time to ensure that they were not being watched. He still saw nothing and no one. After he was sure that they were safe, he looked at his daughter and quietly said, "You must never tell anyone about this, Leigh. They will kill both of us if they find out."

"I know, Dad. We must figure a way out of here. We will need to carefully plan how we can escape. Can you continue to stall on some of the testing?"

"I can certainly try. I think Lippisch is getting a little suspicious, but I also believe that our friendship might trump the timeline that we are on. He is not a Nazi, but he is also in a very difficult position. And von Greim, that arrogant idiot, is a huge problem. His ego is so massive and he has bet his entire career on this. Hitler himself is engaged in this project, and von Greim knows that this is his ticket to the inner circle. Leigh, it is clear that he fancies you. Please do NOT encourage him or somehow think that you can manipulate him in some way. It won't work with someone like that."

"I understand, Dad," replied Leigh.

"Another thing," Edwin continued. "We must not talk about this at home or anywhere there are people around. I've already told you that they have listening devices somewhere in our home. We need to assume that they are listening everywhere."

Leigh thought for a minute before speaking. "Is there anyone on the base besides Lippisch that you trust?"

Edwin paused to think. "No one that comes to mind. There are decent men and women there, but I just don't know any of them well enough to say definitively."

CHAPTER 44

"Jet propulsion?" "How does it work exactly?" asked Parker. Felix Cowgill shrugged his shoulders. "That's a question that requires a technical answer, and I am clearly not an engineer. All I can tell you is that there are no propellers, and that these jet planes can go a lot faster than our propeller planes. And I mean MUCH faster. Our boys won't have a chance up there against them. And neither will yours. They will be able to strike with almost no notice and will be almost impossible to track and shoot at."

Donovan studied his cigar as he listened. He finally spoke quietly: "Frankly, Felix, our intelligence suspected that the Nazis were working on something like this, but we had no confirmation and no context on it. But the idea of jet propulsion isn't all that new. We had reports as early as 5 years ago that the Germans were working on something like this. The difference now is that they appear to be a lot closer than we thought. Do we know how long it will be before they are in production?"

Cowgill again shrugged. "No, we really don't know that. But we must assume that they are close. There are more questions than answers right now," he continued. "Are they reliable? How long are they serviceable for before the engines need to be replaced or maintained? Can they mass produce these? If so, where would they do it? I can tell you this: Our air army is working on similar technology. It's not easy to perfect. It's one thing to get a plane in the air as a prototype. That's actually when the real work begins."

He rose and walked to the window of Donovan's study. With his back to the two Americans, he said quietly, "We have no choice. We must assume that their perfection of this program is imminent. And if they do get these out of production, we will lose the skies. And we will also lose the water. There simply is no way for us to compete against that, let alone defend ourselves against it."

Parker sat quietly, taking it all in. He looked at Donovan, who gave him a slight nod. George's eyes shifted from his boss to their English visitor. "Felix," he began, "Perhaps it's time that we collaborate and share our resources. Now that we know what it is that we are up against, we will both have the same objective: to, at a minimum, stall the production of these planes, if not destroy the Germans' capabilities to bring this technology to the war. We are much better off putting all of our intelligence on the table together and determining how best to proceed."

Cowgill, never turning away from the window, said, "Well, Chaps, I didn't come all the way over here just to have a delicious dinner."

They spent the rest of the evening strategizing how best to proceed. Donovan began by telling Felix about Frank.

He only got a couple of sentences into it before Parker interrupted. "He's a great kid and we sent him in there with no plan and only one way to communicate with us. We have to get him out of there alive."

Cowgill looked from George to Donovan, as if to say, "All right, this one is personal for George."

Donovan, picking up on Cowgill's glance, decided to come clean with Felix, at least as to Frank Sweeney. "This young man – our guy – works for the Irish Independent as a reporter. His cover name is Frank McGuire. We know that he has made contact with Conway but we have no context. We don't know how often he has talked to Conway, or how accessible Conway is to him." Donovan paused. Then: "And our guy happens to be George's godson."

Cowgill: "You mean to tell me that you sent –"

Donovan: "Yes, that is what I'm telling you. We had no other option. The kid was our best and only choice, given the circumstances. We needed someone who was Irish that could pass for a neutral Irish reporter, and we needed someone that we could trust implicitly. And we also needed a guy who knew his way around airplanes. You can find a man that might meet one or even two of those requirements. But Frank was the only one who met all four. Those kinds of young men don't grow on trees."

Cowgill nodded slowly, putting himself in Donovan's position. He reminded himself that the U.S. was far behind them in the intelligence game. Donovan would get the game figured out and then some, but this was really one of the first ventures in the intelligence war for the Americans.

He turned to Parker: "I'm sorry, Old Boy. We will do all that we can to help you bring him back safely."

Parker, his voice tight with emotion: "Felix, I would be forever in your debt."

The room grew quiet as each man processed. Eventually, Donovan spoke again: "Look, of course we all want him back." Then he looked from one man to another. "But we have a mission to complete, and THAT has to be the priority. And it will be. He was sent in to get Edwin Conway off of that project, in any way that he could. Ideally, he walks out of Germany with Conway. But his orders were to kill Conway if he couldn't get him out of there. That was made clear to him, and he acknowledged that order. So, gentlemen, as much as I hate to say it, the mission is still on. Getting our guy out is secondary to getting Conway off of the project."

Felix agreed and said, "We certainly would like to get our asset out as well, although the mission was a bit different than yours. We were simply trying to ascertain what the devil the Jerrys were up to."

Parker: "We can get messages from Frank, and we have. But we have no way of communicating back to him." Donovan anticipated Felix's next comment and said, somewhat defensively, "We were out of time. We had to get him in there."

Felix merely nodded. "War certainly dictates, doesn't it? Well, we can surely put our assets in touch."

Parker asked the obvious question: "But how, Felix? Can you communicate with your asset?"

"Yes, and fairly easily, too. Unfortunately, I am not cleared to tell you about our asset. I know it sounds trite, but I need the Prime Minister's permission to divulge that information, and he was unreachable when I left."

Both men looked disappointed and annoyed at this revelation.

Felix said, "I can tell you this, however. I would say that it is highly likely that they have either figured each other out or they will very shortly."

"So they have been in contact with one another?"

"Not as of yesterday," replied Cowgill. "Although our asset is a bit suspicious of your man's real intentions."

"How is that possible?" asked Donovan, with just the least discernable bit of alarm.

Felix hesitated. "Let's just say that our people are very well trained. Remember, we have been at this for a few more years than you have."

Parker held his head in his hands at that comment.

"There are some other things that we have learned. Maybe you already know some of this, but we should be sure. This project is being led by Colonel Robert Ritter von Greim. He was something of a hero in the Great War, and he reports directly to that mad man, Hermann Göring."

"I know of von Greim," said Donovan. "Von Greim also knows Hitler, because he flew Hitler around between the wars, as I recall."

"You are correct on that score, Old Boy," replied Felix. "What you may not know is that von Greim is what we call a "climber." He desperately wants to be in Hitler's inner circle, and he views this project as his ticket to the dance. On top of that, he is a true Nazi through and through. We think Dr. Conway's German counterpart, Herr Lippisch, is a purist in the sense that he is loyal first and foremost to the airplane and making strides in the world of air travel. He goes along with the Nazis because they happen to fund his passion. The war is something far removed from his world. He is an agnostic when it comes to politics." Cowgill paused at this point to read his two friends' faces. It seemed evident that at least some of this information was new to them. Donovan waved at him to continue.

"Right. Well. As best as we can tell through our contact, Conway is clearly not a Nazi and not even a Nazi sympathizer. Our own people in MI6 are divided about his motive for helping the Germans. One side argues that it makes no sense that he would volunteer to help in this assignment, given that he is supposedly opposed to what the Nazi's promote and stand for. The other analysts argue that he is a widower, having lost his wife a few years ago. He also lost a son. The boy was studying in London and was supposed to go home for the holidays. He apparently got on the train for Dublin. The train only made one stop. He was not on the train when it stopped in Dublin. Not one clue as to what happened to him. That was a few years ago, I believe. Conway has one child remaining, a daughter. She is actually with him in Germany. So what else does he have to live for? The Germans arranged for his daughter to teach English to German children at a private school in Augsburg."

"Which side do you take in this, Felix?" asked George.

Cowgill absently stroked his mustache for a few moments before answering. "I'm afraid that I really don't know, Old Chap. I change my opinion almost daily on this. Most days I wonder if von Greim may have threatened him in some way in order to get him to go to Germany. Maybe von Greim told him that they would harm his daughter if he didn't agree to his plan. Again, we have no proof of that, but, I tend to land on the side that says that it doesn't make any sense for him to volunteer for something like this."

He paused. "However, we also know that he and Lippisch are old friends. Their friendship predates the Great War. So maybe his friendship with Lippisch played a role. We just aren't sure. The only thing we're sure about is that von Greim is a horrible human being who would sell his own mother out if it meant getting into Hitler's inner circle. And the very best way for him to get into that circle and stay there is to get this technology perfected and put into the war."

The three men again sat in silence for several minutes, each processing the information in their own way. All three arrived at the same conclusion, and that was that this jet propulsion business must be stopped.

George finally broke the silence: "What can you tell us about the airfield in Augsburg? We assume that Conway works there every day."

Felix again stared out the window before he answered. He was a little bit ahead of his American counterparts because he had a couple of days to process all of the information that he was now sharing with them.

"We're fairly certain that this is where all of the work and research is being done. First, we have followed Conway on several days. He leaves his home every morning at 7:30AM and arrives at the airfield around 7:45AM. Also, the airfield itself gives us clues. There is very little air traffic into that airfield on one side. The other side looks to run as a true production and assembly facility for the 109's, complete with several takeoffs and not as many landings. So they are completing the 109's and getting them in the air to other air bases on the continent. Having said all of this, the airfield's security is not as strict as you would think." This gave the Americans pause. "Why do..." before Parker could finish his question, Felix continued.

"We think it's because they don't want to draw too much attention to it so that it would become a target to take out. It is by no means wide open, but there are some holes in it, at least on the surface. The facility and grounds are quite extensive. There is more than enough room there for the Jerrys to conduct their research. We think that the group of German scientists that are assigned to this project are some of the more brilliant minds in the country. But it is a relatively small group, because Hitler only has so many resources. Remember, he is fighting a war on two fronts and that requires a tremendous amount of resources."

"You can say that again," said Donovan, grimly.

Cowgill continued: "We also know that they are trying to develop some sort of super artillery gun that can shoot great distances into the air. And then there are their subs. As you know, their U-boats have dominated the Atlantic. And their Panzer tanks. They have launched their third version of those tanks, and they have produced thousands of them. So we believe that they are spread very thin."

Donovan and Parker were impressed. The English were indeed well ahead of them when it came to gathering – and assessing - intelligence. It made Donovan wonder to himself if they just should have approached MI6 about taking this assignment for them, instead of putting a rookie like this Sweeney kid in there. But as quickly as he entertained that thought, he got rid of it. No use second guessing that now. They were in it up to their eyeballs. But that didn't mean that he couldn't ask for some help.

"All right," said Wild Bill. "We agree that we need to move on this. We would certainly be obliged to you if you could re-assign your asset to help with Conway."

"That won't be a problem," replied Felix.

"Good. Let's have your asset reveal your mission to our guy and get the two of them talking. Make sure they both understand that they are to move together on Conway, and to come up with a plan quickly. It is critical that our guy understands that his mission hasn't changed: Get Conway off that project, one way or the other. We would prefer that Conway ends up back with us. But if Frank can't get him out, then Conway needs to be eliminated. The whole war may ride on us stopping this project."

Cowgill, still facing the window, said, "We can certainly agree on that point."

Donovan: "A couple of more things, Felix."

"What is it, Bill?"

"First, we must have very clear communication between each of us and our collective people on the ground. It is so easy in these things to not be clear or to have our instructions misinterpreted, and the consequences to not having everyone with a clear line of communication could be devastating. We cannot afford a slip up here."

Cowgill looked a bit miffed. All he could manage was, "Quite."

Donovan, picking up on the fact that his friend felt he was being lectured, realized he better put some context to his comments. "And your second point?" asked Cowgill, clearly agitated.

The head of the O.S.S. took a puff on his cigar and looked from Cowgill to Parker, and then back to Cowgill. "My second point ties to my first point." Donovan hesitated. Finally, he spoke. "I am very concerned that you might have a spy within your organization. Hence the need to have clear communication, but also the need for only the three of us to know about this."

"Impossible!" Cowgill fairly shouted.

Now George spoke: "Felix, it is not only not impossible but probable that you have someone in your department as a spy. There have been too many leaks and too many lost agents. And I'm not just talking about your agents. We have some missing as well."

Silence, once again, but not as long as before. Finally, Felix spoke. "Just so we have clear communication (he glanced at Donovan as he said it), when I said, "Impossible!" I was not referring to your accusation that we have a spy somewhere in MI6. I have entertained that idea quite seriously for a while now. What is impossible is that I cannot share what we have just discussed with anyone. There are at least two people that I need to tell. One of them is Henry, my assistant, who, by the way, was the man who told me of his suspicions about a spy within our organization. The other is some chap you may have heard of named Churchill, or something like that. He's rumored to have something to do with the war effort."

Donovan chuckled and in so doing, inhaled the cigar smoke that he had just tried to exhale, causing a brief but violent coughing fit. Upon seeing his boss turning red and hacking like a wounded duck, George nearly spit his swallow of the highball out of his mouth. Felix, caught in the moment of seeing both men nearly double over, actually laughed out loud and started for Donovan first, to make sure that he was OK. Donovan put up his hand as he continued to cough, basically the equivalent of the OK sign. Parker was coughing now as well, concerned that the highball would come out of his nose. It took a minute for the three of them to calm down. They all were once again thinking the same thing, and Donovan articulated their collective thought: "That's the first laugh we've had in quite some time," he said. Parker, still chuckling, said, "Glad to provide the entertainment."

The smiles faded as each man collected himself again. Cowgill turned to Donovan and Parker directly. "The trip here has been more than worthwhile. Thank you for a wonderful evening. We all have our marching orders."

Donovan stuck his hand out to his friend. "Let's talk next week. By then we will all have had time to think about how we can help our collective resources over there succeed."

"Agreed," said Cowgill. He paused. "We must stop this project, gentlemen."

After he had gone, Donovan asked George to stay for a nightcap. "All right," George conceded. "But only one."

Wild Bill Donovan was a wine connoisseur. He learned that from his wife, but he was a bourbon man at heart. As Donovan poured the drinks, George asked, rather indelicately, if he trusted Cowgill. The older man didn't hesitate. "I do, George. As much as you can trust anyone in this crazy business, anyway. I've known him a long time, and my contact here has assured me repeatedly that Felix is a man we can trust implicitly with all of our information. After all, at this point, we really don't have a choice."

"That's good to know," answered George. "Because I couldn't help but notice that you didn't tell him everything."

His boss kept making the drinks. "Georgie my boy, just because you trust someone doesn't mean that you have to tell them everything. Besides, I am convinced that they have a spy in their midst. Less is more right now, lad."

CHAPTER 45

Frank sat down with Peter, Minnie and Esther for lunch. Minnie had prepared some melted cheese sandwiches and tea. As they ate, Frank casually brought up the envelope. "Peter, did you happen to see who brought the envelope to the door?"

"No, I didn't. It must have been delivered late last night, because it was there at 6:30AM this morning when I opened the door."

Frank noted that Minnie and Esther didn't ask about the letter. Which meant that they had seen it as well. But it was also clear that the envelope hadn't been opened. So, perhaps Peter just mentioned it to them. They were all too polite to ask what the content of the letter was.

"Thank you for giving it to me," was all that Frank could think to say.

Peter merely nodded. Minnie changed the subject and that was the end of it.

Frank helped with the dishes and then made his way back up to his apartment to wait until 6:00PM. He would get on the train for a bit and move around the city, just to make sure that he wasn't being followed. As he sat in his sparse apartment, he once again tried to summarize all that he had learned and observed since he had arrived in Germany.

He looked around at the small, simple living room. The couch's padding was misshaped, and the small table where he ate snacks was uneven. The same went for the small bed that was in the apartment when he moved in. "Sort of a typical bachelor apartment," he thought. On the other hand, Minnie and Esther had both been so kind to him, always sharing additional food and drink when they could. "They have been so generous with me, especially with a war on," he noted. "Not all of the German people are crazy." Then: "I wonder if they would be this nice to me if they knew who I really was."

His parents would want to thank the Stoffels for taking care of their son. "The odds of that ever happening aren't great," he thought. He made himself some tea and looked out the window at the street. The train was just coming into the station. The screeching brakes were so loud that all conversations would cease for several seconds. "They told me that I'd get used to the noise, but it hasn't happened yet."

There were children playing on the sidewalk and adults hurrying to catch the train. "If it weren't for the food shortages, one really wouldn't know that there was a war on," he mused.

As he nursed his tea, his thoughts inevitably went back to his assignment. And to Leigh. He had never met anyone quite like her. Apart from her beauty, which, he had to admit, attracted him to her from the beginning, she was bright. And funny. Most of all, he loved her attitude. Here she was in a foreign country that was at war, yet she had no hesitation to leave Ireland so that she could take care of her father. That spoke volumes to Frank about her character.

He was falling hard for her, but he couldn't let his feelings for her get in the way of his objective. Leigh's dedication to her father prompted another question that Frank had been wrestling with.

He remained puzzled by Edwin Conway's acceptance of the position in Germany to begin with. He had started to consider the reasons why he would do it and had eliminated several of them. He asked himself for the 100th time: What would make a respected aeronautical engineer leave his homeland and move to a country that would almost certainly end up in a war?

Surely he had to see the writing on the wall when he and Leigh moved here before Germany invaded Poland? After several minutes of more reflection, an idea began to take shape in Frank's head. The more Frank thought about it, the more sense that it made to him.

Of course! All of the evidence had been there from the beginning. Edwin Conway hadn't volunteered to come to Germany. He was *forced* to come. By von Greim. Or von Slime, as Frank had come to call him. Von Greim had made Conway come here. But how? He must have told him that Leigh would be harmed if he didn't come. That's the only thing that made sense.

After all, his wife and son were gone. There could be no other reason. Yeah. That had to be it. But could he get Edwin to admit this to him? And did Leigh even know?

His thoughts were interrupted by more footsteps coming up the stairs. This was followed by a loud knock on his door. Frank automatically tensed. He hardly ever had any guests, and the Stoffels wouldn't likely come to his room so soon after lunch. He tucked in his shirt and ran a comb through his hair as he moved a step toward the door. "Who is it?" he called.

After a moment, a voice said, "Herr McGuire, it is the Gestapo. Please open the door. Now!"

Frank froze. The Gestapo? Why? How...? He collected himself and looked quickly out the window down to the street. Nothing looked out of the ordinary. "Yes, coming," he said quickly.

He opened the door to two men with dark coats. They both had swastikas on their left arms. The taller of the two had a nasty scar that ran across his left cheek. As he took off his special hat, his blond hair was neatly cut without a hair out of place. The other young man was shorter with darker hair than his comrade. The only outstanding feature about him was that he seemed to have eyebrows that ran right into one another.

"Heil Hitler!" they barked.

Frank looked at each of them and said, "Good afternoon."

Scarface handled most of the conversation. "I am Franz Kimler and this is Johan Moeffler." "We are here to check your papers."

"My papers?"

"Yes, Herr McGuire. "It is McGuire, isn't it?"

"Yes, that's my name," replied Frank. "Is there a problem?"

Now Onebrow spoke: "Should there be a problem, Herr McGuire?"

Frank, maintaining his cool, said, "I can't think why there would be," as he handed his papers to Scarface. As Kimler looked at his papers, he sized up both men. They were well built and didn't smile for even a second. All business.

"They are trying to intimidate me," thought Frank, suddenly on to their game. "They have nothing on you. Just keep calm and carry on," as he was taught in the Army Air Force. He relaxed a bit and made sure his Irish brogue was on full display.

"This says you are to be here for six months. Why only six months? We usually see papers for a year or more," said Kimler.

"It's a new assignment for me and my editors back in Ireland wanted to make sure that I was up for the task before committing too much money on me," said Frank.

"And you are a writer, yes?" Now it was Onebrow's turn.

"That's right," said Frank.

"What kind of writer?"

"I write for the Irish Independent, an Irish newspaper back in-"

"I know where the Irish Independent is based. It is my job to know everything, Herr McGuire."

"In that case, maybe I could ask you a few questions, gentlemen."

They looked at each other, temporarily befuddled. "What kind of questions?" Scarface again.

"Well for example, where is a good place to get some good schnitzel around here? It seems like it is difficult to find good food here, and Germany is known for its' great food."

Scarface glanced up from his papers at him with a tired look. "Herr McGuire, we are at war. If you find some good schnitzel, maybe you could tell US."

Frank laughed, trying to make it sound as though three old friends were sharing a joke.

Neither man as much as smiled. Kimler said, "Your papers are in order. Make sure that your newspaper keeps your papers current."

Onebrow now: "We will be back to check on you before your six months are up." He then stepped closer to Frank. Frank looked at him as Onebrow tried to get very close. "I'd be very careful about what I write if I were you." Frank looked at them both and said, "Thank you. I will." With that, they left, not with so much as another "Heil Hitler."

Frank closed the door and tried not to breathe too loudly. He made his way to the window, careful to look surreptitiously for the two men to make their way out of the building. Within a few seconds, they both emerged, checking their notes and conversing. Scarface pointed in a direction and off they went, searching for their next victim to harass.

OPERATION GRAB BAG: A FRANK SWEENEY ADVENTURE

He hated the fact that he had to take that from these punks, but he had no choice at this point. "It appears that this was a random stop," he said to himself.

6:00PM finally came. He went down the fire escape as quietly as possible and waited in the shadows for the train. He waited until the last possible second before the train started to move and then hurried onto the last car. It was almost empty. Just a young mother with two children. The older boy was about seven and the younger one looked to be about two. The mother was busy shushing the younger boy. The older boy stared at Frank with a child's curiosity. Frank smiled at the boy and then looked away. Before long, he got off the train and walked at a quick pace for a couple of blocks toward a different park. He jumped on and off several trains and ended up riding the train to one stop before his normal exit for the flower shop. It was only a three or four block walk to the park where he was to meet Owl.

He arrived in the park five minutes early. It was dark with few lights on. He made his way over to the area that held the statues. He waited in the shadows. And waited. At 7:15PM he was ready to give up. He heard a sound behind him and turned. He saw no one. He heard someone or something. He started to walk slowly toward the sound. He stepped on a twig that snapped. Suddenly there was a flashlight in his face. It hit his eyes and temporarily blinded him. He heard someone running. It took him a few seconds to get oriented. He began to run in the direction of the sound that he heard. More sounds. Faster running ahead of him. He was feeling his way through bushes and limbs. More branches being snapped. He wanted to call out but thought better of it. He kept running. Feeling his way. The sound grew more distant. After a couple of minutes, it was apparent that whomever was there was long gone. After running into a large pine for the third time, Frank gave up. It was evident that the person who ran away knew the park much better than he did. He kicked himself for being so foolish. He looked around quickly to see if he had been followed. He saw no one.

He gathered himself, smoothed his hair, and tried to casually walk out of the woods and back to his apartment. He had had enough excitement and trains for one night.

CHAPTER 46

Von Greim waited in the back seat of his car for his spy to arrive. At 7:03PM the door opened and the man appeared. "You are three minutes late," von Greim hissed. The man had a worried look on his face. "I am very sorry, Colonel, but I had to make sure that I wasn't followed."

Von Greim stared at him. "Then start three minutes earlier!" Do you know how disrespectful it is to keep a man like me waiting?" He was shouting now. His frustration was clearly building. The project was taking too long. Göring would start to ask questions, all the while undermining him to the Fuhrer.

"Well, what do you have for me?" he spat at the man.

"Nothing to speak of, Colonel. He seems to be exactly what he claims to be. We checked with our sources in Ireland and his story mirrors what our sources in Ireland tell us."

Von Greim thought for a few moments as the other man waited anxiously, not saying another word unless he was spoken to.

Von Greim finally spoke. "All right. Have you learned anything else about the project?"

"There is some good news to report on that front," said the other man. It looks as though their first prototype should be ready to test within the next 14 days." At least that is what our sources are telling us."

Von Greim inwardly breathed a sigh of relief. That *was* good news, he said to himself. "This will at least get Göring off my back."

To the other man: "Well don't just sit there! Get out of my car and continue the surveillance. We will meet here seven days from now at the same time. And if you are late again, don't bother showing up. We will find you." He glared at the other man so harshly that he heard the poor fellow's gasp as he leapt out of the car.

"Finally," he thought. "We are almost ready to test. Bringing Conway in from Ireland was brilliant," he congratulated himself. And why not? That idiot Göring would never offer him congratulations. He would instead tell the Fuhrer that it was his idea all along. "I will smash that miserable little man if it's the last thing that I do," he promised.

CHAPTER 47

Frank waited a good distance from his apartment for an hour or so. Seeing no one come or go, he decided to take a chance and go back in. He chose the fire escape as his entrance. He made it into his place without incident. After thoroughly checking the apartment, he made his way downstairs and knocked on the Stoffel's door. No answer. He knocked a second time. After a bit of a longer wait, Peter called out something in German.

Frank guessed what he had asked, and said through the door, "It's me, Frank." After another moment, Peter opened the door and looked at him and smiled. "Hello! Is everything all right?"

"Yes," said Frank. "I was just wondering if anyone stopped by to ask for me tonight."

Peter looked at him a little more closely and said, "Why don't you come in for a minute?"

Frank hesitated, then walked in. He hadn't been in their home before. It was decorated nicely and was very organized and clean. There was a Bible on the table, along with some apple strudel that Minnie had made. Minnie came down the steps and gave Frank a hug. "Would you care for some strudel?" she asked. Frank noticed that there was a couple of pieces left. He also saw four plates at the table. "No, thank you, Minnie. I don't want to eat the last piece," he smiled. "Besides, it looks like you have already been generous with it."

Minnie blushed and said, "I guess I'm just a little behind on my dishes."

After a couple of minutes of small talk, Frank asked if there had been anyone that had come by tonight to ask for him.

"No," said Minnie. "You had two visitors this afternoon, but I'm sure that you recall that."

"Yes, that was a memorable visit," he replied.

Peter and Minnie looked at one another for a second and then back at Frank.

Finally, Peter asked, "Did everything turn out all right?"

Frank, tired and getting a little irritable, let his guard down a bit and said, "Oh, it was wonderful. Being threatened by two Nazi thugs was very uplifting."

Immediately he regretted his comments and apologized. He said, "I'm very sorry. I shouldn't have said anything to you about that. I guess that I'm just a bit tired. Please forgive me."

Minnie and Peter again exchanged a subtle glance that only married people can pull off. She gave Frank a hug and told him to get some rest. Peter gave him a slap on the back and said, "We'll see you tomorrow at breakfast."

Frank returned to his apartment, half expecting the door to be broken down in the middle of the night. Tonight was his first real spy experience and it hadn't gone well. "How could I have been so foolish?" Then, after a moment, "What have I gotten myself into?" he asked himself for the 100th time. "They may very well be on to me. First, I get this random letter. Not handwritten, only typed, so I can't possibly tell who it's from. Then I get an unannounced, supposedly random visit from the Gestapo of all people. Then I take the bait in a dark place to meet Owl at a place of his choosing. Whoever flashed that light in my face did so to identify me. Someone now knows my true identity. How stupid can I be?"

He began to run through a list of all of his contacts in his mind, assessing each one and determining whether each could have leaked something, intentionally or unintentionally to the Nazis. This proved to be futile, because he didn't know all that many people and, so far no one had come to arrest him.

He had, on occasion, wished that he had half the training on this spy stuff as he had with becoming a pilot. The fact was that he had absolutely *no* training on being a spy. That brought him back to his Uncle George and, eventually, to his family.

His Dad always talked about taking a mental vacation for a few minutes every day, where he thought about their cabin up on Poplar Lake outside of St. Croix Falls, Wisconsin. "Great for the mind and the spirit," he would say with a twinkle in his eye. There were so many memories from being at the cabin. The Sweeneys all loved to fish, and the lake had plenty of pan fish, bass and northern pike. Even the occasional walleye would find its way into the boat. The family would roast marshmallows in the fire pit after dinner and the children would listen to their father (and occasionally, their mother) spin yarns about their childhoods. Jack would prod his parents for more stories, even though some of them they'd heard a dozen times before. Jack. Those were such happy and fun days.

He was trying to figure out what time it was in St. Paul. After some calculations, he determined that it would be about 2:30PM back home. It being Saturday, that meant only one thing: the family slept in and had a late brunch that consisted mainly of sour dough waffles that his Mom made from scratch.

Maggie Sweeney's sour dough waffles were the talk of the neighborhood. The other mothers would good naturedly beg her for the recipe, but Maggie always held out. The recipe came all the way from Ireland with Maggie's mother. Of course, bacon would always accompany the waffles. Frank could almost smell the breakfast as he dreamed about it. His sisters would scurry around the kitchen, helping their mother. Evelyn would know exactly what her Mother needed before she was asked.

"I hope Evie is doing all right," thought Frank. "She must miss Richard a lot." Richard Myler, Evie's fiancé, was in the Navy, stationed on a battleship somewhere in the South Pacific.

Tragedy had already visited the Myler family. Richard's brother was a fighter pilot in Europe, and he had been shot down while strafing a supply train. He was officially listed as "Missing in Action." The family clung to the hope that he had survived, but no official word had come as yet.

He thought of Katherine, his other sister. Fiercely independent and very proud of her Irish heritage, Katherine was dating Luis Rojas, a South American doctor whom the family all loved. They might move to Venezuela, the good doctor's country of origin. The Sweeneys weren't all that crazy about the idea, but if that was what Katherine wanted, the family would rally around her. Besides, with Katherine's stubborn Irish mentality, it would do no good to try to talk her out of it.

Frank smiled at the thought of each of them sitting around the kitchen table on a typical Saturday morning in St. Paul. His Dad would lead the family in a prayer of thanksgiving, and his mom would sit down for all of a minute if she was lucky, just because she loved to cook for her husband and children.

He allowed himself another thought. Actually, he didn't so much as allow himself this thought. It was upon him before he knew it. It invaded his mind and took it hostage. It was something that he had fought ever since he was made aware of this mission: Would he ever see his family again? Would he ever make it home? And *how* in the world would he or could he ever make it out of Germany?

The Nazi movement was evil personified. He had begun to hear stories of the persecution of Jews who lived in Germany. Jews who were even German citizens. He hadn't seen anything firsthand in Augsburg of such persecution, but the men at the newspaper talked in hushed tones about what they had heard was going on in other German cities. And, strangely, even Jewish people in and near the city of Augsburg had recently started to just disappear. No one had any idea as to what happened to them. There were really only two schools of thought: One was that the Nazis were quietly showing up at their homes and grabbing them with the idea of taking them and putting them in camps to work; or that these families were disappearing on their own – escaping or going into hiding – before they themselves were nabbed by the Nazis.

Regardless of which theory was accurate, the disappearances were one topic that the Gestapo had made clear was not to be covered or written about by the newspapers. That had come from O'Shea himself.

Frank told himself that this was another reason why he had to make it out of the country. The world needed to know about these abuses. The German people that he had met were kind enough. Minnie and Peter looked after him like he was their own son. He was already so thankful for them and their kindness. The same with Esther.

But the Nazis and that mad man Hitler – that was entirely different. The way they intimidated the ordinary citizens and controlled the local authorities was frightening. Frank tried to picture America with such a "government." "The people would never tolerate such a thing," he thought. "But," he admitted to himself, "I doubt the German people ever thought that this Nazi regime would turn out the way that it did, either."

After a couple of more minutes of reflection, he slapped his knees and said, "All right, back to reality." He thought hard about the mission – his mission. He simply had to succeed in getting Edwin Conway out of the country. Or, if he couldn't deliver on that mission, he unfortunately would need to implement the alternative option. Either way, Dr. Conway would no longer be employed by the German Luftwaffe.

CHAPTER 48

One Week Later

George Parker was in General Donovan's office downloading the latest information that had come in from Lion. It was a positive message because Lion was formulating his plan to move on Dr. Conway. He would implement the plan shortly. That meant that MI6 needed to be looped into the conversation and make sure that the assets on the ground were coordinating efforts.

Peg McFarlane answered the phone at the Director's office on the first ring. "This is the White House calling on the President's behalf for Director Donovan."

"Thank you. I will have the Director on the phone momentarily." She hurried into Donovan's office, knocking as she entered. Donovan looked up from his desk. "Excuse me, Director, but the White House is on the phone. It's the President."

"Tell him I'm busy and that I'll call him back when I get a minute," said Donovan.

Peg looked at him and gasped. Donovan burst out laughing and Parker smiled, but only for a moment.

"I'm just kidding, Peg. Of course I'll take the call immediately." Then, to Parker: "George, stay for a minute. Talks with the old man typically don't last very long."

He called to Peg to put the operator from the White House on the line. That was always the protocol. The President always came on the phone after the person he was trying to reach was on the line.

"Wild Bill!" exclaimed the President.

"Mr. President," replied Donovan.

"I just wanted to talk to someone for a minute who I know doesn't want anything from me. That's such a rarity these days."

"Well, I can assure you that there really isn't anything that I want from you, Mr. President."

"Of course, Bill. I know that. Actually," continued F.D.R., "I'm calling because *I* want something from *you*."

"And how can I help you, Mr. President?"

"I'd like to ask you for an update on our problem with the jet propulsion project in Germany."

"Mr. President, your timing is impeccable, as always. Sitting with me is George Parker, our Special Agent in Charge of this initiative. He has just briefed me on the latest goings on over there. George has received word from our asset on the ground and other sources that the first prototype is imminent. Depending on how the test goes, they could be in production in a matter of months; maybe even weeks."

This news was met with silence.

"However," continued, Donovan, "They will still be desperately reliant on Dr. Conway for a lot more work on the technology. The first prototype is only really a proof of concept, as our engineers call it. It is a significant step, to be sure, but that doesn't mean that they will have these things in the skies overnight, either."

"All the more reason to act, I suppose?" asked the President. Donovan smiled wearily at Parker, who could hear the entire conversation. This was classic Roosevelt. Steering the conversation with small but unmistakable prods.

"Yes, sir. That was the other part of the correspondence from our man over there. He has also communicated that he is going to make his move within a week from now, and, as you know, that means getting Conway out of there, one way or the other."

"Bill, it would be far more preferable to have his mind working for us rather than the enemy."

"Yes, Mr. President. That is certainly what we want to happen as well."

"Good! It's settled, then. Let me know if you need anything."

"Thank you, sir."

"Oh, and Bill…one more thing. Getting Dr. Conway and men like him over here could really jump start our recovery once this thing is over."

"Yes, sir. I couldn't agree with you more."

"Thank you, Bill." A pause. "Did you say that Special Agent Parker is there with you?"

"Yes, sir, I did." Wild Bill looked at Parker, who began to do an amazing impression of a crab trying to backpedal. Although doing so in a chair made it an unusually funny scene, especially when one put his actions together with the absolute look of terror on his face.

"Put him on for a moment."

"Yes, sir."

Parker was already doing the cut across his neck and the violent shaking of his head.

"Donovan, purposely trying not to make eye contact to keep from laughing, said, louder than he needed to, "Special Agent, Parker, the President would like to speak to you."

Parker gasped and then tried to compose himself. He stared at Donovan for a second, as if to say, "When this thing is over, you are a dead man." Donovan, reading his mind, just smiled sweetly and held the phone out to him.

"This is Agent Special Park"…"this is Special Park…" "Ugh…" "This is Special Agent Parker…sir." He looked over at Donovan, whose back was now turned to him, shoulders shaking uncontrollably.

"Special Agent Parker, this is the President."

"Yes, sir!"

"George, I just wanted to commend you on all of the fine work that you have done, particularly on this project. Director Donovan has told me more than once that he couldn't have gotten this project off the ground if it wasn't for you."

"Uh. Well. Um. Thank you, sir."

"I know that this particular assignment has been challenging for you personally, George. But it is one of the most critical missions that we have right now. This one is one of only a handful of efforts that we have in play that can change the game. And it is one of the most urgent, because it is so time sensitive."

"Yes sir."

"This will likely be a mission that, if successful, may not ever be known to the outside world. Take comfort in knowing that we will know, and we will never forget. Just a few of us here, and this young man himself."

"Thank you, sir." Another pause.

Then, quietly: "No." "Thank *you*, Special Agent Parker." And with that, the President of the United States was gone.

CHAPTER 49

Frank arrived early at the newspaper. He was falling behind on a story for O'Shea, and decided to use his tardiness to have a word with his boss. He found him as he always did, sitting behind his desk with a scowl on his face.

Frank knocked on his door. O'Shea didn't move. Didn't look up. Didn't even appear to have heard the knock. Frank decided to knock again.

"I heard you the first time," the older man grumbled.

"Yes, sir. Sorry, sir" More silence.

After another minute, O'Shea looked up and said, "Well?"

Frank paused. "Mr. O'Shea, can I ask you a question?

"I told you: Knock off the Mr. O'Shea nonsense."

"Yes, sir."

O'Shea went back to the project at hand.

Frank, finally realizing that this was as good as he was going to get from the man, started in.

"When we first met, you asked if I was related to a McGuire that you knew back in Ireland." "What was his first name again?"

O'Shea looked up from his work and stared at him for a second. "Why?"

"Excuse me?"

"Why?" "Why do you ask?"

"I just couldn't recall, and the next time I talk to my family I'd like to ask them about it."

O'Shea thought for a second, looking at him. "His name is Sean. Or it was. I don't even know if he is even alive anymore."

"Sean," repeated Frank. "No, definitely not Sean."

It was another crowded and loud Saturday night at the club. Frank arrived at his usual time of 7:00PM. What was unusual was that he was the first person to arrive from the group that always met there.

The place was really filling up. "Herr McGuire!" It was Otto Kruger, his reserved colleague from the paper.

"Hello, Otto. What brings you here?"

"I was looking for something different to do on a Saturday night, and I heard that you and Hans come here a lot, so I thought that I'd try it out."

"Well, it's nice to have you here, Otto. Do you dance a lot?"

"Me? Oh no, I don't really know how to dance. At least not very well."

"Another unexpected interruption," thought Frank. "I must get to Dr. Conway tonight, at least to talk to him."

Mercifully, Hans showed up after a couple of more minutes of small talk between Frank and Kruger. The conversation turned to business. Each shared what stories that they were working on. Kruger had a column about the readiness of Augsburg should the war make its way there.

Hans just completed a piece on the unusually warm stretch of weather and its impact on the gardens and flowers of the city. Both men looked at Frank, waiting for him to tell them about his next contribution. Before he could make something up, he felt a tap on his shoulder. Standing behind him was Dr. Edwin Conway. He had a smile on his face that betrayed a feeling of…what? Preoccupation? Worry? Stress? In any case, Frank stood and shook hands with Dr. Conway. Frank introduced him to Kruger, and he and Hans chatted up the doctor while Frank looked around for Leigh.

He caught her eye as she chatted with people at another table. She smiled briefly at Frank, then turned back to the people that she had been talking to. After another minute or two, she made her way over to Frank and the others. After some quick greetings, she asked her father to help her order some drinks for the table. Surprisingly, Kruger volunteered to help.

After Edwin, Leigh and Kruger made their way to the bar, Frank looked at Hans. Hans simply said, "We need to talk."

Frank looked at his friend. He gauged the serious look on Hans' face and slowly said, "All...right..."

They made their way to the door and made a left down the sidewalk. Neither man said a word until they were sure that they were alone.

They looked at each other and Hans quietly said, "I know who you are."

Frank feigned confusion. "What are you talking about?"

Hans: "Look, Frank, we don't have a lot of time."

Frank, not budging: "Hans, I don't understand..."

Hans: "I know that you are an American pilot and spy. I know that you were sent here to get Edwin Conway out of Germany. You must trust me."

Frank was still silent, his mind racing. "I am admitting nothing to you. I am a journalist from Ireland and I..."

Hans, now whispering more loudly: "LISTEN TO ME! We...don't... have...time... for... this!" "We have to put together a plan and do it quickly! Their prototype engine is almost ready to test – it will likely happen within the next two weeks!"

"What are you talking about?"

Hans looked at his friend wearily. After a moment, he said, "All right, Frank." Hans looked around before he proceeded. "They are working on a jet propulsion engine that will knock everything else out of the sky. If they perfect this, the Allies' planes will be absolutely no match for the Germans. These planes will go 4 or 5 times faster than ours. The Germans will dominate the skies and we will lose the war."

Frank stared at Hans for a half minute. "How do you know all of this?"

"That's not important."

"It is to me, Hans."

Now it was Hans' turn to be silent for a moment.

"What I told you when I first met you was true. I did spend time in Milwaukee as a boy. I was there with some relatives for a couple of years. They lived in Mequon, which is a suburb. There is a strong German population in all of Wisconsin, but especially in Milwaukee." Before he could stop himself, Frank nodded in agreement. Hans ignored Frank's slip, or pretended to, anyway. "That is where I learned my English. And by the way, you have a Midwest accent, somewhere close to Wisconsin."

Frank silently yelled at himself for slipping up on the accent. Hans continued, "Well before the war broke out, I was already back in Germany. My parents were committed Christians – Lutherans – and we could all see what you Americans call "the writing on the wall." "We were told by our relatives in Milwaukee that America had no interest in getting involved in any more wars. So we knew that we had to do something. Both of my parents passed away a few years ago, so it's just me and a sister who is still in Milwaukee. The Nazis think that she is in Switzerland somewhere teaching school. I have nothing to lose in this fight. And that's all that you need to know at this point. You're going to have to trust me, Frank. The less you know, the better."

Frank thought for a moment. Something was missing here. What was it? He couldn't put his finger on it. "What about the other night?"

"What?"

Before he could think any more about it, he heard a young woman's voice: "There you are! What are you boys doing out here? I've been looking all over for you!" It was Esther.

Hans quickly recovered for both of them: "It was so noisy and smoky in there. We decided to get some air while we waited for you."

Esther looked a bit skeptical, but let it go. "Well, come on back in. They are starting to play some wonderful songs to dance to!"

Frank: "Lead the way, Esther!" We are right behind you!"

As they turned to go, the two men exchanged a glance and said nothing. Now that this was in the open, Frank's sense of urgency only increased. He tried to be engaged in the conversations that night, but his mind was elsewhere.

CHAPTER 50

Frank was in a deep, restful sleep. He was dreaming about fishing on Poplar Lake with his dad. And Jack! Jack was there, too! They were in the boat and ribbing each other about the size of fish that the others had caught. Frank pulled in a nice sized bass when Jack's rod began to tip.

"I hate to break this to you, Frank, but your bass is going to look pretty small when I land this one." Frank looked over at his Dad, who was smiling from ear to ear. "That's funny," thought Frank. "I rarely have seen Dad smile like that." As he looked over the side of the boat to see what sort of fish Jack had on his line, there was a dull thumping that started. It was insistent and kept getting a little more urgent with each rap. Then he heard his name being called. "Frank! Frank!"

Frank wanted to ignore it, but the boat – and his brother and father – began to fade from view.

Louder, now: "Frank!" It was a woman's voice. Frank got up, mumbled something incoherent, and, grabbing his robe, made his way to the door. He pushed his hair back. He recognized the voice. "Yes, Minnie, what is it?"

"Breakfast has been ready for you! It's getting cold!"

Puzzled, Frank merely called out, "All right. Thank you, Minnie. I will be right down."

Within five minutes he was at the kitchen table. Minnie had created a very nice spread, especially with war rations going on. Esther came and sat down with them. There were two different jellies, fresh bread and even some sausage. There were also a couple of hard boiled eggs and some strudel for dessert. Frank wondered what the occasion was. Minnie turned on the radio to a radio station that was playing music. She turned it up rather loudly, Frank thought. When he turned to look at her, she put her finger to her lips, motioning for him to stay silent. He smiled back at her in a bit of bemusement, but she didn't respond in kind.

She came over to the table and began writing on a piece of paper that she took from her apron. She started writing in German and then caught herself. Esther began a conversation with her Mother, just to keep things moving. He began reading Minnie's note. "Don't talk. I think there are listening devices here. Two men came yesterday and searched your room. They may have put a device there, too!" Frank took the pad from her and wrote, "How long were they in my room?" She signaled with her hands, "10 minutes."

"These eggs are delicious, Mrs. Stoffel," said Frank, trying to talk as normally as possible. Minnie, trying to play along, said, too loudly, "Why thank you, Herr McGuire. They are very easy to make."

"My mother makes the best eggs, Herr McGuire," said Esther, chiming in. Frank rolled his eyes.

After some more forced small talk, they retreated outside to Mrs. Stoffel's garden. Esther announced that she would clean the dishes. They finally were able to speak unencumbered.

Frank: "What's going on here, Minnie?"

Minnie: "All I know is what I told you. Two men came by yesterday afternoon around 3:00PM and demanded the key to your room. They threatened me if I said anything, but I am not afraid of them."

Frank: "What did they look like?"

Minnie didn't hesitate in her description of both young men: "One of them was a bit taller than the other. The taller of the two was blond and had a scar on his face."

She thought for a moment, rubbing her eyes. "I don't really remember anything different about the other young man, other than that he was shorter than the first man." After another moment: "And his hair was much darker and it looked as though his eyebrows ran together."

Frank immediately gave her more details about the same two thugs that had shown up a couple of days earlier. Minnie put her hand to her mouth and gasped. "How did we every produce such evil young men??"

"They are as bad as it gets," said Frank. "They are the Gestapo, and they are a special group of ruthless men that are specially trained in the ways of the Nazi Party. They are Hitler's henchmen and they are intensely loyal to the Third Reich."

Minnie: "Unfortunately, I am quite familiar with the Gestapo."

She let this sink in with Frank.

Frank again: "You did the right thing by cooperating with them, Minnie. Tell no one what you have told me."

She grew angry. "This is not the country that I know and love! What has happened to us?"

"Minnie, listen to me. For now, just keep doing what you are doing. Do as you are asked. Or told. These are bad people who are doing bad things in other cities in Germany. There will come a time when you may want to…react differently. But for now, just keep a low profile and comply with any directions that they give you."

She looked at him. "Are you referring to what they are doing to German citizens who are Jewish?"

Frank hesitated. This was not going well and he had a feeling that it was about to take another turn.

"Yes, Minnie. That is one of the things that I have heard about."

"And this bothers you, Frank?" Frank gave her a quizzical look.

"I would say "bothers me" would be a very big understatement."

She continued to look at him, then spoke quietly: "The bad things in other cities that you are referring to have started to happen right here in Augsburg."

"I haven't seen any sure evidence of it here," said Frank, warily.

"I can assure you that, as of two months ago, it is happening. It is just happening more quietly," the older woman said.

They stared at one another for a few seconds. Then Minnie continued:

"Given how the news travels, the Nazis know that the Jews are keeping a very low profile, or that they have already tried to move out of the city into hiding. It's better to remove them in a quiet fashion so that the others think that they are safe. They are much easier to capture that way, hiding in plain sight, so to speak. Many are being taken to a camp outside of the city. They are slave laborers, making the parts for the aircraft that are being produced at the airfield."

A longer pause, both still searching the other's face.

Then: "How do you know this?" asked Frank.

Minnie, not breaking eye contact: "Because we have helped some of them hide and escape. They tell me what has happened to their relatives."

Frank looked at her, his astonishment clearly on display. "How?" Where?" He sputtered.

Still looking right through him, she said: "Esther and I are active. My husband is as well. It is better that you not know anything more at this point."

He stood there, awkwardly for a full minute. "Why did you tell me this?"

She looked at him and, with a small smile that lasted only a moment, said, "I have no choice but to trust you. You may be seeing some more people come and go from the house. You noticed the extra dishes the other night when you came by. I can tell that you are a fine young man. I could tell that the minute that I rented you the room. Of course I couldn't say anything right away, because I had to be sure. But now I am sure. At least I better be."

Another small smile. Then she continued, "We are not the only ones in Augsburg doing this, you know. You'd be surprised at the number. But again, it's best that you not know any details. All we ask is that, upon your return to Ireland in a few months, you tell the story of how the Jews are being systematically eliminated here, and that a majority of the German people in Augsburg are ashamed of this and appalled by it." Her voice was getting louder and firmer. She moved a step closer to Frank. "We will not stand by and do nothing!"

They were now inches apart from one another, and Frank, in the same fierce tone of voice that she had displayed, said "I promise you that I will do everything that I can, Minnie."

They stood there still staring at one another, both caught up in the moment and silently affirming the other.

Finally, she said, "All right then."

"Yes, all right then," said Frank.

They walked back inside the home, arm in arm.

CHAPTER 51

Three Hours Later

Von Greim opened the door of the sedan to let his spy in. "I see that you are on time for a change," he muttered.

"Yes sir! I shall never be late again!"

"You had better not be," growled the Colonel, "Or you will find yourself fighting for the Fatherland on the Russian front! Now what else have you learned?"

"The prototype will be tested next week, late in the week. If all goes as planned, they will begin production within a month or two after the test. If it doesn't go well, then there is no telling how much of a delay there will be." Much to von Greim's relief, this news was consistent with what his other spies were telling him.

Von Greim looked at the occupant, who looked back at him and then away.

"That's it? You have no more information than this?"

"Yes, sir. Just that Dr. Conway is working even longer hours and seems very dedicated to seeing the prototype succeed. He and Dr. Lippisch are working very well together and are seen together a lot at the airfield."

After a moment, there was a knock on the door. The Colonel rolled down the window and barked, "What is it?" to a lowly Private.

"Sir, I am sorry to bother you but Herr Göring is trying to reach you and has asked that you call him at once."

"What could that fool possibly want right now?" he asked himself.

To his spy: "All right, leave me. I have work to do." He shooed the other man out of his car.

As he climbed out of the car, Hans Ungrodt straightened, saluted, shouted "Heil Hitler!" and strode away.

From a restaurant across the street, Frank saw it all.

CHAPTER 52

Leigh walked arm in arm with her father. They were in their favorite place in the park, watching the squirrels compete for acorns and other snacks.

Edwin Conway was a bit philosophical on this day. "I've done everything that I can do to stall this thing," he said. There is really only one more card to play."

"What's that, Dad?"

He smiled at his daughter. "For your own sake, it's best that you don't know, lassie."

"Dad! Please! I need to know!"

Her father hesitated. After a few moments, he said, quietly, "I have to think of a way to subtly sabotage the test."

"But how?" asked Leigh.

"I don't really know yet. That's something that I will need to figure out."

"When?"

"I don't know that either, Leigh. But soon. Time is really getting tight."

"But I just don't see how you" – Edward cut his daughter off. "This is why I didn't want to say anything to you. I can't sit here and worry about you worrying about me! You have to trust me, Leigh, and have faith that God will provide an answer."

More silence between them. Then: "I'm sorry, Dad. I know that you're right. I have been praying, and I will continue to do so. I will be available in any way that I can to help you. Just promise me that whatever you do, that it can't be traced back to you." Then, almost in a whisper: "He'll kill you if he finds out that it was you."

Edward paused, then tried to laugh it off. "No, I don't think he'll do that, Sweetheart. He has too much invested in me, and I am too valuable to the project." To himself: "But he will retaliate against me, and I know the options that he has at his disposal. I cannot let that happen. All the more reason for the planning to be absolutely flawless."

CHAPTER 53

Henry Block read the small print in the catalog on page 277. He stopped and re-read it again. And then again. He paused for a moment and then got up to find his superior. After taking three steps toward Felix Cowgill's office, he turned around and grabbed the catalog. Kim Philby watched all of it.

Henry arrived outside Felix's office and, not seeing his secretary around, walked right in. Felix had his back to the door and was finishing a conversation on the phone. "Yes, Mr. Prime Minister. Yes. I will get some more information on it and report back to you tomorrow. Is there anything else?" After more than a minute, with Felix scribbling furiously on a pad of paper, he finally said, "I understand. Yes, sir. I will ring you tomorrow with that information. Cheerio."

Felix spun around in his chair to see Henry looking at him. "Henry! I was just going to come over and see you!"

"Yes, well, ah… here I am, aren't I? Sir, we have heard from our contact in Germany."

"And what is the message?"

"They will be testing the prototype at the end of next week."

Felix caught his breath. "And if it goes well?"

Without a second of hesitation, "They could be in production in about six weeks, give or take a week."

After a full minute with neither man commenting, Felix finally said, "It's time to implement our counterplan."

"Right, I thought that would be your response. I will initiate contact with our resource and give direction to implement Operation Chaos." Another pause. "Sir, a comment?"

Of course, Henry. What is it?"

"I just can't put my finger on it, but I believe that we must proceed as if we feel that we have been compromised."

Felix looked at his man. "Meaning?"

"Meaning that we have someone internally who is giving the enemy very sensitive information."

Felix, a bit irritated, "Henry, we have been through this before. "Do you have any specifics?"

Henry, with a reluctant and weary tone, said, "No sir. No, I don't."

"Well then, we continue with the plan as is. And right now, there are only three people who will know about this in the whole country: you, me, and the Prime Minister himself."

"What about the Americans?"

Felix thought for a moment. "Yes. It is time for us to share everything as it relates to this project with them. And for the record, Henry, Donovan believes that we have a spy in our midst as well."

Henry quietly asked, "Do you really think that we can trust Donovan?"

Felix answered rather quickly. "This isn't the first time that you've asked me this, Henry. I've known the bloke for many years. Here is just a short biography of this man called Wild Bill Donovan: He got his nickname in the Great War because of all of the incredible risks that he took, usually with absolutely no regard for his own life. His men loved him and would follow him anywhere. He is the most highly decorated man in the history of America, including being the recipient of the Medal of Honor, the Silver Cross, the Purple Heart, and too many others to count. The Medal of Honor is the highest single honor that you can bestow on someone in America. Do you know what he did in front of 4,000 people when they gave it to him? He wouldn't accept it. He said that it belonged to his fellow Americans who were buried overseas in cemeteries in France and Germany. The French tried to give him and his unit the Cross of War medal for an incredibly dangerous rescue mission in the Great War. He turned that one down, too. Do you know why?"

"Uh, no…." mumbled Henry, rather weakly.

"Right," said Felix, before continuing. "He refused it because one of the soldiers in his unit happened to be Jewish, and that boy wasn't offered a medal from the French. Donovan nearly blew up and said that he would never accept any medal from the French unless his Jewish soldier got one as well."

Felix paused to light his pipe. Then, looking back at Henry, he continued. "He is one of Roosevelt's most trusted advisors, even though he is a conservative through and through. His assessment of the war was spot on before America ever got involved, and his instincts are first rate. For those reasons and many more that I can't go into, yes, I trust him. I trust him more than I trust some of our own people in MI6."

"That was very thorough. And very convincing," replied Henry. "Well, we certainly can agree on one thing," he mused. "Time is short. Will you be flying over there to meet with them?"

"I won't have to. He and Parker are somewhere over the Atlantic right now. We will meet with them here in the morning."

CHAPTER 54

Bill Donovan could never sleep on planes. He just couldn't shut his mind off while flying. He marveled at George Parker's ability to do that. Donovan glanced over at Parker, who was spread out over a couple of seats, sawing lumber. He smiled briefly as he observed his top man. He really liked George. And more important, he trusted him.

"Can't say that about too many people in this game," he thought to himself. Of course, what he didn't know was that Parker hadn't slept more than a couple of hours every night for the past week. Wild Bill poured himself another highball and found that he was in a reflective mood. He allowed himself a few minutes to reminisce about how he had gotten himself into this mess.

He had made this flight to England countless times before, starting in the mid 1930's. He had met Mussolini. And Hitler. And Stalin. And all of this took place well before Germany invaded Poland three years ago. His old law school classmate at Columbia, who now happened to be the President of the United States, had sent him over to Europe six years ago to assess the early concerns that there was another war brewing. Donovan had also met many of the British leaders at the time. He found Prime Minister Chamberlain to be incredibly naïve. He hit it off with Churchill well before Churchill had resurrected his political career and was relieved when Churchill was named the new Prime Minister. And Churchill gave him unlimited access to all of the people who made up British Intelligence at the time. This proved invaluable in defining and laying the foundation for the O.S.S.

OPERATION GRAB BAG: A FRANK SWEENEY ADVENTURE

He ended up being so close to the British leadership that most of them lobbied Roosevelt to replace Joe Kennedy with Donovan as the U.S. Ambassador to England. Frankly, no one could stand Kennedy. A notorious womanizer and ignorant when it came to recognizing the growing problems in Europe, virtually all of his assessments about Hitler and the possibility of war were proven to be wrong. Roosevelt thought him to be incompetent, but Kennedy's money had helped elect him as President, and he had to park Kennedy somewhere far enough away from Washington so that he wouldn't mess anything else up. "It's probably just as well," thought Donovan. "After all, imagine if I was the Ambassador and poor Joe was trying to put together a spy organization. Roosevelt would fire him after a month, and Churchill would have turned me into a raging alcoholic."

Some turbulence brought Donovan back to present day, albeit briefly. The military transport plane that Donovan had access to 365 days a year was a blessing and a curse. On the one hand, it was ready to go in a moment's notice anywhere, and for any reason. On the other hand, it meant he was, for all intents and purposes, out of communication for hours at a time. The flights over the pond were particularly difficult. Not only was he out of communication, but much worse, his life was in danger. The Germans owned much of the skies, at least at this point in the war. For international flights, there were always three planes accompanying his. Two of the planes (one always being his) would be marked with medical signage as a precaution. The ironic part to all of this was that Donovan never gave his "protection" – or his life – a second thought. He was still active in the war itself, even if he wasn't supposed to be. He actually loved being on the battlefield…even in the battle itself. Roosevelt would throttle him if he knew the chances that Wild Bill continued to take in this man's war. He wasn't a reckless man by any stretch, but his faith was real. He would serve his God and his country until the day he died. It was as simple as that.

As the plane made its descent, he had a few more moments of self-reflection. He had lost his daughter Patty – his only daughter – to a horrible car accident a couple of years ago. Of course, he wasn't there. He was in Europe, doing Roosevelt's bidding before the U.S. got involved in the war. She was just driving down a road in Virginia, not too far from their home. It had rained the day before. Patty must have hit a rough patch and slid off of the road. She ended up hitting a tree. The ambulance rushed her to the hospital, but she never regained consciousness. She was 23. Although they didn't talk about it, he and Ruth were still grieving their loss. It was easier for him, if there was such a thing. He had his work. He had the entire country to think about. And he had a war to win.

Ruth kept herself busy, but it was clear that she had not recovered. "Recovered? Does anyone really ever recover from this?" he asked himself. Their only son, David, was in the Navy, based in Europe as well. Donovan dared not visit him, for fear that he would draw attention to his son as a potential enemy target.

Wild Bill didn't talk about Patty. Maybe it was the Irish influence. Maybe it was just easier that way. He did talk to Parker about her once. It was when Parker was beating himself up over choosing the Sweeney boy for this mission. After listening to his friend for a while lamenting that no one understood what it was like to potentially lose someone so young, Donovan spoke quietly to George and merely said, "Believe me, George I understand what it's like to lose someone young that you love." Feeling awful, Parker immediately apologized. Not another word was spoken.

CHAPTER 55

Frank woke up at dawn. He had been mulling a plan over in his head for weeks now, but seeing Hans with von Slime threw a wrench into everything. He could trust no one. Except Leigh. And the Stoffels. He had to get Leigh out of Germany with her father. He saw no other way through this without talking directly to Edwin. He had to tell him of his mission and work with him on an escape route out of Germany. The part that he may not share would be that he also wanted to destroy the prototype. That would at least delay things for quite a while. But he had to do that before the testing took place. By destroying the prototype beforehand, the Germans would have no results to document and draw from when they got the new one ready. While it wouldn't be a complete do-over, it would buy the allies additional time to fight the war on an even playing field with the Nazis.

He would stop at their home today, unannounced, under the pretense of looking for Leigh. He knew that she always went to the market on Saturday morning, so that would give him some time with Dr. Conway to figure some things out. Of course, this was all predicated on his belief that Conway wasn't a Nazi sympathizer. If he guessed wrong on this, then his plan would take a completely different direction.

He decided to talk to Minnie before he left for the day. He went downstairs and couldn't find her. He finally looked outside and saw her hanging up some wash on a clothesline in the backyard.

He pretended to be helping her as they talked. "Minnie, I just want to tell you again that I am committed to helping you once I leave Germany. If what is going on here is consistent with the other cities, then I can only encourage you to move faster in telling your Jewish friends to get out of Augsburg. Tell them to get out of the country as quickly as they can."

Without looking up from her work, she said, "We are always looking for more recruits. I am disappointed to tell you that few people are – what is the expression the English use? Willing to stick their noses out?"

Frank smiled. "Their necks, Minnie. "Few people are willing to stick their necks out."

"Well, you know what I mean, Frank."

"I do. Tell me, how do you get them out of the city?"

She looked up at him for only a moment. "When the time is right, I will tell you. But for now, there is no need for you to know this. It only puts more people at risk, particularly if you are brought in for questioning from those two awful men."

Frank thought for a moment. "Fair enough. But sooner or later, I will need to know."

"Why?"

He looked at her and waited to catch her eye. "When the time is right, I will tell you," he said, without the trace of a smile. She stared for a moment, nodded, and went back to hanging more clothes.

CHAPTER 56

Edwin Conway was sipping on his second cup of tea when he heard the knock on the door. He immediately put away the work that he was doing, smoothed his hair, and walked through the living room to the door. "Yes?" he called out, somewhat uncertainly.

"Dr. Conway, it's me, Frank."

With a sigh of relief, he opened the door and invited Frank in. "Frank, this is a pleasant surprise. What brings you here?"

"I was in the neighborhood and thought I would see if you and Leigh were up for a stroll today."

"Well, that sounds fine, lad, but Leigh isn't here. She's at the market this morning."

"Oh, right," said Frank.

After a pause: "I was just about to go out and do a little gardening. Care to join me?"

Frank, looking a bit confused, said, "I'd love to."

"Splendid!" said Edward. "You have to look at the green beans. They have really been growing the last couple of weeks. It's so hard to get good vegetables right now, with the hours that I am working and Leigh teaching all day. Come on outside with me and I can show you our progress."

Once they were outside, Edwin calmly and quietly said, "Our home has listening devices in it. I didn't want you to say something that someone could misconstrue."

Seeing his opening, Frank replied, "Well, that seems to be another thing that we have in common, Doctor. You see, my apartment has listening devices in it as well."

Edwin broke off a bean and said, "Apparently they must not like the Irish."

"I'd say that it's a little deeper than that."

"Oh? What do you mean, lad?"

"Doctor, I think you know exactly what I mean."

Edwin looked from the handful of beans that he had handed to the young man. He took another couple in his other hand and gave them to Frank.

"Frank, you must be extremely careful with these beans. They are very fresh, but they are a few days from being ready to be picked. Picking them prematurely can ruin the taste and texture and it will spoil the entire meal. But picking them on the right day will ensure that they will be a part of a very successful and delicious dinner."

"I wish that there was even more sun this time of year," Frank replied. "Because sometimes the meal date has been set, and you have to adjust and hope for the best, even if everything isn't perfect."

Edwin nodded and kept moving. "Now look at these strawberries that are coming in."

Frank glanced around to make sure that they were safe. He didn't see anyone suspicious. "Doctor, I know about the secret project regarding jet propulsion. I am actually a pilot myself. I was sent here to get you and Leigh out of the country."

Edwin stiffened for a moment and then went back to inspecting the berries. "There are a couple of things that I need to do first," he said. "And I should tell you that there are some…complications."

Frank: "I'm not surprised. There always are in these kinds of things. But I have a mission to complete, and you are my mission. So, one way or the other, you are getting out of Germany." Edwin said nothing.

Frank continued, "And by the way, I guess I have a complication of my own to sort through."

Edwin, trying to remain nonchalant: "Oh? And what would that be?"

Frank hesitated. "Well, here goes," he said to himself. "Uh, well. Yeah. Um. I…uh…"

Edwin straightened and looked at him. "What is it, son?"

"I'm in love with your daughter!" Frank blurted.

Edwin looked at him for a moment, and then a small smile formed at his lips. "Well, it's about time that you at least said it. It's been obvious for so long."

"It has?" asked Frank, with a slight look of desperation on his face.

"Lad, I wasn't born yesterday." He looked back at the strawberries and said, "Now, let's move over here to see how the squash is doing."

They were both bending over to look at the squash and Edwin asked, "So what's your plan?"

"Well, once we make it out of the country I am going to ask your permission to marry her."

Edwin rolled his eyes as he kept his head down. "Uh, Frank, I was asking about your plan to get us out of here."

"Oh, yeah, of course. Sorry."

"Focus, boy."

"Yeah, I know. So here's the thing: Don't trust anyone. You need to sabotage the testing of the prototype next week."

"How do you know that the test is next week?"

"I've got some help, at least I thought I did. Is it next week?"

"Yes, it's toward the end of next week. And I already have made plans to sabotage it."

"Perfect," replied Frank. "How?"

"It's probably something that you won't understand, but the technology is such that…" Frank interrupted: "Did I mention that I am a pilot?"

"Yes, good for you. But this…"

"Did I mention that I am a pilot in the United States Army Air Force?"

That gave Edwin pause, albeit briefly. "All right. You moved up a notch in my eyes. You still don't need to know all of the details. Suffice it to say that the type of metal that you need on a plane of this magnitude needs to be able to withstand heat up to 1700 degrees Celsius. And that sort of metal is hard to find. I plan on weakening the metal that we have in our inventory, which will guarantee failure and buy the Allies more time. It will take the Germans weeks to determine why the test failed and how it failed."

Frank looked up and casually looked around. Seeing no one, he went back to inspecting the squash, telling Edwin, "Look, I need a very quick synopsis from you as to where this program is at in terms of maturity, the likelihood of success, and the commitment behind it."

Edwin dove right in. "All right, in two minutes or less, here it is: The Germans have been playing with this technology since the mid 30's, which was a complete violation of the Treaty of Versailles. They had been rebuilding the Luftwaffe even before that. Göring is lukewarm on the project and hasn't funded it as much as they should, frankly. He has only allowed for 35 engineers to even work on this project. He is under the impression that the superior minds of the German engineers with their existing air force will be sufficient to win the war in the skies. So far, he has been proven right. But I also know that the Americans, when unified, can out-produce anyone, and they have some excellent minds of their own over there."

"Where does von Sli –ugh, von Greim fit into all of this?"

Edwin could barely suppress his disdain for the man. "Von Greim views this as his ticket to get into the inner circle. As in, Hitler's inner circle. He will stop at nothing to make this a success. He hates Göring. Von Greim believes the main reason that Göring won't make this a bigger priority is because he is trying to keep von Greim away from Hitler. That may be true in part, but I think that it is more because of what I said earlier. Göring is convinced the war can and will be won with the technology we have today. Plus, the Germans have other weapons that they are working on. There is some sort of massive gun that is land based that can shoot for several miles, and they also have some new submarines that they are trying to launch. There are only so many resources to go around."

"Will they be able to mass produce this plane successfully?" asked Frank.

Edwin didn't hesitate. "In time, yes, they will. Von Greim believes that we are only weeks away from production, assuming that the tests go well. But he doesn't know anything about production and development. I guess it would be possible if everything went perfectly, and we had three full shifts of talented engineers working on it 24 hours a day. But it won't be perfect. I'll make sure of that."

He paused to inspect some more squash, and to subtly look around. Then, the brightest mind when it came to jet propulsion continued. "We on the research side have a saying: It's very difficult to schedule an invention. Understand, Frank: we have design issues, aerodynamic issues, metallurgy issues, weight issues, fuel issues, engine issues...and we haven't even talked about the challenges of mass producing such a plane. But, given enough time and more resources, I believe that this is very achievable."

He continued, "My dream is that this technology will one day be used for good, especially in the commercial world. Imagine being able to fly anywhere in half the time that it takes today, with fewer stops to refuel! Why, this could revolutionize trade and turn poor countries into wealthy ones. People could move and settle into other countries. We could ship products all over the world by air rather than by sea and rail. Tourism would explode! Countries would become destinations for adventures. People would learn and understand different cultures and customs. Why, do you realize..." He looked at Frank, who had a smile on his face. "What is it, son?"

"With all due respect, Doctor...focus!"

Now it was Edwin's turn to smile. "Touché, lad."

"There you are!" Edwin turned to see Leigh, who sprang off of the steps. Frank had been partially hidden by a hedge. When he came out from behind it, Leigh's face immediately brightened and blushed at the same time. "Frank! What brings you here?"

"Hello, Leigh." "I...um. "Well, I..."

Edwin jumped in to save him. "Frank was out for a stroll and decided to stop and say hello."

"How about staying for a light dinner?" asked Edwin with a twinkle in his eye.

"I'd love to, if we can make it quick," said Frank. "I have a deadline on an article that has to be completed tonight."

CHAPTER 57

They met in a smaller, out of the way hotel on London's west end. Donovan and Parker arrived under the cover of night. They entered through a side door with security men scattered throughout the facility. There were two men sitting in chairs on either side of the door that led to the conference room. On either side of the conference room were doors that led to private suites for the two men. One of the security men opened the conference room door for them. As they entered, Felix Cowgill stood up and came over to greet them warmly. On the conference room table was a generous helping of lamb chops, boiled potatoes, and green beans. There was also a couple of pots of tea and a pot of coffee. The men were famished and immediately started their meal. Felix was going to wait to dive into the business at hand, but Donovan insisted on starting as they began to eat. There was a knock on the door and Henry Block came in. After greetings were exchanged, Henry grabbed a plate and helped himself to dinner as Felix began to summarize the latest information that they had received from Germany.

Even though the news was anticipated, Donovan and Parker expressed some...what? Surprise? Alarm? Henry spoke next: "I suppose we shouldn't really be surprised about this. We knew this day would come." Donovan let the comment pass. He was already thinking forward to the mission. "Tell me about the contact between your asset and ours."

Felix took this one. "They are both aware that the prototype testing will begin at the end of next week. To our knowledge, they haven't come together on a plan. We believe that your asset probably is further along in a plan, because, as you'll recall, our contact's instructions were to monitor and report on activity around the project. Yours was to get Dr. Conway out of there and stop them from production. Consequently, whatever plan that they put together will have to be quick. And we all know that the shorter the planning period, the more likely that something goes wrong."

George spoke next: "But communication with your asset goes both ways, right? In other words, you can get information to the contact and the contact can respond?"

"Yes, that's right, George." Henry now. "The process is slow but we can get information back and forth."

"Not that it matters, but how do you do it?" asked Parker.

Henry looked at Felix, who nodded to him. "It's really very simple. There is a very thick catalog of different products that is sent to us. One might be lawn care and the next one might be home products. All correspondence is run through an address in Ireland. Our asset has access to the underground in Germany. Part of the underground includes a hardware store, so we send a thick catalog back and forth regularly. Our contact stops in when a new catalog comes in. Buried in a 300 page catalog under a certain product description is a coded message. That's how information is exchanged."

Donovan looked at George and gave him a look as if to say, "We should have thought of that." Reading his mind, George reminded him that "We had no time, Bill."

Donovan then asked Felix, "Could we get something to our asset over there through your contact?" Felix said, "Absolutely, Old Boy, but, again, we don't have much time."

Donovan nodded in agreement. "Then we need to craft something immediately."

CHAPTER 58

Michael O'Shea was not in a good mood. The editor of the Irish Independent newspaper was waiting for an article from one of his reporters. "McGuire!" "Where is McGuire?"

Frank walked into the building to the sound of his boss' screams. "This can't be good," he thought. "McGuire!" "Wherever you are, get in here!"

Frank hurried in. "Yes sir?"

"Your article on the parks around Augsburg is too long. You need to cut 50 words out, and I need the edit completed in the next hour!"

"I'll work on it right now, sir!"

"Look lad," said O'Shea, softening a bit. "It's well written, but you've got to write in such a way that you know how it will fit on the page."

O'Shea looked back at his reporter and said, "One hour."

Hans Ungrodt appeared from around the corner and said, "Can I help you with your editing, Frank?"

Frank stared at him coldly and said, "No, thank you."

Hans sensed his mood and said, "I already took the liberty of editing it for you. Here, tell me what you think of what I did." As he passed his work to Frank, he was not expecting Frank's next comment:

"I'm sure you've done enough already."

Hans looked at him, puzzled. "Pardon?"

"You heard me."

Hans studied Frank for a minute. Still looking at him, he called for the copy boy and handed him the corrected article. "Please give this to Mr. O'Shea." Then to Frank: "Come outside with me for a moment."

Hans grabbed a couple of papers as they walked outside. "Frank, what are you upset about?"

Frank, pretending to look at the paper, said, "I think you know, Herr Ungrodt. And if you try to stop me, I will kill you."

Hans couldn't hide his surprise. Still, he tried to look nonchalant. "What are you talking about?"

"You know exactly what I'm talking about."

Hans, totally perplexed, said, "I truly have no idea what—"

"I saw you, Hans. I saw you with von Greim, in his car. I saw you get out and give the Nazi salute. And if you even think of stopping me, I will kill you. Do you hear me?"

Hans looked relieved. "Oh, Frank. I wanted to tell you but I couldn't." He slowly let his eyes wander, casually doing a complete 360. "I am what you Americans call a double agent."

Frank, eyed him warily. "It's true," said Hans. "I have been working as a double agent since before the war even started. I was trained as a pilot and before I graduated I volunteered for espionage. Everything that I told you in my so called cover story is true. I did actually live in Milwaukee. I do have relatives there. More important, we don't have time to debate this. I am who I said that I was. Think, Frank! Think! If I was working for the Germans, you would be arrested by now and you would be undergoing incredible torture."

Frank thought for a moment. He had no choice but to move forward. "So help me, Hans, if you're lying to me I'll —"

"Frank, listen to me!" We need to move on from this now! I have a message to give to you!"

"Stop!" said Frank, his temperature – and his voice – rising. "Why didn't you use"—

Otto Kruger walked out the door and looked at both men. "Excuse me. I am leaving to get my car serviced."

Frank smiled and said, "We are just going over the article that I wrote. Mr. O'Shea has told me to reduce it by 50 words and…"

"Yes, I heard him," replied Kruger. He kept walking as he said, "He seemed a little upset."

Frank answered, "A little?" and laughed. Kruger never broke stride.

After he was out of earshot, Hans said, with an urgent whisper: "It says to launch Operation Grab Bag."

Frank froze. "How did you –"

"I just received it last night."

"But how?"

"There is no time for that. Besides, I cannot put my contacts at risk, in case we are captured. All you need to know is that there is a German underground that is committed to defeating Hitler and all of the other evil men who are ruining our country."

Frank said nothing for several moments, weighing his options. If he pulled away from Hans now, he would still have to try to get Dr. Conway – and Leigh – out of Germany by himself. Hans could easily help him succeed in this, his only mission. Hans was German and knew people. He was also trusted by the Nazis, at least some of them, anyway. This was very appealing and increased his chances for success.

But if he trusted Hans and Hans turned out to be a true Nazi, he was dead, and the Conways would be disposed of once they outlived their usefulness. He would be tortured, in order to give up all of the information that he knew about the mission, the army air force, everything. Finally, he said, "All right, Hans. You leave me no choice but to trust you. We need to meet with Dr. Conway and coordinate a plan to get him out. And we have to do it now."

"I'll take care of arranging a meeting with him," said Hans.

"They may have people watching his house, Hans."

"Yes, I'm quite sure that they do. As a matter of fact, they've assigned their best undercover man to it."

"Who is that?" asked Frank.

Hans smiled at his friend. "Me."

CHAPTER 59

Leigh came home at her usual time of 5:30PM. "The kids were a little more challenging today", she thought. After changing her clothes and straightening up the house, she began the process of preparing dinner, not really knowing exactly what time her dad would be home. The nice thing about preparing soup was that she could re-heat it on the stove if she had to. Plus, she noticed that her father wasn't talking and eating nearly as much. "Too much going on at the airfield," she noted. She wondered how he would sabotage the testing. Before she could think too long about it, there was a knock on her door. She looked up to see Hans Ungrodt, and motioned for him to come in. He shook his head no, and signaled for her to come outside. She removed the soup from the stove, took off her apron, and walked out the door. It was dusk in Augsburg, and it wasn't lost on her that Hans had waited until the sun had set to come over.

As she moved down the steps, she looked to her left. Hans stood near an apple tree in the backyard, perfectly hidden from any of the neighbors' windows and street. She joined him and asked what he needed. Before he could respond, she heard a voice call out softly, "Hello, Leigh." She smiled before she even turned around. "Frank! What are you doing here?"

"We're waiting to talk to your dad. We know that he should be home momentarily." As he said this, they could hear a car approach. It was Edwin Conway, arriving home. Hans spoke next. "Let's wait for him to park in the garage, then talk in there."

"But the listening devices," said Leigh. "Dad told me that there were listening devices in our home."

"He is right about that, but I can assure you that there are none in the garage," said Hans.

"How can you be so sure?" Leigh pressed.

"Because I am the one who put them in the house," replied Hans.

Leigh gasped. "It's OK, Leigh," Frank assured her. "We will explain shortly."

They waited as Edwin parked his car, then made their way to the garage. It was a single car garage with two large doors that swung closed and were kept closed with a long two by four. While it could only accommodate one car width wise, it was deep enough to have a full workbench that sat in front of where the car was parked. They all gathered around the workbench area. Edwin didn't seem surprised to see them. He signaled with his hand for silence. Hans assured him that there were no listening devices in the garage and that they could talk freely, albeit quietly. They began to plan.

CHAPTER 60

Von Greim was on the phone with yet another spy. "Tell me, what is the status of the test?" Is it still taking place at the end of the week?" "Yes, sir. Everything is set. It will likely be on Friday. There are some last minute adjustments that must take place, but nothing very concerning."

"Excellent," replied the colonel. "If you keep this up, I will see to it that you get promoted. But you would still report to me. I will have many needs once this project moves forward."

"Thank you, sir," said the spy. "It would be my honor to serve you and the Fatherland in such a capacity!"

"Yes, yes." Keep me informed of any changes." Von Greim hung up the phone and began planning his conversation with Göring after the successful testing of the technology. He would have to follow protocol, at least initially. But after fulfilling his obligation to brief that idiot, he would go around Göring and find a way to talk directly to the Fuhrer. He would not let Göring take the credit – steal the credit - from him. This was his moment. He could leapfrog Göring by getting the jet propulsion…what? Off the ground! There might be something there! The Fuhrer's propaganda machine would like a phrase like that. He'd have to give that more thought. Yes, this would finally be the key to getting him into Hitler's inner circle. And kicking Göring out of it.

He would tell the Fuhrer of the outstanding results. And the results would be particularly outstanding once Hitler understood that Göring had cut short the budget and manpower for this program.

He reached for his phone and dialed up Göring. Göring's secretary answered and, upon learning that it was von Greim, immediately put him on hold.

Von Greim did the slow burn as the minutes passed. He finally hung up and called Göring's office back.

Putting on the most pleasant voice that he could muster: "Yes, hello. Apparently we were disconnected. This is Colonel von –"

"Hold, please."

He cursed a blue streak. He screamed at the phone. He screamed at...no one in particular. But he certainly screamed. Talking to himself: "When I am in charge I will see that that secretary is sent to the front. I will see that he is lined up and shot. I will send him to the worst..."

"One moment while I connect you, Colonel."

"Thank you so much," said von Greim.

Göring came on a moment later. "Yes, what is it?"

Von Greim said brightly, "Hello Herr Göring. It is so good to talk to you."

"What do you want, Colonel?"

"I am calling to tell you that we are ready to proceed with the prototype test next week."

"Well...finally!" retorted Göring.

Von Greim's tongue must have drawn blood, so hard was he biting on it. "Herr Göring, I expect to have excellent news for you and the Fuhrer after the test."

Göring, still making sure that von Greim knew who he was reporting to, said, "Very well. I want you in Berlin next week to brief me on the plans to get this technology into production."

Von Greim: "That might be premature. It would be better to wait to see what–"

"Colonel, I thought you said that you were confident that the test would be successful?"

"Well, yes, I do think that but –"

"Then be in my office in Berlin next week with a preliminary plan to get this into production. He paused. "Unless you'd like me to tell the Fuhrer that you are preparing for a failed prototype test."

Silence. Finally, von Greim said, "I will be there next week, but I must be back in time for the actual testing."

"Very well. Have your aid send my secretary the date and time."

Before von Greim could respond, he heard the click. Göring was gone.

Von Greim slammed the phone down so hard that he broke the receiver. He screamed through the wall to his aid, demanding another phone immediately.

CHAPTER 61

Edwin explained in lay man's terms what he was going to do in order to sabotage the test. They heard him out, but clearly Frank and Hans were thinking of something bigger. And better.

Frank was the first to speak: "Doctor, my mission is to get you and Leigh out of here. That is first and foremost. Second, I want to do all that I can to keep this technology from becoming real. Tell me, is the plan to still test on next Friday?"

Edwin nodded, remaining silent. Hans said, "That gives us less than one week." More silence as everyone retreated to the recesses of their minds, absorbing the task at hand.

Finally, Edwin spoke: "I have dedicated most of my life to the aero plane. There is no greater thrill than to see one's thoughts and studies be transformed into an invention that will change the world. I met the Wright brothers over 30 years ago. I dreamed of this day and worked toward it for decades, even when my colleagues called me crazy. I have spent more time on this project in the last few years than the previous ten combined. We are so close, closer now than we have ever been to achieving this goal that was thought to be unattainable a few years ago."

Everyone gave him time to compose himself and continue. Leigh reached for his hand and held it tight. He looked at her warmly. "Your mother would be so proud," he said. Leigh nodded and hugged him.

"But I also know that the type of aero plane that the Nazis want – the one that I have worked on for so long - will be used for evil. I cannot allow that to happen."

Through clenched teeth he spoke deliberately and slowly. "I will do all that I can to destroy this technology and rebuild it in a country that will use it for good."

Everyone nodded in agreement. Hans spoke up: "Good. That's settled! Frank, let's explain our plan to Dr. Conway and Leigh."

Frank decided to not go into detail. "I think at this point we should just speak in general terms. The test is still five days away. If one of us is arrested, the less that we can talk about, the better."

After a moment, Frank continued: "I will tell you this: we plan to do major damage to the entire testing facility. We cannot possibly send our bombers here. At least not for some time. The Luftwaffe owns the skies over Germany. Waiting until the night before the test to do it will be too late. The security will get tighter the closer we get to the test. We need to strike at night. We can use the cover of darkness to move around and sneak in. We will execute the plan two nights from now. That way, if we have to abort due to something that we had not anticipated, it will still allow time for us to try again before the test day. And it also allows for fewer time for any of us to be discovered and caught."

Edwin Conway looked at Frank. "Can we talk privately?"

"Um…Of course," Frank answered, somewhat confused.

Edwin, to Hans and Leigh: "Sorry, but this is something that I cannot share with anyone else, at least for now."

Leigh looked hurt and Hans was just plain mad. "We can't possibly keep secrets right now, Dr. Conway."

"I'm sorry, Hans, but this is literally a matter of life and death."

Leigh, whose eyes remained on her father's said, "Dad, I trust you. Do what you have to. Come on, Hans. I will make some tea." To Frank and her father: "We will be in the house. Remember the listening devices."

Edwin waited until they were out of the garage. He then told Frank something that he hadn't told anyone…not even his daughter.

CHAPTER 62

The Next Day

Hans Ungrodt sat at home processing his latest communique from his superiors. As he sipped his tea and chewed on bread that was rock hard from being a bit old, he reflected on where things stood for him at this point. It was odd that he had only met one of the men, but he knew the man well. They had met before the war and had managed to keep in touch. Hans had actually reached out to him as it became obvious that the prospect of war was imminent. He took another swallow of tea and contemplated his next steps. The double agent reflected on his latest meeting with von Greim, which took place earlier in the day. He played the role as he always did – obsequious and timid in the Colonel's presence. And von Greim ate it up. So self-deceived was von Greim that he would unwittingly give Hans information, and Hans would then, in a later meeting, oftentimes parrot this information back to him. So vast was the web of spies at von Greim's disposal – and so obsessed was he on the jet propulsion project - that the good Colonel wasn't processing or filtering the information that was coming in. The one thing that Hans did not have success with was finding out who the other spies were. He had some suspicions, but he wasn't able to verify anything. While it was a priority to find these people, it was not THE priority. His mission had morphed from monitoring the jet propulsion project to helping his American friend get Conway off the project and, hopefully, out of the country.

While his cover was of a somewhat bumbling newspaperman, Hans Ungrodt was no fool. He was the perfect candidate to qualify as a spy. His parents had passed away a few years ago, and he had only one sister, who had moved to Switzerland years ago and then secretly immigrated to America, staying with relatives in Milwaukee. Expertly trained in the art of espionage by the Nazis themselves, no one could survive in such an evil place without being very disciplined and street smart. He was a patriot of a different sort. He loved the Fatherland as it once was, but not for what it was today. He lost an uncle in the Great War. Hans hadn't seen his sister since before the war started, but he knew that his sister was no more a Nazi than he himself was. Hans' cousins were the real heroes in his mind. They served in the underground. He wondered if they even slept. They were running a legitimate business with customers and services, but they were also using the business as the primary way to resist the fascist regime that had wreaked havoc on its own citizens and ruined Germany's once honorable reputation. Thankfully, they were on his mother's side so they had a different last name than his.

All of his skills and his access to his network would be put to the test as he worked on his plan to complete the mission. This would not be his last mission, assuming that he survived it. He had much grander plans than getting an aeronautical engineer back to freedom.

His personal goal was to get as many Jews out of Germany as possible. His "partner in crime" was Esther Stoffel, the daughter of Frank's landlord. Between his cousins and Esther's contacts, whom even he was not privy to, they had managed to smuggle over forty Jewish families out of Augsburg and into Switzerland. No small accomplishment, to be sure. The key to what was known as Operation Exodus was to not move too quickly. Great care had been taken to hide the families. They were scattered among many families right in Augsburg. Once their safety had been ensured, Phase II kicked in, which was getting them out of the country. The Nazis were stepping up their searches, however. They were confused – and frustrated – as to how many families had seemingly just disappeared. The Jews left almost all of their belongings behind, mostly to give the false sense that they were on a trip somewhere within the country and returning any day. Food was left on the shelves, grocery lists were made and sitting on the kitchen table, days were blocked out on the calendar, indicating any appointments that they had, cleaning ladies that were scheduled to come…everything was made to look as though they would walk back through the door at any time. If they lived near the train station, even their cars were left at home. Only the most precious – and valuable – items were taken. The rest were either left in plain site or hidden somewhere in the home, with the quiet hope that someday, when this nightmare was over, they could return to normalcy, whatever that would look like. Of course, on the outskirts of Augsburg stood a concentration camp that housed over 1,300 prisoners, many of them Jewish. These prisoners worked on producing parts for the Messerschmitt factory which was on the other side of the airfield where the jet propulsion project was housed.

He worried about the Stoffels. He had a goal of getting Esther out of the country, at least until the war was over. He had already discussed it with Mr. and Mrs. Stoffel. While they themselves had decided to stay and continue to get as many Jews out as possible, they were both adamant that their daughter needed to get out of the country, and they charged Hans with making sure that it happened.

How he was going to break this to Frank was something that had to be thought out, and quickly. Their relationship was rocky, merely because of Frank's uncertainty about Hans' trustworthiness. He had been honest with Frank from the beginning, and he was confident that, if Frank really took the time to think about it, he would conclude that he and Hans were on the same side.

Hans arrived at Leigh and Edwin's home at 7:30PM. It was already dark. Because the weather was cold, it allowed him to wear a long overcoat, which hid the machine gun. He had extra clips in the inside breast pockets, and the two pistols were shoved into both front pockets. Extra clips for the pistols were in his back pockets. All of this would be stored in the garage tonight. But his purpose for getting there before the others was twofold. Clearly, he had to make sure that the weapons arrived safely and without incident. He easily had cover because von Greim was in Berlin meeting with Göring to update him on the project and to lay out the plans for production, assuming that all went well. Hans did tell the next in line of his plan to watch the Conway's house the next couple of nights. That was met with a yawn and an "all right." But the other reason that he showed up early was to confide to Leigh about Esther. Leigh had met Esther at the club a few times. The more the time that they spent together, the deeper the friendship that was forged. They had several things in common, not the least of which were being around the same age and teaching children for a living. And oh by the way, they were both in love with men who were spies.

"Leigh, I haven't told Frank anything about this because he is jumpy and still is uncertain about me. He wants to trust me, but he can't let go of the fact that he saw me leaving von Greim's car. I told him that if I was a German agent, that he would have been arrested by now and would likely be tortured by von Greim himself."

"What are you trying to tell me, Hans?" asked Leigh.

"I am trying to tell you that I need to get Esther on that plane tomorrow night. That means that we have five people and only four seats. That means that you, your father, Esther and Frank will be going. I will stay behind. I need you to convince Frank tomorrow night that this is how it's going to go. Do not say anything to him before tomorrow evening when we see him! I have risked my life for this mission, and I made a promise to Esther's mother and father that I would do this. We will make the drive together over to the airport and I will make sure that you and Esther get there through the park. Esther will stay several feet back while I tell Frank what I am going to do. I can then give Frank the rest of the extra guns that I will have. Then I will duck back into the woods and get back to Esther's house. I'm telling you this now so that you can be ready to support me when Frank is ready to kill me. The bottom line is that the mission will go on and is not compromised. He will still get the people out that he was charged with getting out. He'll just be taking one different person than what he was expecting."

"But where will you go? The Germans will be looking for you if for no other reason that you let my father get away!"

"Esther's parents are one of the key underground families that have smuggled Jewish families out of Augsburg."

Leigh's eyes lit up. "You're kidding! How? How do they get the families out?"

"They work with my cousins at the hardware store. My cousins have a couple of trucks that are specially configured to hide as many as four people at a time. They are taken to the forests that separate Germany from Switzerland. They are dropped several kilometers short of the Swiss border. Once inside the forest, they are met by a series of relay teams that hand off the families to one another after a few kilometers. Each team is isolated from the others so that if one is caught, they can't give away the identities of any of the other teams. We have gotten over forty families to freedom and have yet to fail."

"How long?"

"What?"

"How long? How long does it take to get someone out?"

"The trip from Augsburg to Basel, which is the Swiss border city, is about 375 kilometers. They stop a few kilometers short of the border. That area of the border is heavily forested. People typically get into Switzerland within no more than three days. We should arrive before dawn, which means that I will rest all day and begin the journey over the border that evening. We should cross that night, assuming that there are no problems. We run the trucks a couple of times a week. That's all that we can afford right now, because we actually have a legitimate business on the German side of the border that serves as our cover for going there in the first place. So we need to make real deliveries to real clients. Our men actually wave to the German soldiers at the different check points, who know them by now. It doesn't hurt that we often give them some homemade strudel and coffee on those cold days and nights, either."

He looked at Leigh, who nodded for him to go on. "As far as the method, it's fairly simple. Each team shows up at their given times in the forest every day. If no one is there, they go back to their stations and wait until the following day to do it again. The teams are made up mostly of German and Swiss citizens. There are even a couple of Spaniards who serve as guides. Some are Jewish but most are Christians. They are risking their lives every day for people that they don't even know."

"When would the next one leave?"

"I've already met with Mr. and Mrs. Stoffel. I will be leaving tomorrow night on a special run. Once I get you and Esther to the fence, I will double back and leave my car at my home. I will walk to Esther's house, which will take about 20 minutes, and get there around 1:45AM. The truck will be waiting for me around the corner, and off I will go. I will meet up with all of you in whatever city Frank is recommending. You see, Leigh, we really have no choice. We have got to get your father and you out. I promised the Stoffels that I would get Esther out tomorrow. And Frank must go to escort the two of you. That leaves me…is the term odd man out?"

"Why not just have Esther escape the way that you just laid out?"

"Her mother doesn't want even Esther to know about the specifics. She feels that her daughter has a much better chance of not being caught this way. And she will be in Switzerland in a matter of hours versus a couple of days. If we are caught, the questions will all be geared around how we tried to escape by air. They won't even think to ask about other escape routes. It's too bad, though. I was looking forward to showing off my pilot skills to her."

Leigh looked surprised. "Are you a pilot, too?

Hans looked back, almost amused. "You didn't know?"

"You never mentioned it."

"No, I suppose I didn't. Not to you, anyway. Frank knows, though."

Hans carefully began to unpack the guns and additional clips. He then started to search the garage for a place to hide the weapons until the following night. His eyes settled on a shelf on the other side of the garage that was deep enough to hide everything. He put a couple of buckets in front of them, just in case.

"That should work for a day," he muttered. He looked at Leigh, who was waiting for him to continue. "Before I was trained by the Nazis in espionage, I was trained as a pilot. I completed all of the course work and flight requirements. Right before I was set to graduate, I heard that the Nazis were looking for men to do espionage, so I volunteered. I thought it would give me the opportunity to learn more that I could report back on. You see, I resolved quite early that I could never fight for the Nazis. They are pure evil and they must be stopped. The only thing that is worse than fighting for them is not fighting against them."

Leigh nodded, encouraging him to continue.

"In any case, they needed someone who could understand a plane and get around in one so that when this project became real, it allowed me to understand what exactly they were working on so that I could report back to von Greim and everyone else as to how it was really going. I was given access to the base on occasion, not as a reporter but as a direct report to the Colonel. Of course, no one knew that. I just showed up in my Luftwaffe uniform and went anywhere that I pleased."

"I see. At least we will have a backup if something happens to Frank."

"Yes, I suppose you could say that."

Leigh thought for a moment. "Hans, does anyone else know about you being a spy for the allies?"

"No. Only Esther's immediate family. And of course, my cousins. I only have a sister left, and she is supposed to be in Switzerland. She's actually in America. She doesn't know anything. Why?"

"I just wanted to make sure that we are minimizing our chances of something going wrong."

"Leigh, if you can't trust your own family, then you can't trust anyone. My family – and Esther's family – hate the Nazis. We are embarrassed and ashamed to think of how they have destroyed our country. They must be stopped, and anything that we can do to stop them or at least slow them down is what we will do."

Hans finished hiding the guns and putting rags on top of them. He turned back to Leigh.

"The problem is that they have their spies everywhere. And, they are not at all afraid of making examples out of those people who resist them. As a matter of fact, I plan on volunteering to go back into Germany somewhere so I can do more. It won't be back here, of course, but it's a big enough country so I can help in some other city. For the last few years, I was a newspaperman. For my next act, maybe I will be a production worker that will sabotage some grenades or shells or submarine parts. There's no telling what sort of mischief that I can get myself into!" With that, Hans smiled. And, eventually, so did Leigh.

CHAPTER 63

Frank spent his time processing the latest wrinkle in the plan. After many hours and days of meticulous thought and discussions with Edwin and Hans, the strategy had come together. Time was a great motivator. Over the past few days, he had shared almost the entire plan with Hans, who challenged it, suggested tweaks, and played the skeptic. After hours and hours of discussions and arguments, they had finally arrived at an arrangement that they both felt good about. He opted to keep the one last minute wrinkle that had come up quiet until the last possible minute. There was no need to upset the applecart at this point. He had not anticipated Edwin's news. Frank chided himself for not seeing it sooner. Nonetheless, it was real and he had to deal with it. There must have been a reason that Edwin chose to tell Frank only and not Hans. Or even Leigh. Edwin and Frank had worked out that new element to the plan themselves, at least as best as they could. Frank would wait until they were getting them into the plane before telling Hans and Leigh. It was not ideal but, given the circumstances, he felt that he had no choice.

Edwin, Leigh, Hans and Frank met again in the garage at 8:00PM that night. Frank took control of the meeting immediately. "All right, listen carefully. Hans and I have worked on this plan for a very long time. Here is what we are going to do: We will all go about our business as usual tomorrow. It is critical that we act normally and go through our routines. Talk to the same people, eat lunch at the same time, start and leave work at the same time…we must all stick to our normal schedules. I will be back here at oh nineteen hundred hours -7:00PM - tomorrow evening. Hans, you will need to bring the explosives and the weapons. The wire cutter is already here in the garage. It's best that we are not seen together, so try to get here before 7:00PM."

Hans broke in: "I brought the guns and the clips tonight. It's too risky to carry everything at one time and in one night. I will have the explosives with me tomorrow, and will deliver most of them to you so you can pack them in your car. I will keep one pistol, a couple of clips, and three grenades, just in case."

Edwin looked at Hans for a moment and said, "The life of a double agent, I suppose." Hans merely smiled and shrugged.

Frank continued: "Dr. Conway will go back to work tomorrow night. He will leave here at 7:15PM. There should be no issue getting through the guard station because he has regularly gone back to work after dinner many, many nights. The guards know him and even joke with him. I will be in the trunk – or boot, if they call it that here. They haven't bothered to check his car for months, so we should get in easily enough. I will have the wire cutters in the trunk, the explosives that we will use, and a couple of gallons of gas. I'll also have the machine gun and the other pistol, plus the clips for each one. Don't worry, all of it will be separated and safe in the car. Dr. Conway will park his car where he always does, and I will stay in the car. He will stay in his office and work as he normally would. He will only be able to take one briefcase with him on the plane, so he will begin to compile only the most critical information about the project that he can fit into his briefcase.

Edwin jumped in: "The doors are typically left open there in case they have to scramble a plane quickly. There is a BF 108 sitting there, fully fueled."

Frank turned to Leigh and said, "The 108 was the precursor to the 109. They still use it to train brand new pilots. Because it is a training plane, it seats four, not the two that the 109 seats."

Leigh nodded. She was beginning to see the brilliance of the plan emerge.

Hans picked it up from there: "I did most of my training in that plane. It is very tight in there with four people, and there is no room for any luggage."

Edwin again: "There are no guards on that side of the hangar. The guards are on the other side, protecting the area that leads to the testing area for the jet project. If we can enter the hangar quietly, and get each of you loaded and strapped in, we can fire up the engine and be on our way very quickly. It isn't all that unusual for a plane to take off at night out of there. The trick here is that there are no flights listed on the schedule for tomorrow night. I thought about adding ours, but then we would be drawing attention to ourselves."

Frank nodded and said, "You did the right thing, Dr. Conway. It's best to use the element of surprise whenever possible."

Frank then turned to Hans and said, "You will need to leave your car on the other side of the park that is next to the airfield. Walk through the park – stay off of the streets – and meet me at the twelfth fencepost from the hangar on the east side of the airfield. You must be there at 1:00AM. The runways should be dark, and I will be wearing black anyway, as both of you should. I will cut the fence for you two to get in. From there, we will make our way to the back of the hangar."

Everyone nodded. Frank continued:

"That means that you should leave here no later than 1:15AM. You'll have to navigate the park in the dark, so you'll have to allow extra time for that. The guards will likely be sleeping, even though they aren't supposed to be. Before you get there, I will have had time to check out the plane and make sure that it is ready. But remember, there are only four seats and no room for anything but people and Dr. Conway's briefcase. This is a fighter plane, not a commercial plane. The only reason it has four seats is because it is a training plane for the 109. It will be very tight."

Hans said, "Frank, you told us that already."

"Well, consider yourself warned, then."

"Where will we land?" Asked Edwin. Frank hesitated, then thought, "Oh, why not?"

"We will fly south to Switzerland and land near Lucerne. Hans is arranging things to make sure that we will have people there to meet us. From there we will make our way to London, where we will be de-briefed. That will likely take a few days. At this point we don't know what happens after the de-brief takes place."

Edwin again: "I will have some German beer that will be laced with a sleeping powder that will knock the guards out, at least as many as will imbibe. I have brought them food and drinks before, so that shouldn't be a problem."

Leigh was next. "I will cook some of that sausage that they all like, but I will put some extra salt on it as it cooks. That will make sure that they are very thirsty. Just to make sure, I'll bake some strudel for them as well. We can put the sleeping pill powder in them, too." After a moment: "I wonder if the powder will be effective if it has been cooked?"

"Don't worry about that, lassie. The beer will have more than enough in it to knock them out for a while," said Edwin.

"Were you able to confirm how many guards we are talking about?" asked Frank.

Edwin replied, "At that time of night, six men will be our concern. There will be two at the gate when we come in, but they never come inside. We should give them each a bottle of wine that isn't spiked with anything. I know those two men. They will drink both bottles throughout the evening. Another two will be guarding the work area outside of my office, and two more will be guarding the prototype area that is about a four minute walk from my office. There might be one additional guard in a different area that we may need to ply with the beer."

Hans jumped in. "Remember that there are two towers, one on either side of the airfield. The one closest to the runway that we will use will have at least one guard, probably two."

Edwin: "But remember, I've checked the schedule for tomorrow night and they are not expecting any planes. At least there is nothing on the manifest."

Hans: "Oh, that's right. But that's even better, because that means there will only be one guard there, and he will probably be reading or on the phone with someone. He won't be watching a dark and dormant runway."

Frank: "The trick will be to hold off on giving the guards the beer until as late as possible. We should leave all of it in the car until around 2300 hours...I mean, 11:00PM. We don't want them drinking the beer too soon, because it will wear off on them before we need them to be unconscious."

Edwin replied, "Trust me, Frank, if they start drinking at 11:00PM, they will be out by 11:30PM and won't wake until the morning. I suppose there is a chance that they will wake up when you crank up the plane, but they will be pretty useless, even if they do awaken."

Hans offered, "Frank, you said that you will have the weapons in the car with you. You will need to wait for several hours in the car until Dr. Conway comes out to get the food. When he comes to the car, you'll stay put and he can give you an update on any issues that have come up. You should wait until at least 12:15AM to get out of the car and get into the hangar to check the plane out. That will take you 10 minutes or so...less if you hurry. As I said, I've flown that plane many times. You'll find it to be similar to what you have flown in terms of the basics. From there you should make your way out to the fence. You can take your time and move very slowly so you don't attract much attention. There will probably be the occasional searchlight, but if there is only one guard, he will be shining it toward the active runway on the other side of the airfield. We will be at the fence at 12:45AM to meet you. We will follow you back across the runway to the hangar. Just make sure that you cut a large enough hole in the fence to get...Leigh and I through." Hans looked at Leigh, who tried to smile and nod.

Edwin again: "The plane will be gassed up and ready. I told one of the men to have it ready to go. I told him that von Greim wanted to take it up for a ride after he got back from Berlin. They filled it up yesterday and checked everything. Von Greim is meticulous and has been known to demote a mechanic who doesn't have the plane spotless. Best of all, it is a relatively unmarked plane with neutral colors. That is a policy that von Greim himself started after the war began. He didn't want to attract enemy planes, should they find their way into Germany, and he didn't want any planes – German or otherwise -to follow this plane to the treasure chest, so to speak."

Frank grew very serious. "It is critical that we run this on time! Do whatever you have to do to get there precisely at 12:45AM. This mission is timed down to the minute. The plan is very thorough, but there are still a lot of things that could go wrong. Understood?"

They each nodded. "Good," said Frank. "I guess this is it. We won't all be together again until late tomorrow night at the airfield."

Spontaneously, they came together and grabbed hands and bowed to pray. Edwin prayed for all of them, quietly asking the Lord's blessing on this mission, for His protection, for His wisdom, and for His favor upon each of them. He asked for blessing upon the Allies, and additional wisdom for the leaders of each country as they prevailed against dark forces in Germany, Italy and Japan. Frank, Leigh and Hans listened intently, heads bowed and eyes closed. They all said, "Amen" at the end of his prayer and stood for one more moment before releasing their hands.

They stayed silent for another minute before Leigh squeezed her dad's hand once more and thanked him for praying. A few more moments of silence followed, and then Frank took a deep breath and said, "Look, I've never done something like this, but I'm told that these things never go perfectly. If you are late, I will wait until 1:00AM. If you are not there by then, then we will have no choice but to abort the mission and try again the following evening."

Now Leigh spoke, and she spoke fiercely, even angrily. It was a side of her that Frank had never seen: "No! No, Frank." She was shaking her head and moving toward him. "If we aren't there, you must get on that plane with my father. We will figure another way out of the country. Your mission has always been to get my father out of Germany. Period. The entire war may depend on this! Do not shirk your orders, Captain!" By now she was inches from his face.

After a prolonged silence, it was Hans who spoke next, in a whisper that each of them barely heard: "She's right, Frank."

Edwin: "Now see here, if you think" -

Her eyes were locked on Frank's, oblivious to everyone else in that dark and musty garage.

"Promise me."

Frank stared back, not saying a word.

"Promise me."

"I will not get on" – Hans grabbed Edwin by the arm looked at him, and shook his head.

"Promise me, Frank."

Frank didn't move. His eyes never left hers. Finally, he said, "Don't be late."

CHAPTER 64

Peg McFarlane answered her phone on the first ring. "Is he in?" "Uh…who's calling plea"-

"It's George, Peg. Is he in?"

"No, not yet, George. He's actually at the White House."

"Oh that's just great!"

"Um…Excuse me?"

"When, Peg? When?"

"He should be back here momentarily. He was supposed to have breakfast with the President."

"All right. I will be over there in ten minutes."

"Over where?"

"At your office. I'm not going to barge in on him at the White House."

Across the pond, the sense of urgency was just as…urgent.

Henry Block shared the latest news with Felix Cowgill. Cowgill was calm despite the news. He said only two things: "Let's get a plane ready. I will brief the Prime Minister."

As they boarded the plane, they talked briefly about the mission. Cowgill turned to Henry and said, "I have to tell you, Old Boy, that I had my doubts about Badger's ability to pull this off."

Henry replied, "I'd say that you weren't alone with that thought, sir. Of course, you may still be proven right. It's not over yet."

CHAPTER 65

"I can't believe that the day is finally here," said Donovan.

"No kidding." George Parker was a nervous wreck.

"You know, George, I've been thinking. This latest information that we received. How did it come in?"

"It came from Owl."

"Yeah, OK," continued Wild Bill. "I just wonder…"

"What?"

Donovan hesitated, then spoke again: "Do you think that our Owl and their Badger are the same individual? Wouldn't that be something?"

George, thinking about that for a bit, said, "What would the odds of that be? Neither party divulged a word to the other about any particulars regarding their asset. That would be one heck of a coincidence, Bill."

Before they could discuss it further, Donovan's phone rang. "Yes, Peg. Really? Did she say what – uh huh. All right. Please tell her that I'm on my way."

To Parker: "That was Jane Patterson, the President's secretary. I'm being summoned back. Apparently something big is happening in the Pacific Theatre that requires my attention. I'll ask Peg to get the plane ready for us to get over to Lucerne. We'll probably refuel in London and then get over there tomorrow morning. Have you ever been there?"

"To Lucerne? No, can't say that I have."

"You'll love it. It's beautiful there, although it will have lost some of that beauty due to the war."

"The only reason I'm going is to welcome my godson back. Conway better be worth all of this."

Donovan barely waited to reply. "Oh believe me, Georgie. He's worth it. If he can make it to Lucerne, we will have saved the whole world."

CHAPTER 66

Leigh spent the day teaching, just like she did every day of the week. She said goodbye to each child, just as she always did. "I'll probably never see any of these children again," she told herself. She held back tears as she silently prayed for each child by name as she hugged each one goodbye. To the children, this was a normal, everyday event. They didn't notice that their teacher held on just a little longer than normal. Herr Morgan, her principal, stopped by to say goodnight to her. "Do you have any special plans tonight, Fraulein Leigh?" Her heart skipped a beat. "No sir, just my normal routine…go home and make dinner for my father and prepare tomorrow's lessons."

"Ah. I'm sure that you are quite a good cook!"

"Oh, you are too kind, Herr Morgan," she said.

"I shall see you tomorrow, Fraulein!"

"Thank you, Herr Morgan. Have a wonderful evening."

"He hasn't said goodbye to me like this in – what – weeks?" Just as quickly, she chided herself for reading too much into it. "Stop looking for meaning in things that are just normal events," she told herself. "He's just being friendly."

She made her way to her home, taking the train the two stops that she always did, and arriving within five minutes of her normal arrival time the last two weeks. She slipped into the house, changed her clothes, and began making dinner. Just like every night beforehand, she hadn't noticed the man who followed her all the way home.

The man walked down the street to a payphone, slid the coins into the slot, and reported in. "She just came home. Nothing out of the ordinary. I will continue to watch the house. Herr Conway is due home around his usual time and will likely go back to the airfield after dinner. Word is that he has more work to do on the prototype testing." And with that, Hans Ungrodt hung up the phone and walked back toward the Conway's garage with a bagful of explosives.

CHAPTER 67

It seemed like the day would never end for Frank. He had talked to Michael O'Shea about doing a column on the new pro German movies that had come out recently. Truth be told, they were nothing more than German propaganda, glorifying Hitler and the Nazi regime. The Americans and Brits were portrayed as imperialist nations that wanted to impose their beliefs and will upon the oppressed German people. He could barely stomach the overt attacks on his country. He kept a neutral tone with O'Shea, barely. O'Shea seemed preoccupied with other thoughts on this day. When Frank asked him about it, he muttered a "you wouldn't understand" and told him to get to work. Mercifully, the day ended at 5:00PM and he was back at his apartment by 5:15PM.

There was a note for him from Minnie saying that she would be out for the evening, and to help himself to some leftovers in the small icebox that was in the kitchen. He called around for Esther, but she was not there, either. Frank waited until 6:30PM and made his way out the back door, looking carefully to see if anyone was following him. He walked the back streets about four blocks to the next station, then got on the train that made its way to the Conways.

Twelve minutes later, he got off the train one stop too late and walked the side roads to the small brick home that had the longer than normal garage. It was dark by the time he knocked softly on the garage door. Hearing nothing, he walked in and quickly closed the door behind him. As expected, he found the bag of explosives hidden on the shelf near the guns. Hans had already dropped off the rest of the weaponry and had made his way back to his apartment. The only thing left to do now was to wait for

Dr. Conway to get home. As he waited, he replayed the plan over and over in his mind, searching for weaknesses or something that he had overlooked. He heard footsteps next to the garage and grabbed his pistol. He held his breath as he heard the two by four being removed. He crouched in the corner with the pistol down by his side. As he began to bring his pistol up to aim it, he heard his name being whispered. "Frank? Frank, are you in here?" It was Leigh!

He came out of the shadows toward her. When she saw him, she stepped quickly to him and stopped. He didn't. He held her tightly to him. As they broke apart to look at each other, he bent down and kissed her. The kiss was everything that he imagined it would be. She melted into his arms, and they held each other for a full minute, losing track of their surroundings and the danger that they were facing.

Finally, he spoke: "I wasn't sure if I would see you before the airfield."

"I know," she smiled at him. There was one window in the garage, and Frank was grateful for it. The moonlight showed through the window and lit up Leigh's face to the point where there was a glow about her. "You look like an angel," he whispered to her.

She smiled shyly. "Frank, what will happen to us?" Frank thought for a moment. "I suppose they will take all of us to London after being debriefed in Lucerne, but I really can't say for certain."

He looked at the ground and kicked at a small rock on the dirt floor. "Have you ever been to America?" Leigh, looking a bit surprised, said, "No, never. I've dreamed of going there someday. My mom used to read us books about it. Is it really as wonderful as everyone says?"

Frank thought for a moment. He said, "All I really have to compare it to are England and Germany. I can say for certain that it has Germany beat. England is OK, but it isn't America. America is everything that you've heard about and more."

Then, still kicking at that small rock, he asked quietly, "Would you ever want to live in America?"

She smiled. Frank thought that when Leigh Conway smiled, her entire being lit up. Her eyes sparkled and her straight white teeth seemed to shine. Now she seemed to be searching with her foot for the same rock that Frank was. "I really don't know but one American. And I would have to say that he seems of an acceptable nature."

Their eyes met, and they moved toward each other to kiss again. They didn't even hear the car as it made its way down the alley. The door slamming brought them back to their senses. "It's my dad!" she whispered. "Right on time," said Frank. And then he grinned once more at Leigh and said, "Unfortunately." Leigh smiled and they quickly got in one more hug.

The door opened and then Edwin opened the other door and placed both door jams in place. He made no eye contact with Frank, but greeted Leigh. She moved to the front of the garage as her father parked the car and then shut the doors. Finally, he gave his daughter a hug and went over to shake Frank's hand. "Well, I see you made it, lad."

"Yes, sir. I have everything organized and ready."

They all stood there for a second, and then all three looked at each other and said, "The beer!" Frank stayed in the garage and loaded the weapons into the trunk of the car while Edwin and Leigh made their way back into the house to get the sausage and the beer and wine. As planned, Leigh had doubled the salt that the recipe called for, ensuring that the soldiers would be very thirsty. A home cooked meal was a real treat for the soldiers, and Edwin had brought them Leigh's creations before. They especially looked forward to the home cooked, smoked sausage. And no good German soldier would ever turn down a beer, especially when von Greim was way over on the other side of the country. There were other officers to be worried about, but von Greim was the one who struck fear in all of them.

After 10 minutes, Edwin and Leigh came back to the garage with all of the food and drinks. The sleeping powder would be added to the beer later in the evening, making sure that it remained as potent as possible.

Once the car was packed, Frank reached for the bottles of wine and put them in the front seat for Edwin. This way, in the unlikely chance that the two guards at the gate were going to search the car, any thought of doing so would be curtailed, once the wine appeared. After all, there had never been a security incident of any kind in the many years that the airfield had been there.

The other side of the airfield was more than a half mile away with several larger hangars that were better lit, should any air raids ever occur. It was clear that von Greim was doing everything that he could do to draw attention away from the jet propulsion project. Besides, with the slave labor coming from the nearby concentration camps and their production capabilities, the Germans could re-scale the production of the 109s within days, should these hangars get hit. And, truth be told, this wasn't the only facility in the country that was producing the 109's. All in all, a brilliant plan by von Greim.

As they were ready to get in the car, Leigh asked her dad to pray. All three joined hands as Edwin Conway, one of the most brilliant aeronautical minds on the planet, poured his heart out to the God who made him and everything on the earth. He asked again for protection and favor. The prayer was short but heartfelt. Frank couldn't help but be impressed – and thankful – as he continued to see these Conways in a different setting. Their faith was simple, and very real.

Even holding Leigh's hand during the prayer made him feel woozy. His hand was sweaty, but so, he noticed, was Leigh's. "Lord, protect this very special young woman and keep her safe." He had no idea that Leigh was praying in that very moment the same prayer for him.

As they said "Amen," Edwin gave his daughter a hug, purposely going first so that she could have a moment with Frank. It wasn't lost on Leigh what her father was doing. "This is so typical of him," she thought. To Frank: "Please take care of my dad."

"I will," promised Frank.

"And please take care of you, too," she smiled, as she hugged him.

Frank looked over at Edwin, who was pretending not to be looking. Then he looked back at Leigh, and said, "Remember, don't be late."

"Speaking of being late..." Edwin called.

"I'll see you in a few hours," said Frank.

"Good bye, Frank." One more hug, followed by a quick hand to her eyes and cheeks.

Frank slid into the trunk and quietly called out, "Ready when you are, Doctor."

Edwin, trying his best to look confident, smiled and waved to his daughter. "I'll see you in a few hours, lassie!"

And with that, he backed out into the alley and made his way to the airfield.

Leigh walked back into the house and locked the door.

CHAPTER 68

Hans was finishing his meeting with Esther and her father, Peter, and five other men, along with four women. They were at his cousin's hardware store in a small, cramped office in the back of the facility. A man stood outside the back door that opened to the alley. He smoked a cigarette and his eyes never stopped moving. If he saw any strange movement at all, he was to kick the door lightly, alerting the occupants to the pending trouble.

Hans knew that his cousin Herbert's store was safe from any listening devices. In fact, he knew which homes and offices in most of the city were compromised. He and a few of his peers in the German intelligence were the secret weapons that the Jews and the underground relied on to tip them off. On this particular night, Hans showed up at the meeting with two pieces of paper folded tightly inside of his coat pocket. Peter, Herbert and the other men studied each of the addresses and names on the list. There were approximately 40 names on two pages. After giving them a moment to study the names, Hans cleared his throat and said, "These are all of the names that I was able to find. If there are no listening devices in the home now, there will be. You will need to make sure the network alerts these families to the danger that they are about to be in."

All of the men knew at least some of the families on the list. If there was a family that none of the men recognized, then and only then did they invite the women to look at those names. Keeping the number of people in the know to a minimum was the key to this kind of a mission. Once the men were sure that they had the names of the families that they picked memorized – the addresses were less important because they could always be looked up - the papers were burned in a waste basket. There would be absolutely no extra chances taken and no paper trail left for anyone to follow.

As the meeting was breaking up, Hans sidled up to Esther and asked quietly, "Are you ready?" She looked around casually and replied, "Yes, I think so."

He took her by the hand and they walked to the front of the store and entered another office with no windows. Esther's mother was there. Minnie Stoffel was trying to look confident. Peter joined them after a moment, walking over to his wife and kissing her on her forehead. They tried to smile and reassure one another. Then they looked at the younger couple and opened their arms to them. Minnie and Peter were trying to be brave, but it was so difficult. Their only daughter was leaving the country tonight, and they didn't know if they would ever see her again. She would settle in London initially and eventually make her way to Milwaukee, where Hans had relatives who would welcome her into their home. Minnie and Peter promised to make it there after the war. They would only leave Germany if they felt that it was imminent that they would be caught.

It was unlikely that Hans would get back to Augsburg as well. He really wasn't sure if his superiors would send him back into another part of Germany, or if he would be used in other ways to win the war. Just as another family had done earlier that night, the Stoffels prayed. They prayed in their native language, first Peter, then Minnie, then Esther, and finally, Hans. They called out to the same God that their Irish friends had called to, and that same God heard their prayers in their language, just as he had heard the Conways' in theirs.

As hugs were exchanged, and goodbyes were said, Hans hugged Minnie and whispered to her, I will see you at 2:00AM." She said, "It's all arranged." Peter promised Esther that he and Minnie would see her again, either in London or Milwaukee. He said it with a fierceness that she had never seen before in her father. He was a gentle man, but he was making this pledge to her with everything that he had. A peace came upon Esther. It was a peace that her mother had prayed for as they planned this night. Esther knew that she would see her parents again. She believed her father. She gave them each one more hug, and, turning to Hans, said, "It's time."

CHAPTER 69

Minnie and Peter made their way home from the meeting as they always did: They took the side roads and drove slowly. Once home, Minnie prepared a couple of small meals to give to Hans when he showed up at their home in a few hours. She wanted to write her daughter a long letter as well, but she knew that it was against the rules and it would be used as evidence against her if she was caught. Not that the Nazis needed evidence to shoot or hang anyone. She decided that, just this once, she would take the risk. She told Peter what she was going to do. He, too, decided to write his own letter. Just this once.

Hans and Esther made it over to the Conway residence without incident. Hans comforted her as they made the 15 minute drive. He held her hand and promised her that it would all work out. He reminded her of the plan and what she had to do. It was fairly straightforward. She just needed to stick to what they had agreed on: That, by the morning, she would be in Lucerne and from there, onto a new life in a country that was free. "At least free for now," he thought.

They arrived at the Conway home and quickly parked the car in the garage. They were actually about 15 minutes early, so that made them relax a bit. They had no idea that this was the last time that the mission was going to go as planned.

CHAPTER 70

"Good evening, Men! How are the two finest guards in the German Luftwaffe?" beamed Edwin.

"Herr Doctor, back again for another long night of work, I see," said Jorg, the taller of the two guards.

"Yes, Jorg, there is no rest for the weary," replied Dr. Conway. "But I am not the only man working long hours tonight. Two men before me are also working a long night shift. So I thought I would make the night go a little quicker for you. I have a gift for you!" Bernard, the smaller one, had come around the other side of the car. "That looks like wine, Herr Doctor."

Edwin smiled and said, "It not only looks like wine. It IS wine!"

The men reached and gratefully took each bottle from Edwin. "Thank you, Herr Doctor!" That was most kind of you! To think that we have beer AND wine tonight!"

"Beer?" asked Edwin, trying not to sound nervous. "Who brought you beer?"

Jorg answered, because Bernard was too busy trying to open his bottle. "Why, Dr. Lippisch is here tonight as well! Did you not know? When I saw you pull up, I just assumed that you two were going to work late together! Ya, Dr. Lippisch arrived about 10 minutes ago!"

"Well, that's wonderful. Thank you, Jorg, and enjoy the wine." Bernard, still working on the bottle, absently raised the gate for him to go through.

As he drove toward his office, he called to Frank, "Did you hear all of that?"

A muffled voice from the back of the car shouted, "Yes. Don't worry. It will work out."

Edwin drove another mile or so inside the airfield to the parking lot. He parked where he always did. There was only one civilian car in the entire lot, and that belonged to his friend, Dr. Alex Lippisch. He got out of the car and, seeing no one around him, pretended to look for something in the back seat. Frank could hear him much better, now that the engine was turned off.

"What do we do now?" asked Edwin.

"Let's stick with the plan. Like I said, we have several hours yet. Go about your work. Step one is to find out how long he is planning on working tonight. We have a saying in our Army Air Force, Doctor: Stay calm and carry on."

"Stay calm and carry on," Edwin repeated. "Right. I will come out in roughly three hours to get the sausage and beer. I'm going to crack the trunk open for you. You can always quietly shut it if you need to. Will that work for you?"

"That should be fine. Even if you do that, it's not the best with these gas cans. Can you place them in the back, on the floor?"

"Yes, of course. I'm glad that you said something. Why don't I put them right next to the car on the ground? No one will be out here."

"No, that's too risky," replied Frank. "We've already been surprised here once. Let's not take any chances."

"All right, son, we will do it your way." He popped the trunk and quickly retrieved the gas cans and put them on the floor in the back seat. Then he thought better of it. "I will put them on the floor in the front seat, so that it's at least a little further away from you."

"Thank you, Doctor. That should be fine, as long as they are out of sight."

"They will be. Try to rest or…something. I'll be back out in three hours to get the food and beer."

"Roger."

"Pardon?"

"Oh, sorry. I meant to say, OK and thank you."

As Edwin moved toward the office, he asked himself, "Who the devil is this Roger?"

CHAPTER 71

As Frank waited in the car and tried to think of some contingency if this Lippisch guy was going to stick around, he thought back to the first meeting with his uncle and Bill Donovan. They mentioned Lippisch, the famed airplane designer. He and Edwin Conway were the one-two punch that the Germans needed on this project to make their dream a reality.

Edwin had mentioned Lippisch when he briefed Frank on the project. It was evident that they got along well and shared the same passion of creating an entirely new and better way for people to travel. As Frank recalled, Edwin thought that Lippisch was not a Nazi, but was still a pragmatist. It was obvious that the Nazis were committed enough to this program to fund it and give him the resources that he needed in order to birth this technology. Who was Alex Lippisch to say no to such an offer? This was where the two engineers parted ways ideologically. Edwin could not and would not stomach such incredible technology being used by a country who had a mad man running it. "If Lippisch was such a decent guy, how could he not side with Conway on this?" he wondered.

"Well Frank," he said to himself, "you may get the chance to meet Dr. Lippisch tonight and ask him in person."

CHAPTER 72

Edwin had more or less snuck into his office so as to avoid his friend Lippisch. He thought that there might be a chance that Lippisch would leave after an hour or two. While Edwin came to work at night frequently, it was not the case with Alex Lippisch.

Lippisch had come in to work out a couple of last minute answers to demands that von Greim had made. Assuming that the testing went well, he knew that the Colonel would want to accelerate the timeline for eventual production.

As much as he loved his work, he also had a wife and four children at home. The hours were long enough at the airfield, and he wanted to spend at least some time with his kids. They were growing up way too quickly, and the war had only accelerated this propulsion into young adulthood. Still, tonight he had to make an exception.

His biggest fear was that his twin boys who were 11 now would one day be called to serve in the war. He had rationalized that the technology that he and Conway were working on would accelerate the close of the war, thereby sparing his twins the horrific experience of killing other people.

In addition to preparing a presentation on the initial production of the engines, Lippisch had to work on another demand from von Greim. The Colonel had insisted on seeing some early indications of the wind tests and how the plane held up under such extreme conditions. His crew of engineers were not ready to complete any such tests, but he could do some rough calculations and formulate some assumptions, based on those calculations.

In a rare conciliatory effort, he had promised his wife that he would be home by 10:00PM. "After all," he thought, "The next few nights leading up to the test will likely require me being here much later than 10:00PM. At least I can still get home at a reasonable hour tonight and get a good night's sleep."

Edwin looked across the building and was relieved. His strategy had worked! Lippisch's office lights were off at 9:45PM.

He knew he was a bit early, but at 10:45PM he couldn't wait any longer.

Frank was still in the trunk and a bit on edge when he heard footsteps approaching. He slowly pulled his gun out of his coat pocket and waited, hearing the steps get louder. "Don't worry, it's me," said Edwin. Frank breathed a sigh of relief. "You're early, Doctor."

"I know, but I couldn't wait any longer. Let's get the beer out. If you can help me carry it to the door, I can wheel it in and begin mixing in the powder." Within five minutes everything was ready to go.

As Frank retreated to the car, Edwin moved everything inside and began slicing up the sausage. He took one bite of it. He could taste the extra salt, but it was still good. "She'll make Frank a very good wife," he thought. He got emotional just thinking about it and had to make himself focus on the task at hand.

He began to go from guard to guard, offering each a plate of sausages. They were quick to partake. Edwin would then say, in a conspiratorial tone, "I also brought some beer in. There isn't a lot of it, so you may want to get some sooner rather than later. I know how much the other guards like it, so it will go quickly." That's all it took.

Over the course of the next 45 minutes every guard ate heartily, and drank even more. Except one. And he was unfortunately, guarding the greatest treasure of all.

CHAPTER 73

Hans and Esther waited in the garage for Leigh. There was still plenty of time. They heard the door to the house squeak open, and then a short gasp. "Who are you? What are you doing here?" It was Leigh's voice.

"Good evening, Fraulein. We saw your father on his way to the airfield and we were doing our final checks for the evening."

A second voice joined the conversation: "Ja, and we were wondering if your father made it home yet." There were two men. "How did…Where in the world? Think, Hans, think!" he said to himself. He heard the conversation continue.

"I will ask again: Who are you?"

"Who we are is not important to you. But, to show you that we are reasonable men, I am Sergeant Kimler and this is Sergeant Moeffler."

Leigh looked closely at them. They were almost assuredly the two Gestapo men that had shown up at Frank's apartment, unannounced.

"And what are you doing here?"

"We are doing our job, and that is to keep track of your father's whereabouts. He is a very important man."

"He is not here. He often works late, especially the last several nights."

"So you must know what he is working on?"

"Whatever he is doing is none of my concern. He has made that quite clear to me. I am not to ask him any questions."

"It is cold tonight, Fraulein," said the first voice. "Perhaps we can come in for a drink?"

"I don't think that would be a good idea. I am just getting ready for bed."

"All the more reason, then to just have a small drink. Then we shall leave."

Silence for a moment. Then: "Very well. You may come in for a drink. I'm not sure that it's such a great idea, though."

"And why is that, Fraulein?" Second voice.

"When I see him on Saturday evening, I wonder how Colonel von Greim will react when he hears that you two demanded to come into our home at this late hour insisting on having a drink with me. Especially since you lost track of my father tonight."

A long silence followed.

Finally: "Good night, Fraulein."

"Good night, gentlemen."

As they turned to go, First Voice said, "Oh, and Fraulein?"

"Yes?"

"We at the Gestapo use threats and will follow through on them. It's a very strange coincidence, but people who threaten us often tend to eventually disappear. No one ever hears from them again."

Second voice: "Rest well, Fraulein. Heil Hitler!"

Her heart racing, she waited for them to leave. They made their way to the street. A minute later she heard a car start up and drive off.

She started back into her home but was stopped by Hans' voice calling softly to her in the darkness. She looked once more to the street and then walked quickly to the garage. Hans was standing by a tree with his pistol still drawn.

"I know those men," he said with disgust. "They were the same men who confronted Frank. They spy on your father occasionally. They are nothing but thugs that are trying to make a name for themselves. You handled them brilliantly."

By now the reality of the situation had struck her and she began to shake. Esther came out and joined them, giving Leigh a hug. "You showed such courage!"

"I think I was more angry than courageous," replied Leigh.

Then, to Hans: "It's time to go. You don't want to be late." Hans agreed and said, "All right, Leigh, hurry up and change your clothes. Remember, we are all supposed to be in black."

Leigh looked at him directly and said, "I'm not going. I was speaking to you and Esther. You need to hurry."

Hans looked at her, stunned. "What? Of course you are coming. Come on, Leigh, hurry and get changed. Esther, please help her." Esther moved toward Leigh and Leigh stepped away quickly.

"Hans, you are not listening to me. You and Esther are going tonight. The mission is totally dependent on getting my father out of the country, not me. There are four seats on that plane."

Hans started to say something but he was quickly interrupted by Leigh.

She continued: "Instead of you escaping via the roads tonight, it will be me. You must get Esther to Switzerland. Mr. and Mrs. Stoffel will feel so much better knowing that you are with Esther. So it will be the four of you on that plane – you, Esther, Frank, and my father. I will make my way to Esther's house and be in Switzerland in two days, three at the most. I shall meet all of you in Lucerne, and it will be a wonderful reunion there. Now, get going!"

Hans stepped toward her. He was angry. "Listen to me, Leigh. You are coming with us right now. You are going to change clothes and get in that car. Now!" he hissed.

"Hans, I will tell you this only once more. You and Esther are getting on that plane. If I have to, I will start to scream right here and now. It will draw the attention of our neighbors, who will phone the authorities. I don't think any of us want that to happen."

He stared at her. "I have never…"

Esther was weeping. She was so confused. All of this was new information to her. She had thought Hans was going with her all along. She didn't know that the plane only had four seats, and immediately felt terrible that she was the cause of all of this commotion.

Turning to Hans and Leigh, she said, "I am going to go back home. I will help my-"

"No!" both Leigh and Hans whispered in unison. The three stood quietly for a moment.

Finally, Hans said, "I don't know why you are doing this. Frank will have a fit and want to shoot me for not bringing you. And I think I might let him."

Then to Esther: "Esther, this is my fault, not yours. I didn't tell you that the plane had only four seats. I was never going to be on that plane. I was going to circle back and – well, you heard the plan."

Leigh reached into her pocket and said, "Please give Frank this. It's a letter from me to him. Now go!"

Hans waited, wrestling with this huge last minute change.

Finally, he said, "All right, Leigh. Now look, you have to be at Esther's house at 2:00AM. The truck will be" -

"Yes, Hans, I know. You were very thorough in how it all works. We are just substituting me for you. I am fine. Frankly, I am the safer one of all of us because I am taking a proven route with veteran underground people. And whatever you do, don't forget to give Frank the letter."

The three hugged, prayed, and then parted ways. Leigh went back into her house. This time she did change into black.

CHAPTER 74

All of the guards had taken the sausage and, more importantly, the beer. Within 45 minutes, each of the men slumped over and were completely out. All except one. Gerald Krantz was the guard assigned to the one prisoner who was housed at the airfield. A slight man with thick glasses, Krantz was a soldier rank – the equivalent of a private in the U.S. Army. He wasn't a great soldier, but he wasn't a bad one, either. Krantz didn't volunteer for this assignment. He was in the wrong place at the wrong time. A few years ago, the prisoner landed at the airfield with an officer in the Luftwaffe. Krantz was guarding one of the research areas and was approached by the same officer with a pointed finger. That same finger waggled him forward. He immediately came to the officer and stood at attention. "Take him to the cell." That was the first and only time that he spoke with the officer. But he never forgot the officer's name. It was Colonel von Greim.

Truth be told, he liked the prisoner. But he had a job to do, and the last thing that he wanted to do was disappoint his superiors. He didn't drink the beer because he was somehow morally superior to the other guards. The reason really was quite simple: He didn't like beer.

Try as he might, Edwin was not going to be successful getting Krantz to have a pint. He realized this once he went down to the lower level to check on him. Krantz thanked him for the sausage and told him the prisoner was fast asleep. He did, however, believe that Krantz would still get thirsty. He walked back up to his office, where he found Frank quietly going through files that Edwin had left out for him. Frank had a small camera that he continually clicked on to take pictures of the key material.

Edwin told Frank about the problem guard downstairs. "What kind of German is this man? A kraut who doesn't like beer? Impossible!" He took the last of the sleeping powder and dropped it into a large mug of water and returned downstairs.

Krantz sat quietly outside the cell, reading a book. When he heard the door open, he started to stand. But when he saw that it was Dr. Conway, he sat back down.

"Did you enjoy the sausage, Soldier Krantz?"

"Very much, thank you, Dr. Conway. But I think it has made me quite thirsty," as he eyed the mug.

"Ah, yes. I thought so," replied Ewin. I brought you some water."

"Oh! Thank you!" He took the mug and returned his eyes back to his book, swallowing half of the mug in one draw. "Would you like some more sausage? The other guards left a couple of pieces for you."

"No, but thank you, Doctor. It is such a wonderful treat to get good sausage. As you know, the food here is not so good."

"Yes, I would have to agree. Someday you should come to my home. My daughter is an excellent cook and she would enjoy cooking a traditional Irish dinner for you."

"That would be wonderful, Herr Doctor, but I doubt that I would ever be allowed off of the airfield for something like that."

He took the second gulp and drained the mug. Then: "Doctor, you should tell the other guards to not drink too much beer. After all, Colonel von Greim is going to land here in a couple of hours."

Edwin stiffened. "He is in Berlin, Gerald."

"You mean that he *was* in Berlin. He left earlier this evening. A couple of my comrades upstairs told me that he decided to fly home tonight, rather than wait until tomorrow. He should land around 1:30AM or so, assuming that there were no delays. He probably will go right home, but we cannot take that chance. The men are going to have to look in their best form, just in case he decides to come over to this side of the airfield."

"Yes, I suppose so," replied Edwin. "I think I am going to go home shortly. I will speak to the guards and remind them about cleaning up the lab area. Goodnight, Gerald."

"Good night, Doctor. And thank you again for the wonderful sausage." Thankfully, he let out a long yawn.

Edwin walked down the hall and opened the doors to the main floor. As he shut the door, he turned and sprinted up the stairs. He hurried to his office and told Frank the latest news.

"You're kidding!" was all Frank could say. He looked at his watch. "It's almost time for me to make my way to the fence anyway. Leigh and Hans should be there in 15 minutes. I have already checked the plane and it looks like it is completely ready. We won't know until we get it started up, but given von Greim's requirements, the plane will likely be in excellent condition."

"This isn't going according to plan, lad. First, Alex – Dr. Lippisch - shows up, we encounter a guard who won't drink beer, and now we find out that von Greim is arriving in less than two hours."

"We need to stick to the plan, Doctor. The good news here is that everything is still on schedule, for the most part. We've lost some time with the guard downstairs, but I think we will be back on track once Leigh and Hans show up. In the meantime, please continue to go through your files and cram as much important material into your briefcases that you can. I will be back here in about half an hour, assuming that they are running on time."

"Good luck, Frank. Stay low!"

CHAPTER 75

Frank grabbed the machine gun and the pistol and made his way toward the fence. It was about a half mile from Edwin's building to the point area of the fence that he and Hans had agreed on. The searchlight was sporadic. Edwin had confirmed that there was only one man up in the tower – one of the guards had told him that as he devoured the sausage. He quickly made his way over the dark runway and dashed directly for the fence. Once he got to the fence, he started counting posts. He jogged to the twelfth post, made sure that he had the right one, and began cutting as quietly as he could. There was very little noise at this time of night, but he also knew that that could change at any time. It took him only two minutes to cut through enough of the fence to allow for Leigh and Hans to make it through. Then, he waited. After five minutes, he heard some rustling coming from the woods. In the moonlight, he could see the silhouettes of two people. As they got closer, he could make out the shapes. He was relieved to see that it was one man and one woman. He looked at his watch: 12:45AM. Right on time. He didn't care in that moment about the mission. He was just relieved that Leigh had made it. She wouldn't be happy with him after he told her, but she would just have to understand.

As they approached, he stepped through the fence and reached his arms out to hug Leigh. "Frank, it's me, Esther." Before he could say anything, Hans said, "We had a problem."

"Where's Leigh? Esther, what are you doing here?"

Hans spoke next: "Frank, we don't have time for this. The short story is that Leigh insisted that she get out of the country through other means. Esther's parents will help her get out tonight."

"She did what?" he thundered.

"Keep your voice down! She found out that the Stoffels were desperate to get Esther out. She didn't tell anyone. I had agreed to bring Esther and Leigh with me tonight. In order to not expose anyone else, I decided to not tell a soul about this change, not even you. Of course I knew that the plane only held four people, so my plan was to drop the girls with you, make sure that you got on the plane without any issues, and then go back to the Stoffels. The truck is coming to their home at 2:00AM. There are secret compartments that can handle up to four people at a time. Esther broke in: "My parents are staying in Germany to continue to work in the underground. There is a special run tonight just for Hans...well, it's now for Leigh."

Hans took over: "Frank, you must listen to me. Leigh threatened to scream and attract the neighbors if I didn't agree to this. She realized that there were going to be five people and only four seats on that plane. That's why she decided to do what she did." Hans paused, holding Esther's hand.

Then, back to Frank: "She gave me this and insisted that I give it to you." Hans handed his friend the envelope. "You'll have to read that later. The four of us need to get on that plane. The heat is being turned up. Your two friends who visited your apartment a while ago showed up at the Conways' tonight."

"What? Why? Is Leigh OK?"

"Yes, yes. I told you that she is fine, remember? They were just trying to find Dr. Conway and keep track of him."

"All right," said Frank. "We have a couple of problems on our end here."

"OK, said Hans. "What are the problems?"

Frank took a deep breath. "First of all, von Greim is flying back here tonight. He will likely land in less than two hours."

Hans said nothing for a moment. But then he couldn't help himself. "He's supposed to be in Berlin."

"Yes, well, apparently he decided to fly back tonight. Who knows? Maybe Göring couldn't take any more of him."

"All right," said Hans. "We are going to have to accelerate our departure time."

"Yes," agreed Frank.

"What's the other problem?"

"The second problem is a little more complicated."

"I'm listening, Frank."

Frank looked at his friend and said, "You've confessed your adapted plan. Now I have to confess my adapted plan to you."

"What are you talking about?" asked Hans.

"Well," said Frank, "We still have five people and only four seats. It will be clearer when we get back to the hangar. Come on."

CHAPTER 76

Edwin collected the most important of his files and jammed them into a rather large briefcase. He burned as much as he could of the remaining documents in the trash can outside of the entrance. After several trips back and forth, he checked the time. 15 minutes had elapsed. Was that enough time? What if it wasn't? What excuse could he give for going back down to see Krantz? He would just have to take that chance. He walked quietly to the door and made his way even more quietly down each of the steps. Turning to his right, he got to the corner and made one turn. Gerald Krantz was sprawled across his desk, snoring loudly. Taking no chances, he tiptoed by him and reached for the spare set of keys that were hanging on the wall behind him. He grabbed them as quietly as possible and walked the short distance to the cell. He looked at the prisoner and smiled.

"Hello, Dad," whispered the young man behind the bars. "Hello, son," said Edward, equally quietly. "Are you ready?"

"You have no idea," said Jimmy Conway.

CHAPTER 77

Frank led Hans and Esther back across the runways to the research building. They entered the door tentatively and were relieved to find that all of the guards were still unconscious. Per the plan that they had mapped out, Edwin had gone around and confiscated all of the weapons from the guards while they were still out.

As they entered the hangar, Edwin and Jimmy came through the door from the basement. The five of them came together quietly. Edwin pointed to his office and they all tiptoed in.

"I'd like you all to meet my son, Jimmy. Jimmy, this is Hans and Esther. And over here is the brains of the operation, Frank McGuire. It is Frank McGuire, isn't it?"

"It's actually Frank Sweeney, but I can tell you more about that in Switzerland."

"At least Sweeney is just as Irish as McGuire." replied Edwin.

"Where's Leigh?" asked Jimmy.

"Yes," said Edwin. "Where is Leigh?"

Then it dawned on him. They had five people and four seats. Six with Leigh. He started to say something, but nothing came out of his mouth.

Frank looked at Hans, then back at Edward. "Leigh is going to meet us in Switzerland."

It didn't take Edwin long to find his voice. "WHAT?" he boomed. "Where is my daughter? I demand to know right now!"

To Frank: "You lied to me!"

Hans quickly jumped in and explained what happened. "This is not Frank's fault, Doctor. He knew nothing about this until 15 minutes ago."

Now Frank spoke: "I am going back to get her and go with her through the underground. "I promise you that she will be in Switzerland within three days, maybe sooner. I will see to that."

Looking at his face, Edwin could see that Frank was resolute in his commitment to bringing Edwin's daughter safely back to him.

After a moment, Jimmy said, "Dad, we've waited years to be together. We can wait two more days. Jimmy reached out to shake Frank's hand. "Thank you for getting us all out of here."

Frank shook Jimmy's hand and nodded to him. "All right," said Frank. "We've had a few surprises tonight, but the basic plan is still intact. The latest surprise is that von Greim is flying into this airport tonight, not tomorrow. He could be landing in as little as 15-30 minutes from now. We need to be wheels up in no more than 20 minutes, and we need to do it quietly. Doctor, have you had time to sabotage the area?"

"Yes," said Edwin. "Frank, I'm sorry. I shouldn't have" –

"Forget it," said Frank. "I want every bit as much as you to have her here. Let's stay focused. Hans will be flying you out of here. That's a blessing in disguise because he knows the 108 a lot better than I do."

Edwin walked a distance away and thought. He turned and said, "I want to switch places with you, but I know that you won't allow me to do it. I also know that you have your orders, so there is no point in arguing with you about it, because I won't win. So, let's get going. Just promise me, Frank. Promise me you'll have her in Lucerne in three days."

Frank walked over to him. Edwin looked like he had aged 20 years in the last two minutes. His eyes were full and a single tear slowly spilled out of each eye. His upper lip trembled and he continued to swallow. "I promise you, Doctor."

Edwin just needed to talk more. "I don't want to trade one child for another. I want both of them! I just…" His shoulders shook and he buried his face in his hands.

Frank grabbed his shoulders and said, softy, "Doctor. Please look at me." Edwin slowly regained his composure and his eyes worked their way up to Frank's face. But it was a face that he didn't recognize. Gone was the face of a young man – a boy, really. It was replaced by a warrior who knew that he was going into battle. "I promise," the Warrior repeated.

CHAPTER 78

They hurried to the plane, still trying to move quietly. There were two seats in the back for Jimmy and Esther. Jimmy had grabbed some of the sausage to take with them. He was famished and was used to meager helpings of airfield food. They managed to grab a couple of mugs that were in the mess hall and washed them thoroughly. They filled the mugs with cold water and set them on a small table a few feet away from the plane. All five then pushed the plane out onto the cement. As the others boarded, they shook Frank's hand and thanked him. He nodded and wished them luck, reassuring them that he and Leigh would see them in a couple of days. Edwin stood by the plane and waited for Hans.

Hans stored what he could of Edwin's files and was ready to hop up to board the 108. He and Frank talked through some final thoughts. As he was getting ready to board, Frank said, "Hans, something has bothered me for quite a while and I couldn't put my finger on what it was until tonight. I know that now is not a great time to talk about this, but why didn't you end up using the signal when we first met? That would have allowed me to trust you a lot sooner."

Hans was focused on the flight plan and wasn't paying close attention to what Frank was saying. All he said was, "All right, OK."

Frank repeated the question, and Hans finally focused. "What are you talking about?" asked Hans. "The signal, Hans. The signal that Donovan and Parker worked out with you."

"Frank, I have no idea what you are talking about. We need to get this thing in the air." As he turned back to the plane, he said, "And I don't know any men named Donovan and Parker."

Frank said, "They must not have used their real names with you, just for additional protection. We Americans are like that, I guess. After all, look at me, I didn't use my real name, either."

Hans slowly turned around. "Frank, surely you know that I don't work for the Americans?" Frank was stunned. "Of course you do."

"No, Frank," said Hans, firmly shaking his head. "I work for the Brits."

"What? You're not Owl?"

"Owl? Who is Owl? Like, the bird, the owl?"

The blood drained from Frank's face. Hans caught him just in time as his knees began to buckle under him. Before Hans had even finished his sentence, Frank knew. Edwin was standing there, looking at him with complete confusion on his face. "Frank, are you all right? What's the matter?"

Frank, trying to regain his composure, said, "Nothing. I'm fine. With everything going on, I forgot to eat anything today. And I don't think I even had any water, either."

Hans was already making his way over to a sink with a couple of mugs on it. He returned with both mugs full of cold water. Frank drank the first one and held onto the second for a moment.

After less than a minute, he said, "You're right. You need to get in the air right now." He stood up, gathered himself, and led them to the plane.

"Here, Frank." Hans handed him the keys to his car. I left it on the other side of the park, just where I said I would leave it. You better hurry and get it. Leave Dr. Conway's car where it is. There's no point using that because you'd have to get through the gate, and we both know what sort of trouble that would cause."

"Got it."

Edwin began climbing aboard. "I'm praying for you, Frank." Jimmy and Esther waved to him, and Hans said, "We'll see you in Lucerne at the park right by the lake."

Frank merely nodded, still processing what he had finally put together.

As he turned to go, Frank saw a plane's lights in the distance. Frank gave Hans the high sign to wait. Frank cranked open the windshield. "Now what?"

"There's a plane coming! It must be von Greim!"

Hans instinctively turned to look but couldn't turn around far enough to see anything.

"Hans, wait for it to be on final approach, then hightail it out of here. I will signal you when to crank the engine, and wait for me to signal you when to get to the runway. We want it to be too late for von Greim to order the plane back up in the air from the runway. Besides, there's a chance that they won't see you if you don't use your running lights." Hans gave him the thumbs up and relayed the information to the others. It took another two minutes for the other plane to get into final approach. When von Greim's plane was only 100 feet off the ground and making enough noise, Frank gave the signal to Hans to start the plane. He did. Frank gave him the "go" sign and Hans raced to the runway with no lights except for the moon. Within seconds the plane was barreling down the runway and off the ground. As the wheels were being cranked up into the belly of the plane, the singular sound that was competing with the plane's roaring engine was the sound of von Greim's plane slowing down and making its way to the hangar on the other side of the airfield.

Frank raced to Edwin's office and lit the match, then crossed over to the other side of the building and did the same to Lippisch's office. From there he ran over to the lab and lit the fuse under the prototype jet propulsion engine that Edwin had dedicated the last several years to. He had about 20 seconds to get out of there. A couple of the guards were beginning to stir. The phone next to the prototype lab began to ring. Smoke had already started to fill the area and began billowing. A lone siren now. He ran to the runway. The single searchlight. Within seconds, more searchlights. He dodged and weaved across the runway, hurling himself into a gulley or just lying very still, face down as the searchlights sought him out. As he got up to move, the explosion hit, throwing him forward ten feet. He landed on his shoulder and rolled, coming out of the roll perfectly and resumed running. Voices now. Screams. Confusion. The searchlights were moving almost frantically and in no pattern. More screaming. Boots on concrete. More shouts in a language he didn't know. More explosions. Tires screeching. Finally, he made it through the fence and raced to the woods.

CHAPTER 79

Robert Ritter von Greim finished Göring's briefing on the war and the increased role that the new weapons would be playing over the next 12 months. "The man is such an imbecile," he said to himself for the hundredth time. "Everyone knows this war will last at least three more years, although no one wants to tell the Fuhrer that. But I will. Once we start mass producing these jet machines, only then will we know how long the Allies will last. It will only be a question of how long they can hold on. The Fuhrer will then realize how important I am to the war effort, and to him. Göring will then be revealed as the idiot that he is."

As they began final approach, he decided that he would stop at the lab and see if anyone was around to speak with about the prototype.

"Conway has been working almost every night the last couple of weeks," he observed. Not so much with Lippisch. He made a mental note to check with his spy who was following Lippisch around. It made him question Lippisch's loyalty to the Party. It might be time for another talk with him. He seemed more interested in the technology than the ideology. Von Greim expected all of his people to be completely loyal to both. He knew that he would never convert Conway. But Conway would soon be of less use to him than before. Conway would never leave Germany alive. As long as he had his son and daughter, he wouldn't – what did the English say? Rock the boat.

He looked to see where they were and decided not to make the pilot change course to the other runway nearer the jet propulsion lab. "I could make the change when I was 50 feet off the ground, but this fool can barely fly this thing," he grumbled.

As the wheels touched down, the plane bumped along the runway. "Terrible landing!" he roared.

Within seconds, he realized that that was the least of his problems.

CHAPTER 80

There was bedlam at the airfield. Von Greim's car raced through the gate and made its way to the research building. It was too late, and he knew it before he even got out of the car.

"Are any of the engineers in the building? I saw Dr. Conway's car in the parking lot."

One of the guards stepped forward and answered, "He was here earlier tonight, but we don't know if he was killed in the blast or not."

"And Herr Lippisch?"

"He was also here, but left earlier in the evening. The log says that he signed out at 9:45PM, sir."

"Call the Gestapo. They have two of their men assigned to watch Conway and Lippisch. Find both of them immediately."

"Yes sir! We will find the Gestapo men immediately."

"NO! You imbecile! Tell the Gestapo men to find Conway and Lippisch immediately!"

"Yes sir!" The soldier breathed a sigh of relief. He was not going to be the one who ended his career by telling von Greim that Edwin Conway likely escaped with his son.

He heard von Greim yell at another soldier: "Lock down the entire airfield. No one comes in or out without my permission."

"But sir, the fire engines..."

"Yes, you idiot! Of course let the fire engines in!"

Von Greim had a bad feeling about this. He turned and found another soldier. "Where is Captain Martin?"

"Sir, Captain Martin was off the base tonight. He was tending to his wife, who you'll recall is on her deathbed."

"Do you mean to tell me that there were no officers here this evening?"

"No, sir, not at this area of the airfield. Across the airfield at the normal facilities, there are four officers. You'll recall, sir, that this part of the airfield was purposely low profile because –"

"I know it has been kept low profile, you fool! And I know why it was kept low profile! Get Captain Martin here immediately!"

"Yes sir!"

"What is the extent of the damage to the laboratory?"

"We don't know that yet, sir. We need every available fire truck here to get the fire under control."

Von Greim was apoplectic. "Get the fire out! Now!"

The poor soldier, who knew long before the conversation started that he was dealing with a moron who couldn't think under this sort of pressure and chaos, merely "yes sirred" the Colonel to death. The sooner he could be dismissed, the sooner he could contain the fire.

"And no communication about this to anyone outside of my chain of command. If this gets outside of my chain, I am going to hold you personally responsible. What's your name?"

"Sergeant Horst Mueller, sir."

Von Greim ran toward the laboratory.

With that, Sergeant Roderick Blum looked around and breathed a sigh of relief, knowing by the look of chaos in the Colonel's eyes that von Greim would probably never remember a Sergeant Mueller. The darkness hid his face well enough. And the Colonel would certainly never recall a Sergeant Roderick Blum, since Blum never gave him his real name.

CHAPTER 81

Leigh had watched from across the street as the two Gestapo men had pulled their car up to her home and raced through the door with guns drawn. She could hear the sirens in the distance.

"It must have worked!" she told herself. "They must be looking for Dad! That means that they couldn't find him at the airfield! Or, it could also mean that they are looking for me. Either way, I need to leave. And now."

She snuck along back streets, running and walking the two miles to Esther's home. It took exactly 25 minutes. She arrived well before 2:00AM. Peter and Minnie were shocked to see her.

They greeted her warmly and gave her a cup of tea. "Who were you expecting?" she asked them.

"To be honest, we thought it would be Hans," said Minnie. "We knew that there were only four seats on that plane, and that someone would have to stay and come here to get out through our methods. We knew it wouldn't be Frank or Edwin, or you. And we knew that it wouldn't be Esther. Or at least we hoped. We were really expecting it to be Hans, because that is what he told us would happen."

"Well, it's me," said Leigh. "But if you don't mind, I'd like to wait for a few minutes after 2:00AM to see if anyone else shows up. Just to be sure, I mean." Peter looked at Minnie and said, "We can only spare a few minutes. Everything is arranged with the boys at the store." They talked briefly about the evening and everything that had happened.

"Unfortunately, all we can do is speculate, but it looks promising, yes?" said Peter.

"Yes, it certainly does," said Leigh, with as much confidence as she could muster.

Minnie spoke next: "We will take you to the hardware store. With all of the sirens, it is too risky to have the truck be here at this hour. Too many people are up and talking about what is happening, and they will see the truck."

Peter said, "I agree. I will put the signal out for them to drive back to the shop." With that, Peter stepped outside the back door toward the alley and walked to the rose bushes in the backyard. He draped a single white towel over them. That was the signal for the truck to keep moving past their home in the alley and return to the shop. He stepped back inside the home and nodded to Minnie that the signal had been placed.

Before they could go on further with their conversation, there was a loud knock on their front door. They each looked at one another. Minnie got up to walk into the living room to answer it. Peter motioned for her to stop. There are many advantages to being married to the same person for a long time. The Stoffels communicated without saying a word.

Minnie quietly took Leigh's hand and led her upstairs. Inside the spare bedroom, she opened a closet door and pushed aside a rack of Frederick's suits. Then she pushed a latch that wasn't visible to someone who wasn't looking for it. The back of the closet opened up to a small, windowless room. She ushered Leigh in there with a silent "shush" sign, hugged her, and put everything back in its place. She then hurried back downstairs to join her husband. The pounding started again. Peter went to the door as Minnie was just at the base of the steps. Taking one last look around, and being satisfied with what he saw, Peter opened the door. He was hoping that it was Hans or one of the others that were trying to escape. It was not.

CHAPTER 82

Frank hurried in his effort to get to the car. People had come out of their homes and were pointing and talking about the smoke and red sky that was coming from the direction of the airfield. They were talking excitedly in German and English. Frank could make out a few words and phrases. "A plane crashed!" shouted someone. "No. A plane wouldn't make that big of a fire," said another. More arguing and more sirens getting closer. "Take advantage of the chaos," he reminded himself. "It won't last very long."

He kept moving at a walking pace, not wanting to attract any attention to himself. He made it to Hans' car and drove away. He stayed on side streets and could hear even more sirens that belonged to all of the police cars and fire engines that were racing toward the airfield. He smiled in satisfaction. "Even if I don't make it out, at least we knocked a giant hole in their program," he thought. "And von Slime is done."

He knew that he shouldn't, but he would never forgive himself if he didn't. He stopped at the Conway's to see if Leigh was there. He knocked softly on the door, and then more loudly. He tried the door. It wasn't locked. He made his way into the entry way and living area and called softly: "Leigh? Are you here? It's Frank."

He reached into his pocket for his pistol and kept his hand on the gun, all the while leaving it in the pocket. He found the standing lamp next to the door and turned it on. The room was empty. He called again to Leigh, but there was no answer. He searched the house and found nothing out of the ordinary. He checked the garage to see if she was there. Nothing. "OK," he thought, "She must be at the Stoffels."

Then he remembered the letter. He took a flashlight from his pocket and ripped opened the envelope.

It was written in cursive. Frank realized that he had never seen her handwriting before. He read:

My Dear Frank,

Thank you for all that you have done to get my father out of this awful place. I will forever be in your debt. I could not come tonight for two reasons. First, as we agreed, Dad is the priority. His removal from this project may end up saving the war for the Allies.

Second, Esther's parents were insistent to Hans that she get out now. When Hans came to me and told me that he would be circling back, I knew what I had to do. Please forgive me for not telling you. I couldn't live with myself if I took Esther's place on that plane. And please don't blame Hans. I gave him no choice.

I guess that there is a third reason. My dad has never told me, but I am sure that the Nazis threatened my life if he continued to refuse to come to Germany and work on this project. I don't know for certain, but I have a small hope that they are holding Jimmy somewhere as further insurance that Dad completes the project. The only reason that I am guessing that this is a possibility is because every once in a while I would catch my dad speaking about Jimmy in the present tense. People who haven't accepted someone's death will do this, but it felt different to me. He has never referred to my mom in the present tense, so why would he with Jimmy?

When you and my Dad talked privately the other night, my hopes rose because he referred to his discussion with you as "life and death." So, if I am right, we would have six people trying to get out of the country, which would make it completely untenable.

I know that I am breaking protocol by writing so openly. But I trust Hans. There is so much more to say, but I must go now. Hans and Esther will be here at any moment. I hope to meet up with all of you at the appointed place that we discussed. If I don't make it, please do take care of Dad...and Jimmy, if in fact my hunch is right. I will do all that I can to find you, my darling. And if that shouldn't happen, I will always remember you. You will be the very last thought that I have when I leave this earth.

I do have one last question: Are you related to a Jack McGuire?

Lovingly,

Owl

Frank read the letter over a second time. Then a third. He thought back to his meeting in London with Donovan and his uncle. It never occurred to him that they would recruit a woman. And not just any woman, but the daughter of the very man whose project they had to learn about. They must have gotten to her right before Leigh and her father left Ireland for Germany.

"Those guys are brilliant," was all he could say. He walked out of the garage and got to the car. He also realized that he had to dump Hans' car somewhere along the way. He couldn't leave the car anywhere close to the Stoffels' home. Nothing would be easier for the Nazis to put together than Hans and the Stoffels. He began to pray that Leigh would be there to meet him.

CHAPTER 83

After Frank had ditched Hans' car in a small parking lot next to a grocery store, he jogged the remaining mile to his apartment. He stopped a block away to catch his breath and calm his body down. It was almost 2:00AM. He walked the last block and stopped before the house to listen. He didn't hear anything, and all of the lights in the shop were out. It didn't feel right to him. There was supposed to be a rendezvous at 2:00AM, hopefully with Leigh there. He decided to keep his pistol in his pocket, but his hand on the gun just in case. He walked the short distance to Peter and Minnie's house and tried the door. It was unlocked. He knocked softly on the door. No answer. He knocked again, a little louder. Something was definitely off. He decided to enter the home. As he made his way into the entry way, he called out softly, "Hello? Peter? Minnie?"

He reached for the light switch. The entry way lit up. Before he could even look around, he heard a voice say, "Good evening, Herr McGuire. What brings you here at such a late hour?"

"Who are you?" asked Frank. Now it was a second voice. "You have met us before. Do you not remember?" He then got a good look at the two men. The two young thugs from the Gestapo!

Scarface was sitting in a chair in the corner of the living room. Onebrow was standing in the other corner.

"I remember both of you. What are you doing here?"

"We are asking the questions, Herr McGuire."

Neither had their guns drawn.

"Where are the Stoffels? What have you done with them?" There was a muffled moan coming from the kitchen. Frank looked and saw two set of feet facing each other, both tied at the ankles.

Scarface came straight to him and stood a foot away. "I told you! We are the ones asking the questions! Not you! Now where were you?"

Frank stared at him and then began walking to the kitchen to see who was tied up.

"STOP!"

Frank kept walking to the kitchen.

"I SAID STOP!" It was Scarface.

Frank had gotten enough of the way to see that it was Peter and Minnie. Both had been tied up. Peter had been struck in the face more than once. He smiled at them assuredly and gave them an "It's OK," look. He then turned back to face the two Gestapo men.

"I was working on a story. You'll recall that I am a reporter. And I really don't appreciate what you have done to my friends."

They ignored his comment about Peter and Minnie and focused on Frank's comment about working on a story. "We don't believe you, but since you mentioned it, we have a story for you, Herr McGuire."

"Really? What would that be?"

"We seem to have uncovered the people who are hiding Jews and then getting them out of the city."

Frank: "Oh? And who would that be?"

Scarface again, with a triumphant smile: "Why, the Stoffels, of course. We have letters from each of them to their daughter. Apparently she is trying to escape tonight. We suspected them for quite some time."

Frank, playing along as he waited for the train to come: "Wow, that's impressive. And what sort of evidence do you have beyond a confidential letter from her parents?"

Onebrow jumped in: "You still haven't answered our question. Now tell us immediately where you were this evening."

"Well, all right. If you must know, I was helping Edwin Conway escape."

Scarface, shouting now: "We are not in the mood for your jokes!"

Frank stared at him and shrugged his shoulders.

Onebrow scoffed. "We thought that you might be looking for Miss Conway."

"Why would you think that?"

"Tell me, Herr McGuire, did you find her?"

"Who says that I was looking for her?"

Onebrow, getting more frustrated: "Maybe you can help us, then. You see, there was an explosion out at the airfield earlier tonight."

"Really? That sounds like quite a story. Can I interview you about it?"

Frank could hear the train in the distance. It was probably less than a minute away from arriving.

Onebrow sensed what Frank was thinking.

"Do you have a train to catch, Herr McGuire?"

Frank said nothing.

Scarface now: "We cannot seem to locate Dr. Conway. And since we can't find him, we thought that we should ask his daughter. Or you. You seem to spend quite a lot of time with them."

Frank: "So, you can't locate either one of them?"

Scarface, moving a little closer to him now: "That is not what I said. I said that we could not locate the doctor. I never said that we didn't know where his daughter was. We know that she is not at her home. She is here. Do you know how we know this?"

Frank said nothing and just stared at Scarface.

The Gestapo man continued: "Because we saw her come in here several minutes ago. Do you see the couple out in the kitchen? Perhaps we have Miss Conway tied up somewhere else in the house. Or, worse."

Frank didn't move an inch. He stared directly into Scarface's eyes and said very quietly and slowly, "If you have hurt her, I will kill you."

"You dare to threaten the Gestapo?" he roared. Scarface reached back to slap Frank across his face. Frank grabbed his arm in midair and held it there. Still not breaking eye contact, Frank whispered to him, "I don't have time for this. Where is she?"

Scarface was dumbstruck. Frank didn't know if it was because he had moved so quickly or if it was because no one had challenged a Gestapo agent before. He stepped back from Frank and said, "Perhaps you would like to fight me?"

Frank's eyes never moved off of him. "I told you. I don't have time for this."

Scarface said, "Very well, perhaps I should just shoot you." He reached for his weapon. Frank never had taken his right hand out of his pocket. Just as the train's brakes screeched, he fired his gun through his jacket, hitting Scarface in the chest.

Onebrow gasped in surprise and started to move backward as he reached for his gun. Frank fired again and hit him in the middle of his forehead. He was dead before he hit the ground. The train came to a full stop. The screeching of the brakes had covered the sound of both shots perfectly.

Scarface was on the ground, gasping and going into shock. Frank got down on one knee and pointed the gun at his head. "For the last time, where is she?"

"I...don't..know..." he sputtered. "But...on the other hand...maybe I do..." Frank looked into his eyes and saw only evil. He took the gun from the ground where Scarface had dropped it and then moved to Onebrow, and removed his gun as well. He looked at the dead man. It actually was an improvement, because Onebrow now actually looked like he had two separate and distinct eyebrows.

"Peter and Minnie, everything is OK," he called. I will untie you in a minute."

Scarface was fading fast. Frank bent down and looked into his face. "This is your last chance to do one decent thing in your life. Where is she?" Nothing. "Who else knows you're here? Who sent you here?"

The man on the floor was struggling now. His breathing sounded more like a man with a strange wheezing laugh. He looked at Frank and spoke his last words. "Heil Hitler."

He had taken two lives tonight. Maybe even more, if some of the guards hadn't been awake enough to get out of the building at the airfield. He didn't feel awful about it. He didn't feel anything right now. He had to finish the mission. And he had to find Leigh.

CHAPTER 84

The fire was a long way from being out, but it was starting to be contained. They had found Alexander Lippisch at home. They immediately brought him back to the airfield, where he met with von Greim. It was evident that he was astonished at what had happened. He even wept when he saw what was left of his laboratory. "This will set the project back for at least a year," he wailed. "Did Edwin make it out? Is he all right?"

Von Greim looked at him with disdain. "He's not here."

Lippisch looked relieved. "At least we can start again," he said.

Von Greim smashed the table so hard that Lippisch literally jumped from his chair. "Dr. Lippisch, how can such a brilliant mind as yours also be so incredibly dense?"

Lippisch looked at the Colonel, still confused.

"Does this look like an accident to you?" The Colonel leaned in. "Edwin Conway is gone. Nowhere to be found. His son is gone, too. Does that make the picture a little more clear for you?"

The look on Lippisch's face went from confusion to understanding in a matter of seconds.

"Edwin did this?" Then: "Edwin did this…" Finally, "Oh, Edwin…"

Von Greim called all of the guards together. They met in what was left of a conference room.

"You all have a choice. You can either be shot by firing squad tomorrow morning or be sent to the front. The only way that you will not be shot is by telling me exactly what happened tonight."

It was going to be a long night.

By the time that they had figured out that they were missing the BF 108 – the four seater – von Greim knew it was pointless to even try to find it. Edwin Conway and his son and whomever else was with them were long gone.

He called an aide and told him to find Hans Ungrodt. Ungrodt would have a lot of answering to do. And he would make one of several excellent scapegoats.

CHAPTER 85

Frank untied Peter and Minnie. Before they even had the rag cloths off of their mouths, Frank was shouting, "Where's Leigh? Where is she?"

Minnie: "Are they dead?"

Peter: "Are they dead? Did you get them?"

Frank: "Yes, yes they're both dead. Where is she?"

Peter: "OK, all right. OK, all right."

Minnie: "They're dead? Both of them?"

Frank, trying to talk more quietly now: "Listen to me, listen: we are safe. We are OK. I killed them both. I have their guns. They can't hurt you. OK? Now where is Leigh?"

Minnie started to cry. Peter held her and whispered to her. He looked at Frank and almost whispered: "She's upstairs in the guest room closet. First door on the right. There is a false wall at the back of the closet. Just move my suits away. You'll figure it out. I need to" –

Frank: "Yeah, yeah. I know. I'll get her and then we'll come down. And then we need to get out of here."

Frank bounded up the stairs and began calling for Leigh. Once she heard Frank's voice, she began shouting.

Frank found the closet and searched for a latch. He found it quickly and opened it. Before he could even move, Leigh leapt into his arms. He held her tight. She had been crying. And now she began again. They both started talking at the same time, asking each other rapid fire questions.

Frank said, "Look, we will have plenty of time to talk in the truck. Everything is on plan. Different, but the plan is still working. We need to get out of here and fast. We have two dead Gestapo guys in the living room."

Through her tears she told him that she could hear the two Gestapo men threaten the Stoffels. The two thugs kept pressing them for the whereabouts of the Conways, but they held fast.

"I know, I know. Let's talk about that on the way." He helped her out of the closet and she held onto him as they started for the stairs. She stopped and looked at him urgently.

"Frank, why are you here? There should have been room for you on the plane. Was…was I right about Jimmy?"

Frank smiled. "Yes. Your brother is very much alive and can't wait to see you!" Then she started to cry all over again. And Frank couldn't blame her.

CHAPTER 86

Colonel Robert Ritter von Greim was now officially beside himself. And things were about to get worse with the knock on the door. "Yes, what is it?" he barked.

Sergeant Blum – or was it Mueller? Appeared. "Colonel, we cannot locate Edwin Conway's daughter, whom I think you know. Her name is" –

"I know what her name is." Then to himself: "Dr. Conway would not leave the country without his daughter. She is obviously with her father, you fool."

The sergeant continued, "We also cannot locate Hans Ungrodt. He lives by himself and has no immediate family in the country. That's one of the reasons he was selected for the espionage assignment. He was said to be developing a relationship with a girl named Esther Stoffel. We have sent two men to her home to see if she knows anything."

Von Greim merely grunted.

Blum went on: "The Stoffels are a quiet family that own a flower shop and appear to be normal loyal citizens. They also rent out a couple of rooms to a couple of young people. There is a young man and a young woman who rent from them. The young woman works at a department store and the young man"-

"Sergeant, why are you boring me with this?' von Greim asked angrily. "Just find Ungrodt. Send someone over there to interview the Stoffel girl and see if she knows where Ungrodt is. He can't have just vanished into thin air."

"Yes, sir."

A cold chill went up von Greim's spine. Hans Ungrodt was a pilot.

"Get someone over to the Stoffels right away."

"But sir, I told you, we already have two men that should be there by now" –

"Then get two more! Move! Now!" he screamed.

CHAPTER 87

Frank started to move the bodies into the trunk of the Stoffels' car. They needed to move quickly. While he was moving the bodies, the Stoffels and Leigh were cleaning up the mess in the living room. The bullets remained in each of the SS men's bodies, thankfully, so there was very little blood splatter. There was some blood where Scarface fell, and there was a bit more where Onebrow bought it, but all in all, it was manageable. Minnie went down to the basement and brought up a couple of dark rugs that could cover the floor where both men dropped. As they all looked at the scene, they agreed that it didn't appear at first glance that anything had happened there.

Leigh turned to the Stoffels and said, "Thank you so much for protecting me. Did they hurt you badly?"

Peter quickly said, "No. They got in a couple of punches and that was about it. After they read our letters to Esther, they seemed to sense that someone else would be coming through the door, so they decided to tie us up and gag us so we couldn't warn anyone."

Leigh hugged them both and thanked them repeatedly.

Bringing everyone back to the present, Frank said, "We have less than ten minutes to get out of here. And Peter and Minnie, you are coming with us. Don't even bother arguing with me. Tonight has changed everything."

Peter looked at Frank, then looked at his wife. "He's right. If we stay, our mission will be brought to light. We can do no more here. If we are caught, we will be tortured and forced to give up other names in the underground. Grab our money and your jewelry. Everything else is replaceable."

After a moment, Minnie quietly said, "I agree. We can be with Esther and Hans. We have no more family here, and the underground can continue because no one knows as much as we know."

Leigh helped her grab all of her essentials. Peter grabbed a book of family photos. They left within eight minutes. Ten minutes after that, two new Gestapo agents showed up at their home looking for Hans.

Frank could hear Minnie sniffling and crying quietly in the backseat. They were leaving their home, maybe forever. He could hear Peter whispering to her in German, no doubt encouraging and reassuring his wife. Underneath her friendly exterior, Minnie Stoffel was a mentally tough and fiercely loyal woman. She hated to leave, but she also knew this day would come. If she stayed, she would be jeopardizing everything that they had built, and, more importantly, she would be jeopardizing the lives of everyone associated with the underground. She had to leave. Her mind told her that. But her heart told her something different.

Frank decided to try to take Minnie's mind off of the current situation as much as possible. He told them as much as he could on the short drive...the sleeping powder working perfectly, the guards being knocked out, getting Jimmy out of there, the surprise of Esther showing up (he skipped over most of that), and the escape in the plane. Last, he told them in greater detail about how much of the facility went up in smoke. "We did our jobs. We're pretty sure that we got Edwin out of the country, and we did major damage to the jet propulsion project."

Leigh wanted to know about her brother. "Frank, how did Jimmy look?"

"Well, seeing as though I had never seen him before, he looked...fine." That brought a chuckle from the backseat.

Leigh persisted: "You know what I mean."

"He looked...healthy. Maybe skinny. But it looked like they at least had been feeding him. Your dad had told me that he had laid out the plan to him a few days ago. He slipped him a note when the guard wasn't looking. Jimmy understood and signaled that he was all for it."

After more questions and a review of what the next couple of days looked like, they arrived at the store.

CHAPTER 88

Dale and Christopher Spodan, Hans' cousins on his mother's side, were ready and didn't complain about the last minute signal that changed the plan. They did not complain about them arriving at the shop fifteen minutes late. Nor did they complain about the Stoffels unexpectedly leaving the country – and the underground. They didn't even complain about having to get rid of the car with the bodies in it. All of it would be taken care of. The two couples were shepherded into the hardware truck and placed in the secret compartments. The compartments themselves were borderline ingenious. Being in the hardware business helped. There was a false bottom on the bed of the truck. The cousins simply carved out a space below the bed of the truck that wasn't visible to the naked eye. Unless a guard really took several minutes to get underneath the truck and look up, the compartments were virtually undetectable. There were small holes carved into the bottom and the sides of the compartments to allow for good air flow. It was anything but luxurious. Since the time spent in these "travelling coffins" was long, every effort was made to make each person as comfortable as possible, given the circumstances. There were even some small pillows and blankets for the escapees, because it could get chilly at night. Given the alternative, no one complained.

Peter took great care to tell Dale and Christopher about the remaining names of the Jewish people that he was responsible for. The two men promised to memorize the names and quiz each other on the trip to ensure that the names – the people – were not forgotten.

The two couples were loaded into the compartments in no time. Dale told them the signal – three hard knocks on the back of their cab – would indicate that they were coming up to a check point or that there was potential trouble brewing. And with that, they were on their way.

They knew that there were road blocks and check points that were in the process of being set up around the city. The remaining members of the underground communicated as best as they could what areas in the city to avoid. Dale and Christopher considered how best to mitigate the potential check points, but arrived at the conclusion that there was more risk taking alternative routes than there was in taking the most direct route to the border. A lot of the Germans recognized them and their truck, so traveling a different path would raise suspicions. The best protection that they had were their familiar faces and their words. Beyond that, all that was left to defend themselves were shovels, rakes and cement bags. Getting caught with guns would be extremely detrimental to their health. The only gun in the truck was sitting in Frank's one remaining pocket in his coat. The other pocket had been blown apart when he shot Scarface. He also had two grenades left, but he was hoping that those wouldn't be needed. He had already concluded that being taken as prisoners was not an option. They all knew too much about too many things. Plus, having Leigh in their possession would give the Germans leverage to get Edwin back. And there was no way that Edwin would not come back for his daughter. They had two more days to go.

He couldn't help but think about the previous evening. He killed two people, maybe more if the guards at the airfield didn't get out of the building in time. He felt no guilt about the two Gestapo agents. They were pure evil. But he did feel for the guards. Most of them had a job to do, just like Frank. However, the Gestapo guys seemed to enjoy their jobs, and there was something wrong about that. He had heard about the Gestapo. But seeing it firsthand was different. There was no doubt in his mind that they would have killed him if he hadn't shot them first. He took some solace in the fact that the noise of the planes and the fire itself probably woke most of the guards up. Edwin collected and threw all of their guns outside, so, after realizing that they had no weapons, their natural inclinations would have been to get out of there quickly. At least that's what Frank told himself.

Leigh. He was so thankful that he had found her and that the Nazis hadn't had a chance to torture her. He vowed that she would not leave his side until this mission was over. If they did make it to Lucerne, he would ask Edwin for his blessing. He was going to marry that girl. "Mom and Dad will love her, and Katherine and Evie will, too. Nothing like having another sister in the family."

Leigh was lying quietly in her compartment. She hadn't realized how exhausted that she was. As she thought about everything that had happened in the past 24 hours...being confronted by the two Gestapo men that ended up dead later that night...the relief in finding out that her suspicions were right about Jimmy...saying goodbye to her dad, not being sure if he would make it, or if she would ever see him again...her relationship with Frank and falling so deeply for him...and now, in all likelihood being hunted by the Nazis. All of it came crashing down on her. She began to weep quietly. They weren't tears of sadness as much as they were tears of...what? Just being overwhelmed. She prayed. She prayed in Thanksgiving for Jimmy being alive. For Frank coming into her life. For the work that the Stoffels had done to save so many Jewish families. For the courage of Dale and Christopher. She closed her prayer with this: "Thank you, Father, for protecting us through this process. I ask for your mercy and protection in the coming days. Help us to make it to Lucerne, and help Dale and Christopher to make it back safely. May the evil found in this country not prosper and may it be destroyed. Preserve the remnant of the faithful people here. May they be strong and trust You and seek You in all things. In the name of the Savior I pray, Amen." Within a minute of her prayer, she was asleep.

CHAPTER 89

Von Greim began to assess the situation. He cared less about the damage to the project than he did about the damage to his career and reputation. He could possibly keep the lid on this. It *was* possible that Conway was killed as the result of some additional work that he was doing in the lab. After all, the destruction was significant and there was very little left of some of the bodies. It would be impossible to identify some of them. And that went for Conway's son as well. Lippisch survived only because he was at home. Yes. That might work.

But what about Conway's daughter? She may have run off with Ungrodt. No, that wouldn't do. She was fond of that other reporter, the Irish one. He would have his people look for him as well. What was his name? Ah, yes. McGuire. Frank McGuire. He went out and called for the sergeant that he had been dealing with before. The man came hurriedly over. "Yes sir?"

"Sergeant, have someone pick up Frank McGuire. He is a reporter for the Irish Independent Newspaper. He is a friend of the Conway girl."

"Yes, sir." The sergeant paused. "Sir, the man named McGuire was the other tenant that I was trying to tell you about."

"What?"

"Frank McGuire is the other tenant at the Stoffels' home."

Von Greim turned white. "Find him! Find both of them!"

"Yavolt!" shouted Sergeant Blum, as he turned on his heel. There was a small smirk on his face. He knew that von Greim was really in trouble now.

CHAPTER 90

On their way out of Augsburg, they made it through two hastily set up checkpoints without incident. They drove all night and ended up a few klicks from the border. Dale pulled the truck onto a small dirt road that was well camouflaged by huge pine trees. They all thanked Dale and Christopher. Hugs were exchanged and directions were given to the next meeting spot.

They gathered together and Peter prayed for each of them. After one last round of hugs, Dale and Christopher Spodan headed to their local store.

Their last bit of directions included the name of the guides that would meet them on the trip: Timothy or William, or possibly Sam.

"What do they look like?" asked Peter. "We can't tell you that," replied Christopher.

"Really? After all of this you can't tell us?" asked Minnie.

Dale's turn: "You don't understand, Mrs. Stoffel. We can't tell you what they look like because we don't know what they look like. We never are sure which person we will get. If you get Timothy, he's married, so he may have his wife with him. Her name is Donna. The other two men aren't married, at least we don't think that they are. We don't even know if those are their real names."

"Can't get more compartmentalized than that," reasoned Frank.

With the sun having risen, the Stoffels and Frank and Leigh headed into the forest. They had changed into clothes that the brothers had brought so they would be more comfortable hiking.

They followed a loosely navigated path, stopping every few minutes to silently listen for friend or foe. After two hours, they crossed a bend and a young man stepped onto the path well ahead of them and raised his hand. They froze for a moment. He looked around and then waved them on.

Frank said quietly, "I'll go first. You all stay back in case it's a trap."

Leigh said, "I'm coming with you." Frank was firm. "No, Leigh. I have a gun and one grenade. Peter has the other grenade. Stay here with the Stoffels."

She reluctantly complied. They did move slowly after him but kept a distance of over one hundred feet, constantly looking behind them and to the sides to see if they were being surrounded.

As Frank approached, he started to take a good look at the man. He was in his mid 20's, average height and well built. He spoke excellent English. Frank stopped about 10 feet in front of him. The other man smiled at him and said, "I understand why you are being cautious and I applaud you for it, but we need to keep moving if we are to meet the next party."

Frank did not allow himself to relax. He said, "What's your name?"

"To you, my name is Timothy. If we get caught, my name is Timothy Borruel. I am from Spain. This is my wife. Her name is Donna." A small, attractive dark haired woman appeared from behind a tree. We are married and we are your guides. You are on a two day hike and you are our customers."

"What are your partners' names?"

"To you, they are William and Sam. You will meet one of them next."

"What are the names of the fellows who brought us here?"

"I don't know their real names. Their cover names are James and John. We call them the apostles."

"All right. Good enough," said Frank. He waved the others up.

They waited for the others to come. Minnie started to introduce herself and Timothy held up his hand: "It's better that we don't know any of you."

After an awkward pause, Frank said, "OK..."Tim" and "Donna." Lead the way."

Tim and Donna smiled and began moving down the path. Donna turned and said, "Please stay back about 10 meters. It will be easier for you to dive into the woods if you need to. And if you need to do that, the older couple should run to your left and the younger couple, you should run to the right."

Frank turned to Leigh and said, "It appears that they have thought of everything. I'm impressed." Leigh nodded in agreement. "This is not their first time at this, that's for sure," she said.

They marched on for another three hours, Timothy and Donna staying ahead and not talking to them.

Finally, they stopped to rest near a large rock. Timothy reached beyond the rock and pulled out four chocolate bars and thermoses. The thermoses had fresh water in them. He had two separate thermoses for Donna and him in a canvas bag that he had brought with him. "Drink all of the water in your thermos and put the wrapper for the chocolate bar in your pockets" he instructed. "Then give me back the thermoses." They did, and all four fit in the canvas bag.

"We have two more hours to go," he announced. "Then we will drop you off to the next party."

About an hour and forty five minutes later, Timothy stopped them and briefed them on their next guide. "His name will be either William or Sam. Stay on this path and you should see him in ten to fifteen minutes."

Leigh said, "I think we've seen this movie before."

Timothy and Donna both smiled and wished them luck. All four thanked them profusely and wished them well. The couple nodded to them and then took a side path. They were out of sight in less than a minute.

The group walked on for another two kilometers. They came around a bend and saw a young man sitting on a rock. He immediately waved to them and stood. Frank exercised the same discipline with the team and made contact with the stranger. The same conversation was exchanged as the first time. "Rest for ten minutes. We will take a break in two hours. Then we will walk for another three hours. After that, we will camp for the evening." After exactly ten minutes, "William" stood up and said, "We need to leave." He was a tall young man, maybe 6'3 or so. He had a ready smile and it was evident that he was a natural leader. But, like Timothy and Donna, he kept to the rules and didn't say much.

273

After the first break, they walked a little more closely to him. He didn't object. Frank thought, "He must be OK with this. On the other hand, he hasn't said hardly a word the entire hike, so how would we know?"

After another three hours and fifteen minutes, they stopped. Frank thought that they must have made worse time, since they walked a bit longer than what the schedule called for. William led them off the path for about 10 minutes, until they came to an open area. Buried between two trees was a canvas tent. They quickly assembled it. "Many hands make light work," said Frank, remembering a phrase his father always told the kids. It was big enough for six people. Frank took one end of the tent and Peter was next, followed by Minnie and then Leigh. William said that he would sleep outside and guard the tent. They didn't risk a campfire. More chocolate bars appeared, as well as a couple of loaves of bread, followed by more water. They were all exhausted and fell asleep by 8:30PM.

Frank awoke first. He quietly made his way out of the tent. Light was just starting to break. He went over to check on William. When he approached the figure on the ground, he jumped a bit. The man lying outside of the tent was not the same man that had said goodnight to them the previous evening.

CHAPTER 91

Frank pulled his gun out and slowly and quietly got closer to the man lying there. He took a closer look. This man was older and looked shorter than William. He had salt and pepper hair and hadn't shaved in a few days. Frank looked for a weapon but didn't see anything. He gently kicked him in the side. The man woke to see a young man pointing a gun in his face. The man did an eye roll and said, in a perfect British accent, "Put that away," and promptly rolled over on his other side.

Frank stood there, a bit shocked. He recovered and said, "Hey, hey…"

The other man rolled over again and said, "All right, take it easy Old Boy."

Frank said, "Don't tell me, your name is Sam."

He rubbed his eyes and said, "Actually, my real name is Thomas. Thomas Paul, if you really want to know. But that's neither here nor there now, is it?"

"Are you our last guide on this trip?"

"Yes. And put that gun away. Guns make me nervous."

Frank rolled his eyes and said, "We are on our last leg of a very long trip and an even longer mission. How did we get stuck with someone like you to get us over the border?"

"I don't know, but I can tell you after talking to you for less than a minute that I know a lot more than you do. Some spy you are."

"What's that supposed to mean?"

"You don't even know where you are."

"What?" What does that mean?"

"You crossed the border last night. You're already in Switzerland, lad."

"Huh? Are you sure?"

Thomas was getting up now. "Of course I'm sure. But that doesn't mean we are out of the woods…literally and figuratively."

"What do you mean?"

"What that means is…Oh hang it all, I'm not going to explain this four times to four different people. Let's get the others up."

Frank hurried into the tent to wake the others. They were already stirring.

"We have a new guide, everyone. Come on out as soon as you can."

It took two more minutes to gather everyone outside the tent.

"This is Thomas and he is going to update us on the situation," said Frank.

"Right, well, here we are, aren't we?"

"What in the world does that mean?" asked Frank.

Ignoring him, Thomas proceeded. "You crossed over the Swiss border sometime early in the evening yesterday. But you are not out of danger yet. Just because the Swiss are officially neutral, that doesn't mean that they don't have spies for both the Allies and the Germans lurking around. And believe me, they are looking for you. We will divide up from here. We will look very conspicuous if we walk out together. Frank, you and the girl will walk out together. "Her name is Leigh," said Frank, evenly.

"Yes. Quite. In any event, I have some different clothes and equipment for both of you so that it looks like you are campers and not just hikers. We're winging this a bit because we didn't know that there would be four of you, now did we? I will walk out with the older couple, who will continue to be hikers. More like three friends who went for a lengthy hike in the woods. We will go ahead of you. You follow close enough to us, but when we clear the woods, meet us on the train, NOT in the train station. We will catch a train to Lucerne that leaves at 8:30AM. It will take a little less than ninety minutes to get there." Next he held up three tickets, giving two to Frank and one to Peter. Turning to Minnie, he said, "You and I will buy two tickets when we get to the station."

Then he looked at Frank and Leigh and continued. "Wait until the last minute before you get on. We want to minimize the likelihood of being followed. Keep your eyes open at all times for people who could be following you. Know that the Nazis use men AND women very effectively to spot or follow people. We have about an hour's hike left. Let's get that tent put away where you found it. Sorry, but no breakfast until you get to the station. Remember, we are not together so don't look for tea or food at the same place." He then handed out an ample supply of Swiss francs to each person.

"This will be more than enough for breakfast and for something on the train. You won't be able to spend all of this on food. When you get off of the train in Lucerne, go directly to the park by the lake. It's about a five minute walk from the train, toward the downtown area of Lucerne. You can't miss it. Those are the only instructions that I have been given."

Leigh couldn't help herself. She had to know. "Did the others make it to Lucerne?"

Thomas said, "I have not been briefed on anything other than what I have just told you."

Minnie and Peter looked hopeful and encouraged. "Let's go. We are almost finished with this trip," said Peter.

Thomas stepped in front of them and got very serious for a moment. "People, listen to me. This is very important. You must look at this leg as the most dangerous and important part of the entire trip. You must not let your guard down! There will likely be some very professional spies in the city, watching the train station specifically. They probably won't have your pictures to go on, but they will have general descriptions. The last thing I have are a couple of cameras that you will need to share. You are on holiday. Take a lot of pictures. Wear the hats that I have given you. And the sunglasses. There are canvas bags here as well for you. Put the cameras in the canvas bags and take them out to take a lot of pictures. Use a portion of the money to buy mementos like tourists do. Buy some postcards. You get the idea. Pay close attention. You are all actors in a play. Play your part!" He paused and looked at each person. "Any questions?"

The other four shook their heads. "All right. Let's go." To Frank, quietly: "Keep that gun handy."

Thomas, Minnie and Peter led the way. About an hour into the walk, they stopped. Thomas walked back to Frank and Leigh and said, "We're ten minutes away from leaving the woods. Give us ten minutes and then come out. We'll see you on the train."

He pulled Frank to the side, looked around again and said, "You and the girl are the most vulnerable, because they will likely be looking for two couples. I had to do it this way. The Stoffels are sitting ducks by themselves. I'll take care of them but you need to take care of the girl."

"Her name is Leigh."

"Right, you told me that before. Leigh." Then: "Look Old Boy, it came down to the fact that you are the best equipped to defend yourself. And her. Leigh, I mean."

The next exchange was totally nonverbal but clearer than their actual conversation.

Frank gave him a "What's your deal?" look.

Thomas, gave him a head shake and a shrug that said, "I have a couple of things on my mind here. I am improvising because we didn't anticipate the older couple. Sorry."

Frank nodded an "I get it, we're all tired here" look.

Thomas shrugged knowingly.

With that, they looked at each other. Finally Thomas shrugged once more, nodded at Frank, and said, "Good luck. See you on the train."

Frank said, "We'll be there."

As he started to walk away, Thomas turned one last time to both of them and said, "Keep your eyes open. It is highly likely that the Nazis will be there in some form or fashion."

Frank said, "Roger that."

Thomas made his way back to The Stoffels. They listened to him for a moment, nodded, and looked back to Frank and Leigh. They gave the young couple a small wave and smile. Frank and Leigh returned the wave. The Stoffels then turned and followed Thomas.

Frank and Leigh waited for what seemed like an eternity. Leigh wanted to talk about the last few weeks and explain everything to Frank from her perspective. Frank stopped her.

"Please don't tell me anything. As much as I want to know, remember that we aren't safe yet. The less both of us know about the other's situation, the better. At least for another couple of hours. After that, we can talk to our hearts' content."

They talked quietly about the final leg of the journey. Leigh asked Frank what Thomas had said to him. Frank merely told her that they were just doing some last minute planning.

She looked at him and asked if Thomas had said something to Frank about her dad and Jimmy not making it out of the country. Frank shook his head firmly. "If he had told me that, you would have been able to read it on my face immediately. We need to remain optimistic about it. As far as I'm concerned, no news is good news."

After waiting another couple of minutes, Frank turned to Leigh and said, "OK, let's go." Leigh grabbed his hand as they started down the path that would lead them to the train station. Her hand fit perfectly in his. Just like that first time in the dance hall when their hands came together, Leigh's was a little damp. Frank was sure that his was as well. After a few minutes they emerged from the woods, subtly looking around to see if they were being watched.

CHAPTER 92

Von Greim was putting the final touches on his narrative of what happened. Of course, all of it was a lie. He knew it, and maybe Lippisch knew it, but von Greim could get him to go along. He would threaten him with no more funding for the project. He would stick with his story, telling Göring that Edwin Conway and his son were both killed in the explosion. After all, several of the guards were killed as well. There wasn't very much left of some of the bodies. He died during some final testing of the prototype that apparently went horribly wrong. To put the icing on the cake, von Greim could blame Göring himself. After all, Göring is the one who called him away from Augsburg for the meeting in Berlin. "Yes," he said to himself, "This could work. But I must control the message right now, starting with everyone who survived the night and everyone that I have instructed so far."

CHAPTER 93

Frank and Leigh made their way into town and looked for a place to eat. They were both famished. The good news was that they didn't have to pretend much about being a couple. That was coming very naturally to them. They found a small café and ordered some coffee, eggs and sausage. They were served the coffee first, along with some fresh bread and butter. After only two minutes, they were asking for more of both. They asked the waiter to take a picture of them, which he willingly obliged. Frank waited until the waiter left again. Then he turned to Leigh and said, taking her hand, "Remember, we are supposed to be a young couple in love." She blushed, which made him blush. "Oops," he said to himself. Then to Leigh: "Sorry. That might have been a little forward."

"Frank," she began, "I have to tell you something. I don't...um...I mean...What I am trying to say is that...I...really...haven't dated very much." Her eyes were looking at the table and they were filling up fast.

There was silence at the table. Finally she looked up at him. Frank was smiling.

"Do you think this is funny?"

He kept smiling. "Yes, I do. Do you want to know why?"

Those beautiful brown eyes locked in on him. There was hurt in them. "Why?"

Frank gave her a smile that spoke reassurance and empathy. "You say that you haven't dated much? I may have you beat. I'm not sure that I've even dated at all."

He leaned in and whispered to her, "So, the way I look at it, you are at an unfair advantage, Miss Conway."

Those brown eyes lit up. "Really?"

"Really what?"

"Really you haven't dated?"

"Nope. At least no one more than once."

Now it was Leigh's turn to smile.

Frank again: "I was wondering if you could show me the ropes." Another blush. "Man, she looks so adorable when she blushes," he said to himself.

Peter and Minnie were sitting with Thomas across the narrow street from Frank and Leigh. That put them only about 50 feet apart. They had bought a hat for Peter and sunglasses for both of them. The three of them were certainly in character. There was a lot of conversation and laughter.

They were situated where both tables could see each other, which was good. As good as they looked, what was actually taking place at the table was far different than three friends laughing and joking. The Stoffels were asking Thomas questions, and it was clear to them that he didn't want to answer too many of them. He had sunglasses on as well, so Thomas was able to keep his eyes constantly roaming. The Stoffels were natural listeners and were other-oriented people. When he did engage them, Thomas was interested in learning about the underground, but both Peter and Minnie felt that that topic was off limits, especially to someone that they had known for less than three hours. Thus, the canned laughter and effusive arm waving.

Frank looked at his watch. With only fifteen minutes before departure, he decided that they would keep up the charade and go to a novelty store to look at some souvenirs. Just as they were about to look for the waiter to give them the check, a man in white shorts and a white beach shirt with dark glasses and an oversized hat sat down at their table. "Hello, Frank. And Leigh, how nice to see you again."

CHAPTER 94

Leigh stared at him, not placing him right away. But Frank knew immediately who he was. "Otto, the outfit isn't quite a fit on you. And the glasses are a little much, don't you think?"

Otto Kruger, his fellow reporter at the newspaper, stared at him. "I didn't like you from the start, McGuire. Or whatever your name is."

"McGuire will do for now," answered Frank. "And for the record, Otto…I didn't like you, either."

"You'll like me even less when I turn you in. And don't try anything. I have a gun under the table that is trained on one of you. You can guess which one."

"That's funny. Because I have a gun aimed at you as well. But before we make a scene, tell me something. Was it you that reported on me to the Nazis?"

"Of course it was, Frank. I watched your every move. I was the one who told the Gestapo to go by your home. I was the one who told them that I had my suspicions about you. And I was the one who insisted that they keep an eye on your girlfriend, here."

"Very impressive," said Frank. "Tell me: why did you decide to look for us here?"

"Believe it or, we don't have unlimited resources. We have a person at every border town between Germany and Switzerland."

"Only one?" That doesn't seem very…comprehensive."

"Like I said, even the Party has limitations these days. The good news for me is that I have captured both of you. I will be a hero!"

"Yes, perhaps you can get a promotion and report directly to von Greim."

"Oh, please. After what happened the other night, he's finished."

"What did happen the other night, Otto? We never did hear."

"Why should I reveal anything to traitorous spies?" He waited a moment, and then said, "But, for you, I will make a concession. You may want to prepare yourself, Leigh. No one made it out alive." He looked her in the eye and said, "Your father and brother were both killed in the blast."

Leigh gasped. All she could say was, "No!" She covered her face in her hands. Frank reached out and lightly touched her arm. He then looked at Kruger and back at Leigh.

He said, "Leigh, look at me." Her eyes met his. He said, quietly but firmly, "He's lying."

Otto looked at Frank and said nothing.

Frank stared at Otto and said, "You're lying."

"Herr McGuire, why would you say such a thing?"

Frank ignored him and leaned over to Leigh. He whispered to her: "Remember what I told you. I was there."

"What are you saying?" barked Kruger

Frank now turned to him, but he was still talking to Leigh.

"Think about it, Leigh. If your Dad had died, why would they even bother looking for you? Your dad and Jimmy both made it out. They need to catch you so they can bargain with your dad for him to come back. Jimmy is safe with him, so you are the only leverage that they have now."

Frank smiled at Kruger. He continued, "Otto's trying to make you give up all hope so you will confess to something. He's so foolish that his attempt at lying has just confirmed for us that .they are both safe."

Otto smiled back at Frank. But there was no humor in his face. He had been caught and he knew it.

"I may as well tell you. It really doesn't matter, because you will never be a problem for us again. Edwin Conway is nowhere to be found, nor is his son. Conway's portion of the lab was almost completely destroyed, and Dr. Lippisch's area was also heavily damaged. Best case is that we lost a year on the project, but we will re-build it. You see, this is a minor setback. We will never be defeated."

Then to Leigh: "Your father will come back once he knows that we have you."

"And how is the good Colonel faring through all of this?" asked Frank.

Otto smirked. "Von Greim is starting to spread the word that the two Conway men were killed in the blast...that Dr. Conway was doing some last minute testing on the prototype engine when everything blew up. The Colonel can say what he wants, but it certainly doesn't sound that way to me. A few of the guards didn't make it, and there wasn't much left of the bodies, so I suppose that it's possible. But I think he knows that they escaped. You were correct, Herr McGuire. Why indeed would there be such a priority of finding you two and bringing you back?"

Leigh had quickly regained her composure after listening to Frank. Inwardly, she breathed a sigh of relief. She got right back into the game, looking at Kruger:

"See, here's your problem, Otto," said Leigh. "You have to bring us back. Alive. So, we know that you're not going to kill us."

"Did I say that I needed to bring both of you back alive? Forgive me, but I misspoke. I only need to bring one of you back alive. And that would preferably be you, Leigh. They don't care nearly as much about this gentleman," he nodded at Frank. "After all, what do the English say? That spies are a dime a dozen?"

Frank stared at him and said nothing.

"Besides, Leigh, you and I have a special kinship of sorts. Who do you think got your brother off of that train over four years ago?"

Leigh's eyes flashed at him and her hands balled into fists. "How dare you, you..." her voice trailed off.

Kruger just chuckled. "It wasn't that difficult. I merely did what your father did to the guards. Sleeping powder can knock a person out within minutes. All I had to do was put some in his tea when he reached up to get a book. He was out within fifteen minutes. We got off before we got to Ireland. Someone so unconscious can look like he had too much to drink. I helped him off the train. We had a car waiting, and the rest is history, as they say. Although I do feel a bit badly that I never had a chance to visit him in his cell. Your father had access to him almost every day. That was the deal that von Greim cut with him in order to get him to Germany. Plus, we knew that we had you here as well. All three Conways in one place where your father could see both of his children every day. That made for a much better work environment for him. It wasn't all that difficult, but it helped me land a job as a spy at the newspaper."

Then to Frank: "I suspected you from the start."

Frank rolled his eyes. "Ok, Sherlock."

"Who is this Sherlock?"

Frank ignored him. Leigh said quietly: "I actually feel sorry for you, Otto. You are a very small man who has wasted his life for an evil cause."

Otto smiled. "I can tell you one thing, Fraulein Conway. I would rather be a part of changing the world than being a citizen of a country that can't make up its mind."

Leigh didn't hesitate. "You will lose, Otto. The entire world has risen up against you. That madman that you call your leader will die a coward's death. It may not be this year or the next year, but there is no way that the world will allow him to succeed. You may want to rethink which team to play for."

Kruger kept his smile pasted on his face. "I like our odds. You see, Leigh, the difference between this new Germany and your country is that we will stop at nothing to succeed."

Frank knew that he had to do something. "Otto, look at me. You are not leaving here with her."

"My dear Frank, who do you think my gun is aimed at? If you shoot me, my gun will assuredly go off and kill this lovely young woman who is seated less than a meter from me. Not to mention that this young woman and you appear to be in love. Such a pity, that. Falling in love in the middle of a war is really not very wise."

Frank's mind was racing. He didn't want to look at his watch. He tried to subtly look for a clock and found one over the small bar that led to the indoor seating area. The train was leaving in five minutes. He and Leigh had to be on it. As he wrestled with what were limited options, Otto spoke again:

"Now let me tell you what we are going to do. Frank, you will first put your gun away. Then, we will walk to the car that I drove here. It is a two minute walk to the car. Leigh, you will drive. Frank, you will sit in the front seat. I will sit in the back with my gun pointed at Leigh's head. Once we are at the checkpoint into Germany, you will be taken to a holding cell. There you will be separated and then interrogated individually. I suggest that you quickly give up any ideas of gallantry. Believe me, you will spare yourselves considerable pain and, in your case, Leigh, probably some permanent disfigurement. Frank, if you would be so kind as to slowly put your gun in your napkin and slide it over to me, we can get on with this."

Frank glanced at Leigh. She was trying to remain stone faced. He had already concluded that there was no way that they were going to cross back into Germany. He would rather die trying than willingly go and be tortured. More important, there was no way that he was going to let anyone touch Leigh. He opted to just try to shoot Kruger right now and hope that he could hit him in such a way that he would not have the strength to pull the trigger on his gun and hit Leigh.

No one paid any attention to the waiter, who was putting the bill on the table. "Thank you, Miss. And thank you, gentlemen. I wish you a lovely day. You can pay at the register in the front of the restaurant."

Otto never felt the needle that entered his brain as Thomas continued on in his little speech about the way that the bill should be paid. It happened so quickly and so quietly that no one else around them even noticed. Otto's body went limp but Thomas leaned into him to hold him up. There was a small speck of blood at the base of his neck. Leigh dropped her napkin and as she reached down to get it, she grabbed the small handgun that was still in his hand and hid it in her napkin. She then took the napkin and emptied the gun into her bag, all in one motion. No one noticed.

Thomas looked at the table and pretended to be cleaning it. "I saw him drive up in his car. No doubt that his keys are with him or in the car. Almost everyone in the restaurant is catching your train in three minutes, or are going to hike in the woods. We have three men here who are working the perimeter. They will come and take your table. I will serve them champagne. We will make it look like they are all drinking way too much, especially so early in the morning. Once the train is gone, they will stumble off and carry this man to his car and be gone in a matter of minutes. We can dispose of the body and then make our way to Lucerne in his car."

Frank, pretending to look at the bill, said, "He told us that he is here alone, that there is one person assigned to every border city, and catching us would be his ticket to fame."

"Good to know that he was working alone," said Thomas, who appeared to be wiping crumbs from the table. "We will spread some rumors that he defected and came over to our side. If I don't meet you in Lucerne, I will probably see you in London at some point. Get up and stroll slowly to the train. Minnie and Peter should be boarding right now. They've probably witnessed this whole thing, so make sure that they are settled down. Go now!"

Mumbling a quick thank you, Frank and Leigh got up and walked at a leisurely pace over to the train. After a minute, they were aboard and found their seats.

CHAPTER 95

They arrived in Lucerne right on time. "The Swiss and their trains," Frank thought as he looked at his watch. They disembarked and kept to their plan of segregation, slowly making their separate ways to the park near the huge lake on which the city sat.

The two couples wandered around for ten minutes. Then three well-dressed men approached them. "Captain Sweeney?" Frank looked at both of them and said nothing.

"I'm Sergeant John Dierberger. Sorry to make you wait, but we had to make sure that you weren't followed. I have orders to bring you and your party to meet with General Donovan and Mr. George Parker."

"How do I know that this isn't a trap?" asked Frank.

"Now the second man spoke. "Sir, I am Sergeant John Eggerding, and this here is Corporal Pete Ehrett. There are ten men on the perimeter. We are all here to protect you and get you to the General."

Corporal Ehrett said, "Sir, it's a seven minute walk and you'll be able to see the General. He will be on the fifth floor of the hotel. He will signal you."

"That will be acceptable," replied Frank.

They followed the three men through the park. Frank looked around and saw about ten men slowly and subtly surround them on the perimeter as they walked. He wondered how many more there were that he didn't notice.

After a few minutes, Sergeant Dierberger asked Frank to look up to the fifth floor at the hotel across the street. He did. There was Donovan and his Uncle George. Both were smiling broadly and waving to him to come up. Frank smiled and gave a short salute. He ushered the others to the hotel. Then he turned and grabbed Leigh's hand, kissed her, and breathed a huge sigh of relief. He held her tight and said, "We made it. Let's go see your Dad and Jimmy."

CHAPTER 96

Von Greim was in his office when he heard a knock on his door. "Enter!" he barked.

It was Sergeant Blum...or was it Mueller?

"Sir, Herr Göring would like to speak to you."

"I've told you before. Tell that idiot that I am busy and that I will call him later."

There was a long pause. Von Greim looked up from his work. "Well, what are you waiting for? Tell the fool that I will call him back."

After another moment, Sergeant Blum said, "Sir, Herr Göring is not on the phone. He is standing right behind me."

With that, Blum turned and left the room. A broad grin emerged on his face as he walked out.

Von Greim gasped and stood up immediately, knocking over the coffee on his desk.

"Herr Göring...I...I wasn't...I didn't expect...I wasn't expecting you!"

Herr Göring walked in slowly and stopped. He whispered, "No, you weren't expecting me, were you Colonel? Heil Hitler!"

EPILOGUE

The reunion in the hotel was one of tears of happiness and relief. Donovan and Parker were joined by Felix Cowgill and Henry Block. Leigh jumped into Jimmy's arms and she hugged her father hard. All three of them wept over one another.

A similar scene was taking place on the other side of the suite with the Stoffels.

Frank and Hans hugged each other briefly and said "You made it!" to each other, just at the same time. After a few minutes of comparing notes over the events of the last couple of nights, they made their way over to their superiors, where introductions were made. Parker's back had been turned away from Frank. When he turned and saw his godson, he left Felix in mid-sentence and ran to meet Frank. He hugged Frank tightly as tears fell from his eyes. "I am so thankful that you made it. I prayed every day for you, lad. Every single day! Your parents will be so relieved!" He hugged Frank again.

"It's all right now, Uncle George. We're all fine. Mission accomplished!" They walked back to the other men, arms draped over one another. More introductions were made followed by toasts to Badger and Lion.

"Hey, what about Owl?" It was Leigh, who had come over with her father and brother.

Parker hugged her. "Leigh, you're all grown up!" To the others, he said, "I met her when she was nineteen. Look at her now! A veteran spy!"

Donovan looked at her and said, "So this is Owl. Well done, young lady! Well done!"

More introductions followed as the entire group came together. A large dinner table was arranged with leg of lamb, Irish stew, potatoes of all kinds, and even some steak. A feast if there ever was one.

During dinner, Donovan was holding court, entertaining all of them with his many stories from the Great War. He also weighed in on the current war. "We will be victorious again, but it won't be easy. Fighting two wars against two formidable enemies will tax all of us, to be sure. But make no mistake: we will win."

Parker was engaging in side conversations while his boss worked the table. "Jimmy, your courage over the last several years is admirable. I don't know if I could have done what you did. To live in a cell with all of those Nazis. Amazing."

"Thank you, sir. But it really wasn't bad, considering I got to see my dad almost every day. The hard part was not being able to let Leigh know that I was alive."

Donovan turned to Edwin. "Dr. Conway, it is such an honor to meet you. I have followed your career for many years now."

"Thank you, sir. I am familiar with your record. All of Europe owes you a great debt for your service in the last war, and I have a feeling that that debt will only grow as the result of this one."

"Thank you, Doctor. We could really use your help in helping us perfect the jet propulsion technology."

"Yes, we all could," said Felix, not wanting to be cut out from this remarkable man and the technology that he had spent the last several years working on.

"Gentlemen, I would love for this effort to benefit all countries who are committed to liberty and freedom."

"I think we can all agree on that," said Wild Bill.

George Parker leaned over to Frank. "You're not angry with me?" he asked.

"Angry with you? Why would I be angry with you?" asked Frank.

"Maybe because I put you in an almost impossible situation with very low odds of success?"

"On the contrary, Uncle George! I want to thank you. This mission introduced me to the woman that I am going to marry!"

"By the way, where did you meet Leigh?" asked Frank.

Leigh heard the question.

"We met right before Dad and I were to leave for Germany. Mr. Parker asked me to help them determine what this secret project was all about. In essence, I sort of had to spy on my dad, which wasn't very comfortable," she said. "I think he knew what was going on, though. Sometimes I would leave his briefcase unlocked. Then, after a while I noticed that he would purposely leave it unlocked. I wasn't very good at this spy thing, at least not initially."

"You did great!" said Parker. "Without you, we would still be trying to figure out when this test was going to take place."

Frank said, "We didn't do a very good job of coordinating our efforts, Uncle George. I thought Hans was Owl. You could have knocked me over with a feather when I figured out that Leigh was actually Owl."

Leigh laughed. "I almost let you catch me in the park that night."

"So that was you?"

"Yes. I'm sorry. But I can explain that. I guess that we have a lot to talk about."

Frank smiled. "Yes, we do. We'll need to take our time to get through all of it."

The debriefing took three full days. Once they were finished, Donovan turned to Felix and said, "It looks like we have a pretty solid combination with these two young men."

"It would appear so, Old Boy. Maybe we can use them together again at some point."

Donovan turned to Frank and said, "Because of the great work that you did on this mission, you are officially retired from the Army Air Force."

"Retired at 24?"

"That's right. You are coming to work for the O.S.S. Take a couple of weeks off and get home to your family. Then report to your Uncle's office in D.C."

"Yes Sir!"

One Week Later

The flight to Holman Field in St. Paul took about 5 hours from Washington, D.C.

They all got off the plane and looked around.

"Welcome to Minnesota!" said Frank. All looked around, excited to have finally arrived. It had been a long seven days. Leigh was so excited – and relieved to finally arrive - that she started to cry. Frank held her tight and whispered to her in assured tones.

30 Minutes Later

The front door at the house on Hague Street in St. Paul flew open. Michael and Maggie Sweeney hurried out of the house and raced the short distance to the street to greet their son. And their future daughter in law. And her brother. And her father.

Evelyn and Katherine flew out of the house right behind their parents. Hugs and shouts of joy were abundant. Jimmy hadn't stopped smiling since hugging his sister in Lucerne. And he wasn't about to stop now. Edwin was beaming and hugging everyone as if they had known each other for years. On the long flight home, Frank had told Edwin, Jimmy and Leigh all about his parents and siblings, and the Conways had loved hearing all of his stories.

A second car pulled up, and out stepped the Stoffels with their daughter and their future son in law, the soon to be Mr. and Mrs. Hans and Esther Ungrodt. More hugs and laughs were exchanged.

The last person out of the second car was George Parker, who was all smiles. He and Michael exchanged a firm shake, and then they did the unusual. They hugged each other and wept. "Thank you for bringing him home, Georgie."

"I kept my promise, Mike," he sobbed. "I kept my promise."

Maggie came up and hugged George as well. She was a complete puddle. "Thank you, George! Thank you!" George couldn't speak. He could only nod as he tried to compose himself.

More tears flowed, but they were happy tears, for a change. Neighbors came out of their homes, waving and applauding. Some waved flags and others merely shouted their congratulations.

And for a brief time during these horrible days of war, all was right with the world, at least in St. Paul, Minnesota. For laughter and joy had finally returned to the home of Michael and Maggie Sweeney.

ACKNOWLEDGMENTS

Any errors contained herein are mine and mine alone.

First, a couple of things about this book. Most of this story is fictitious, but not all of it. Some of the characters are real. For example, everything about Michael Sweeney is pretty much accurate, although he was actually much older than portrayed in the book. He was my Great Grandfather. Frank and Leigh were my maternal grandparents. Both were gentle souls who were salt of the earth Americans. Frank actually worked at Sweeney Detective for several years. He was involved in thwarting an attempted robbery of one of the agency's trucks. It didn't end well for the bad guys.

Jimmy is a character that I created. He was named in memory of my cousin, Jim Myler, who left this earth way too early. He was a Sweeney through and through…a gentle man who just may have been the nicest guy that I have ever known. He and his family will always be very special to all of us.

The character of Bill Donovan was real. Wild Bill was indeed the father of American Secret Intelligence. This man was an incredible patriot and warrior. There have been several books written about him. One of the better ones is "Wild Bill Donovan, the Last Hero," by Anthony Cave Brown. "The Last Hero" reference is actually from President Eisenhower. These were the words he chose to describe Donovan, shortly before Wild Bill's death. He died from vascular dementia in 1959. He was a remarkable man who used every minute of every day usefully. Indeed, read about him and you will be amazed. And inspired.

Colonel Robert Ritter von Greim, Hermann Göring, Alex Lippisch, and Kim Philby are also historical figures. Philby was a Soviet spy inside of MI6. He did incredible damage to freedom around the world, and the information that he gave to the Soviets resulted in scores of deaths. Incredibly, it would take over 20 years to confirm that he had betrayed his country. He secretly fled to the Soviet Union in 1963.

Germany's jet engine program was also real. It was called "Project 1065" within Nazi circles. It would have been a game changer in the war if they could have gotten it perfected and into production much sooner. There were a few planes that were in service in 1945, but it was too late to impact the outcome of the war. God clearly spared our nation. And the world.

You may have noticed that there aren't any curse words or sex in this book. I just firmly believe that one can write a book that is filled with adventure and intrigue without having to put all of that stuff in there. Someone once told me that "Cursing is for the conversationally crippled." I like that. I recall reading "Band of Brothers," a marvelous book by peerless author Stephen Ambrose that later became a miniseries. The book was based on real men and real events involving Easy Company from the 101st Airborne Division. The book and series follow the exploits of these incredibly brave young men as they parachuted into Normandy and waged war in the Battle of The Bulge, among other missions. The main character is Colonel Dick Winters, who is worthy of more than one book in his own right. One of the few beefs that he had with the miniseries was the language. He said that none of his men talked like that, and that that sort of language would not have been tolerated. I doubt anyone would disagree that, while there was profanity and promiscuity that took place back then, it was certainly a lot less prevalent than it is today. And in my opinion, it has impacted our society for the worse. So there.

My first and last acknowledgement on any sort of earthly "accomplishment" belongs to my bride of over thirty five years, one Sharon Lee. She is an absolutely amazing woman who has put up with me and my schedule for a very long time. I got the better end of the deal, although I think there are days when she would be in violent agreement with me on this statement. Sharon is one of those people who is far more talented than her spouse, but willingly and gladly chose to take a back seat to all of this malarkey to do the most important job in the world: to be at home to teach our three children. In addition to all of this, she really helped me with the editing of this book. With the kids now mostly on their own, she recently completed her second Masters and is now mentoring and counseling women of all ages and also teaches personal health classes to people of all shapes and sizes. She is one of those rare souls who leaves a lasting impact on everyone that she touches. I love you, S.E.

Thank you to our three children, Katie, John and Callie, for all of their support in this effort. All three thankfully take after their mother. In other words, they are bright, intelligent, and good looking. And very kind. Callie, thanks for reading the manuscript and your suggestions on dialogue and the design of the book cover. Last, and most important, I thank the God Who made me for giving me the wherewithal to actually write this book. To Him be all praise and glory.

ABOUT THE AUTHOR

Will Ponner is a lover of history, particularly anything to do with World War II. He is an appreciative admirer of the Greatest Generation. Will makes his home in Stillwater, Minnesota. He and his wife have three children, all of whom live in the land of Sky Blue Waters. This is his first book in the Frank Sweeney series. He can be reached at willponner58@gmail.com.

Made in the USA
Lexington, KY
25 January 2019